C000126837

The Third Heaven

Ian Pateman

Grosvenor House
Publishing Limited

The book cover design by Ian Pateman

This book is published by
Grosvenor House Publishing Ltd
Link House
140 The Broadway, Tolworth, Surrey, KT6 7HT.
www.grosvenorhousepublishing.co.uk

This book is a work of fiction. Any resemblance to
people or events, past or present, is purely coincidental.

A CIP record for this book
is available from the British Library

ISBN 978-1-83975-119-6

"You, who by understanding move the third heaven, listen to the argument that is in my heart, which I know not how to say to others, so strange it seems to me." Dante Alighieri, *Canzone*

FLORENCE APRIL 1378

"Life is a hard and weary journey towards
the eternal home for which we look, or if we
neglect our salvation, an equally pleasureless
way to eternal death." Francesco Petrarca

Spring of this year finds me withered and fruitless, come
full circle and returned once more to the city of my
youth. I sit here in my room, surrounded by my few
books and my earthly possessions, mouldering in the
autumn of my life, feeling in every way, in every fibre of
my being more feeble than at winter's last passing. And
yet, I find – as though it has come about by some
miracle - that I am still alive. For this small blessing I
know I should and must be grateful but in such knowledge my heart is suffused neither with pride nor joy. Of
the many and varied dreams of immortality I once harboured in my foolishness, in my youth, all have long
since been thwarted; not one of them remains.

Others I have known on this journey have been far less
fortunate in the allocation of their days. I have seen many
pass, friends and enemies, young and old, and still it
seems to me the events of the world (the world of men
that is) turn their fickle and unfathomable patterns around
me. Today, for instance, it has not escaped my vague, old
man's attention that the whole city is cloaked in mourning: all around bells ring out the slow *cadenza* they
assume to announce the coming of Death, and in the

street below the proud and pious are making silently to their churches, there supposedly to pray.

I will say here only that I am sceptical of their motives, though perhaps it is I who moves with ungracious spirit, and that they go indeed to offer prayers for the one whose soul has departed this earthly existence, not - as I surmise of them - in the vain hope of salvation of their own. Nevertheless, my curiosity having been aroused by the uncommon stillness in the streets (and once awoken curiosity being a restless and insatiable thing), I asked of the old widow who is mistress of this house and who for a small consideration keeps my table and tends to my needs, whose death it was that had brought about this halt in the commerce of our normally busy little street. Absent, the familiar creak and clack of carriage wheels upon cobbles, the cackle and bleating of beasts, of fish-wives braying; the barks and cries of vendors piercing the air, vying for the citizen's coin; absent too the perpetual stridor of voices and footsteps rising from the street below to enter through my window as accompaniment to the silent and solitary studies I now pursue to occupy my days. Missing all of these small yet necessary and comforting facets of God's Creation, I asked the old woman when she came to bring my morning provender what was amiss.

"Have you not heard the news, *Messer* di Buoninsegna? The Holy Father; He is dead," she informed me breathlessly, for she seemed to find the matter to be cause for excitement, or perhaps it was merely that she had been winded by the climb to this attic, high above the traffic of the world, where I abide.

"Taken of a sudden by some affliction of which no-one knows the cause, though there is much rumour of poisoning or the like," she added. "Everyone is shocked and saddened by it."

I cannot say that I shared in her excitement, nor in the outward sorrow of my fellow citizens, if this singular death was indeed its cause. My hardened heart no longer has it in it to grieve at such inconsequential news as her words conveyed.

"Is that all? Then there has been no great loss to the world at large, nor to any of us in particular," I offered in reply, to the woman's palpable consternation.

"Soon enough another will be found and elevated in his place, in whom equal qualities will doubtless have been fortuitously discovered." It amuses me sometimes to provoke her in this way. She is always too concerned for the future redemption of the souls of others, particularly so of mine. As is usually the case, she was less amused than I by my heresy.

"But it is the Holy Father. He is dead," she repeated, as though I had not heard her, a tactic I have observed she uses frequently when she does not want to hear the things I have said, and then she turned and scurried away, huffing and tutting, and muttering some words to the floor about perfidy and my assured eternal damnation.

"He is still but a man, and to be mourned neither more nor less than any other," I taunted at her retreating back. She made no reply, at least, none I could hear, though I could still make out her agitated footfalls shuffling about on the floor below.

And what of this news, be it sad or not, that pious Pope Gregory XI, Pierre-Roger de Beaufort is dead? Can it really be so, and that within but a month of his return to Rome in triumph, having freed the Holy Church, or so he proclaimed (and with it of course his own precious crown), from the combined tyranny of his fellow Frenchmen, and from the maws of that infamous place, the Papal court of Avignon, a place the poet Petrarca described, and rightly so, as the Babylon of the West? A high-testing ground for every kind of lust he called it - as I have seen and can also give witness - where prelates feasted at banquets, clad in silks and jewels and fineries, served by half-naked whores and catamites, and rode on horses white as snow and shod in gold.

Must I mourn then for such a man, who sat in high residence condoning such laxity, when I believe his heart to have been cloaked in the same gaudy cloth? Should we not be glad for him, not mourn and regret his passing? Should we not celebrate his assumption into the higher realms, there to take his allotted place at his blessed Saviour's side? Unless, of course, he has been sent more rightly to suffer and to redeem his perjuries in the hot, steaming kitchens of Hell.

But enough! Of what significance is that to him or to me now, or of my spiteful conjectures? Better then, that like those who proceed solemnly below my window I should simply pray to God to rest his soul. Then perhaps my own corrupted soul might likewise accrue some late and small redemption through such an effortless act of grace.

You see the comings and goings of my fellow men no longer touch me. I have seen so many souls brought into this world only to perish - sometimes peacefully, more often than not locked in the agonies of a most dreadful, awesome death - that I can no longer impel my soul to regret each individual passing. Long have I ceased to try to fit such futile suffering into some great and pro-vidential pattern. In the course of my life I have seen the bodies of countless men, women and children too, lying twisted and sore-ridden, littering the way-side where they had fallen, lying beside the rotted corpses of dogs and sheep; or their flesh pierced by arrows, or their bodies hacked limb from limb, or swinging senseless from rows of make-shift gibbets stretched along the road as far as the eye could see. I have seen them too, burning at the windows and thresholds of their homes, their flesh peeling, their exposed entrails steaming, their eyes boiling in their sockets, their choking voices crying out to their God for mercy as they were offered up as sacrifice to the one thing which in my divers journeying I have seen always to shape and govern the lives of mortal men.

I speak, my friends, not of the ways of the just and vengeful God of which the Good Book and the scholars rightly tell us, and in whose name, perversely, so many of those atrocities had been perpetrated. I speak, not of God, nor of His laws and strictures, but of something far more human in its workings - that passion to which all mortal things are diversely subject. Mortal fear, in all its devious machinations, and which base passion drives us in our ignorance of its hold upon us to commit every one of our numberless acts of shame.

Yes, in my time on Earth I have seen and known well the touch of Death. Reflecting on my life, it seems to me now that I have felt his presence as accompaniment to almost my every doing, although - as my continued existence will testify - his business has been always with those numberless others about me, not with my own ever-anticipating self. Now though, I too wait for him to greet me personally, and as do my fellow men, I too await his coming with dread.

From experience of his ways I do not expect his visit to be conducted either with sympathy or politeness. I know he will be impatient to meet me. I have kept him waiting long.

But tarry a while longer I pray thee, gentle and silent Death. Go visit some unfortunate and less needy other; be not too impatient to embrace me in your wings. I am not yet done with this flesh that I have borrowed, nor with this other death, which our time on Earth undoubtedly is. Grant me then but a few days more that I might complete what I have come to see as my mortal purpose. I promise I will not resist you when I deem my proper time is come.

In this I would make one last demand of my already protracted days. Being now so decayed in the flesh, and subject too to the vagaries of a replete yet failing memory, grant me the grace to set down a chronicle of my days, both for Posterity, and for the greater glory of God. So it is that I intend (taking up this onerous task where others would be more content perhaps to accept the approach of blissful oblivion), to record here some few of my many travels, and the meagre lessons I learned while embarked upon them; to tell of the strange omens which visited me in my youth, and of the time I spent in Florence and Padua, assisting there in the great works of my master, and of the terrible journey which events, and indeed my own fear and ignorance, forced me to undertake in the middle of my fifty-seventh year; to relate too some of that which happened on that journey, both concerning the passage I made from Pisa to Genoa by sea, going then willingly in search of reward and honour, and of how I eventually came from there to Nurnberg, driven against reason and desire by passions much less worthy, and in which city I arrived some two years later, wearied and touched for all eternity by the train of events, both curious and frightful, that I had witnessed.

Thus saying, and being equipped at least with the wit to know where a thing must commence if not the pre-science to know where it will end, I must take you back in time, to place you and my story at the point where it begins. Thus, will you discover me first in the nonage of the *trecento*, in the autumn of the year of Our Lord thirteen hundred and one. When, as a child of ten (though one acknowledged by all to be bright and precocious and more than a little capricious in his childish ways and miens), and finding myself full of the curiosity and enthusiasm which only the short-sighted ignorance of youth can bring, I would run each evening as darkness fell, and would hurry through the alleys and passage-ways of the town to join in the heavy chorus of footsteps echoing through the timber joists and frames as the whole populace of the town - the dogs and children, the mothers with babes-in-arms, the hawkers and peddlers, the traders, the *sottoposti*, the guildsmen and aged scholars, the layabouts and ne'er-do-wells, forsaking for once the more worldly pleasures of the inns and hostelries, and even the proud Priors and *gastaldi* and other officers of the commune who deigned to join us, drawn too by their vain curiosity - bustled together across the old wooden bridge which spanned the turbid waters of the river Arno to stand and watch and wonder at the strange new visitor which had come that year to illuminate the night skies above my native Florence.

-OO-

PART 1

THE ALTAR OF VANITY

FLORENCE, OCTOBER 1301

"This hairy star does not concern me, it menaces rather the king of the Parthians, for he is hairy, and I am bald." Vespasian

It came to us each night to rend the earth-shadowed sky with its brightness, hanging motionless against the heavens, silent and forbidding as the hand of God. Now with the passage of so many years I cannot begin to describe it adequately, for in my words, as in the futile efforts I have ever made as a *dipintore* to portray it on gesso and plaster, I fear my powers of depiction will fail me again in the face of such a task. Then, however, it had been for me a presence of such strength and beauty, its fulgent image had lingered in my thoughts and had gone with me constantly, illuminating both my day-time and my night-time dreams. The sight of it each evening suspended there like the Sword of Judgement, its hilt infused with the glory of God, its blade exuding trails of fiery, and doubtless vengeful fumes, served only to confirm my troubled dreams and fantasies and to fill me anew each day with trepidation and awe.

Could this be the long-awaited Day of Retribution, I wondered; the dawning of the Millennium of which so many, both wise and foolish, had threatened and promised, and which one day must surely come? Was this the hand of God, or of His hordes of angels come to bear our iniquitous souls to Purgatory, to weigh them in the balance of His mercy, reaching down from the skies to gather us to His judgment?

Do not suppose for one moment though that I was alone in my state of fearful reverence. Whenever I went upon the hill there were many about me who were equally as fearful of the visitation as was I. The other children laughed amongst themselves bravely and waged grand and sweeping battles in which they rallied together under the names of stars and constellations. Whenever they had to speak of it directly though their voices were hushed in deference to its presence, and they pointed at it as they would at the flesh of a sinner laid open on the pillory, similarly drawn by its gaudy fascination but with their hearts not wholly free of doubt and fear. As for the adults, many of them said little or nothing; they simply stood, or wandered in awed silence, or they gathered in groups to talk in lowered voices - of the blazing star, of the torch of the Sun - speaking of it as though it were an enemy, or at best an emissary sent by the Evil One. For beyond its visible attraction they saw too that the star brought light where darkness more rightly held dominion, disturbing the natural order of the world they believed they knew. They feared too that other things, dreadful things would follow in its wake - sickness, floods, plagues and destruction, the death of princes and kings; these were the things I heard intimated often as being the rightful concomitants of such heavenly luminaries, though none I heard speak dared voice his fears out loud.

And I, in my prideful ignorance, as I came to see it did not harm us, I too came to doubt such arcane wisdom, and to wonder from what source these blasphemers had acquired their assured and righteous knowledge of such assuredly unknowable things. As did they, I acknowledged that the new star did not fit easily into the scheme of things as ordained in the world by God Almighty, neither did it seem part of the sublime Nature created and maintained by Him for our pleasure and sustenance here on this perfect and wholly comprehensible Earth. Yet, innocent that I was, and in defiance of my own ever present trepidation, I came to take it for nothing but a Divine and therefore benevolent token, not as those around me did in the light of their blind superstitions, as an omen of catastrophe, and of dire, demonic and temporal things.

-OO-

But who exactly was that child of whom I am talking as though he were familiar to me, who ran each night through the streets of Florence to witness an inexplicable manifestation in the sky? Was that child really me, of my blood and flesh, and of my soul? If pressed to answer now, I would have to say I think not, or rather that I find it hard to comprehend that the child of whom I tell was really I. My understanding of who and what that juvenile creature was is as far removed from how I see myself now as it could possibly be, free as that little stranger was of all the experiences and preconceptions which trouble and weigh this old man down.

And yet it must have been so, that I was he, for I do still possess his tarnished memories. I can feel the ground, hard, and the wooden bridge, resonant, beneath his feet; can sense the wonder in his veins as he gazed in awe at that terrible apparition; can share too the excitement and expectation he felt at the commencement of the apprenticeship his father had recently procured for him in the workshop of a certain Giotto di Bondone, artisan and dipintore of Florence, who was being hailed then as the finest craftsman in all of Tuscany, and who was soon to be hailed as the greatest amongst all living men. Truly it was a significant and eventful time for me of which I tell, but whether it is right I should seek to find significance, not only in the events themselves, but in the numerical perfection which hindsight permits me to detect in the age I was then, I cannot say.

Ten - the perfect symbol of the perfect age? Is that how I saw myself then, or rather as I choose to see myself then and still? The child as the perfect and unblemished pupa which, of necessity, would unfurl and grow, being bound by (while at the same time aspiring to deny) the natural laws of the world of which he was undeniably a part; a creature of that world, metamorphosing through life's various stages, blindly acquiring and discarding all my bright, deceptive carapaces of knowledge and understanding, into the imperfect and tainted imago I have since become?

Or is all of that mere hindsight, or nonsense; an old man's foolish efforts to assign some sense and meaning to his childish ways and miens? Then again, perhaps it really was so (and who can say now if I am right or wrong?), or perhaps I was no more, nor less, than what my simplest words can say - a child of ten, innocent, yet bright and precocious, and blessed with a modicum of talent, and with good fortune certainly, who ran each night to watch a star fall across the sky.

-OO-

One evening towards the end of October, when the star was approaching its zenith, having grown brighter and greater each day since its arrival during the preceding month, I happened to observe my master on one of the slopes above me, accompanied by several youths from the commune. The young men were gathered in a group around him, and as he conversed with them, he pointed repeatedly towards the heavens, apparently discussing with them the apparition which hung there locked in its slow fall across the skies. I must admit I felt envious not to have been included among such privileged company. But what else could I have expected? I was but a child, and one largely ignorant of the mechanics of the world in which he lived, let alone of the vast, unfathomable heavens which turned above him, and who had but recently been apprenticed to serve in the *bottega* of the greatest dipintore in all of that lower realm. I was not even certain my master knew or remembered my name.

As I stood and watched in envy, the youths all turned as one towards the city below, their attention having been drawn there no doubt in order that they might refer the temporal to the celestial for the sake of their discussion, and as their gazes fell in my direction, Messer Giotto - being an observant man by nature - noticed me staring mournfully at them from out of the crowd. I dare say I presented myself as a very sorry figure that evening, standing alone among that great gathering, the disappointment and frustration I was feeling in my soul sketched out clearly upon my face. This my master could not have failed to notice - even had he not developed such powers of observation as he possessed under the guidance of his own master, Cimabue, and had he remained but an untutored shepherd-boy scratching images of his flock on the hillsides of Vespignano, which had been his own humble beginnings - and feeling sorry for me I suspect, he motioned for me to come and join them where they were.

"And what is your opinion young Messer Buoninsegna?" he asked immediately I came to where they were standing. A warm glow of pride flushed through my body that he had indeed remembered my name.

"Is our new arrival," he said, motioning upwards at the *cometis stella*, "a portent of evil or of good?" The scholars of that time had taken to calling our visitor the *cometis stella* - the star which appears to fall but does not fall - and to the human eye its motion across the heavens did indeed appear endless, yet despite this apparent motion its movements there could not be discerned by the eye alone.

"I do not know, sir," I replied, still flushed, and trembling visibly, or so I feared, at being given this opportunity to prove to others the ignorance I readily admitted to myself. "But bad, I would think," I added hastily, for fear I should be taken for one without opinions of his own, yet for all that, offering not my own, optimistic interpretation, but echoing instead the common fears I had heard voiced all around me. Although I suspected those fears to be grounded more in superstition than in fact, I also knew them to have been validated, not only in the teachings of the scholars, but by the words of the most good and Holy Book. I had no more wish to reveal myself to my master as a blasphemer than to be taken by him as a fool.

"So! Bad, you would say?" he said, nodding thoughtfully. "What should we make then of John of Damascus' assertion that comets are not to be found among those stars which were made in the beginning of Creation but are formed only at the time they appear, by Divine command, in accordance to His need, and are then dissolved? Would you claim rather that God is capable of creating something which is evil? Or do you perhaps dispute the wisdom of the illustrious Fathers, knowing other or better than they?" At this the youths all started to laugh, and I to blush, and to regret having been invited to join their numbers if it was only to be the butt of this all too philosophical discussion.

"No sir, I did not mean...," I started to reply, to defend myself, and to excuse my already proven ignorance, but found instead an unexpected ally in the one who but moments before had been the very instrument of my embarrassment.

"Why is it," Giotto said, turning to the others, "that guilty dullards such as you all undoubtedly are laugh so readily at the faultless ignorance of another? Even I, possessed with my small learning and my knowledge of books am almost as confused by this problem. It is a matter of some confusion."

At this they all fell silent, apart from one Domenico, who after me was the youngest among our present company, and who was likewise apprenticed to the *bottega* of my master. Thinking this reversal still part of my master's jesting, he laughed out loud again, and as reward received a reproachful look from Messer Giotto. At this the youths standing nearest to him began again to giggle and snort, and then to jostle the unfortunate boy, who - to add injury to his innocence - had been blessed at birth with a *valgus* so pronounced it made of his left leg a sweeping bow, which gross deformity forced him to hop and hobble in a most ungainly fashion. Experiencing in some measure the humiliation he was currently suffering I resolved that, if for no better reason than our shared age and insignificance, he and I should be friends.

"Aristotle also claimed comets were but transitory phe-nomena," Messer Giotto continued once some semblance of order had been resumed. "And that, being ephemeral bodies, they could exist only in the sublunary sphere. He said too that their coming portended droughts, and plagues, and famines, and other such calamities. Origen however refuted this opinion, citing the Treatise of Chaeremon the Stoic, and claimed that on occasion, when something good was about to happen, a comet would appear, and it should be no wonder to us that at the birth of Christ a star - or maybe a comet such as this - had arisen to guide the three Kings to their Adoration." As he spoke he again pointed to where the fiery sword of the comet rent a hole in night's velvet canopy, his arm stretched out with authority, his body held taller and more compact than it actually was, or so it seemed to me, and our own juvenile and bemused faces followed its command as one to see where he was pointing, though every one of us had seen and had wondered at the thing many times before.

I was fascinated though by the unfamiliar things my master was saying, especially so by the idea of the wise men from the East having been led to the birth-place of the infant Christ by an apparition such as the one we were at that moment witnessing. My fancy on this however was interrupted by the voice of a large and swarthy youth whose true name I can no longer recall but who came from Fanano, or some other such God-forsaken place in the mountains which lay to the north of my own birth-place, Pistoia. But I do recall vividly that he was an arrogant sort, employed by my master as a *pictor*, and how he liked nothing better than to bully and boss us young apprentices whenever the opportunity arose.

Amongst ourselves and behind his back we younger boys called this braggart Paraveredus (which as you know is a saddle-horse for a lady, of comely appearance and sure-footed), a name he had acquired both through virtue of his size and strength, and of a certain other reputation, the details of which I believe I have no need to elaborate upon. Therein, I suspect, may be found the reason why I am no longer able to recall the name under which he was born. By the time I arrived at the *bottega* he had already been employed there a number of years, and the epithet had by then become a commonplace among all and sundry. Also, he had died young, may God rest his soul (a victim, it was variously said, of the pox, or plague, or of an irate husband's blade), and before he had put his name to any work of his own of distinction which might have helped stimulate my memory to its rightful purpose. Perhaps, therefore, I never knew him by any other name.

"In Fanano the common folk believe all human commerce to be governed by the positions and motions of the stars across the heavens, and that the coming of a comet portends nothing less than the death of kings," he said stiffly, and with conviction, as though he was taking his authority from the Good Book itself, though personally I could not tell from his tone whether he was siding with popular belief or disparaging it. His father, from what I had heard of him, was a merchant in wools and textiles, a man of some means and standing but formerly but a shop-boy, and then a factor, and only recently made wealthy by the profits of his trade. Yet for all his humble beginnings the son often assumed (when not boasting for political ends of his affinity with the *popolani*, the working people) the pretensions of one who was nothing less than an aristocrat by right of birth.

"That may well be," Giotto replied, echoing the tone the young man had used. "The positions and motions of the fixed stars have been known for many generations, and the appearance of a new star among them would seem to violate that order." He looked around at us as though seeking confirmation of what he had said, and one or two braver heads nodded tentatively in reply. "But is that reason to assume they presage always some form of human calamity?" he asked of us all.

"But they say it is often so!" the saddle-horse retorted indignantly.

"Do THEY indeed?" Giotto almost roared, and then he smiled, looking at no one in particular, although his eyes sparkled playfully above the protrusion of the thickened carbuncle of his nose, shining out from their profound setting in the amorphous plum pudding of his face. For all the beauty he created in the world, it is my sad duty to confirm that my master was himself not a handsome man, nor was he one to trouble to dress himself in frills and finery despite the monies his renown had brought him. He was of short and sturdy stature, and went about always in a coarse linen smock, presenting himself carelessly to the world as a figure of caricature almost, with his ever-rubicund visage and but a few fine, unruly threads of grey hair sprouting at the edges of a high-domed pate. Whatever, it was no secret among us in the *bottega* that he tolerated the ways and indiscretions of this Paraveredus only on account of the great skills the youth displayed in his work. Some even said that it was he, Giotto (whose grosser exterior concealed an at times frivolous and irreverent spirit), who had coined the coarse cognomen by which we all called him, and which, being our master, and therefore entitled to call us by whatever name he chose, he used often to his face, and which the youth in his arrogance took always as flattery.

"Might it not be," he continued, "that their frail human reason, being fearful of change and uncertainty, and having been made more fanciful perhaps by the thin mountain air they are forced to breath, makes the connection between cause and event only when such heavenly signs are followed by calamity, and that it neglects - possibly through the intoxication of rejoicing - to recall the numerous occasions when they are not?" At his thinly veiled sarcasm we all began to laugh and on this occasion we were allowed free rein to our levity.

For his part, Paraveredus - for Paraveredus he will always remain in my memory, and through my words, I fear, will remain so also in yours - was not so amused, and decided not to pursue his argument. As for myself, I was by then of the confirmed opinion that Giotto also believed the star to be a good omen but that he chose to keep this inclination to himself, hoping through his arguments to stimulate our young minds to their own conclusions. Perhaps though, it is so that I came to that opinion only from wanting to see nothing but good in my new master, and to share with him every one of his ideals and beliefs. In any case, his brief dialogue with Paraveredus had given me time in which to regain my composure and to formulate a reply to the question he had earlier asked of me. After the chatter of noise and laughter had subsided I asked him politely if I might speak.

"Sir, I have listened to your arguments, and have found the possibility of truth to exist in both accounts. But should we not seek our answers in original causes, not in what is merely the visible manifestation of what the eye is unable to see?" I paused, amazed at my own eloquence and audacity, and fearing that at any moment such wisdom as had shaped my words might as readily desert me.

"May the Lord not create something which is good," I continued quickly, before such a disaster could befall me, "even though its purpose is to portend something which in our trepidation and our ignorance of its true and higher reason we can perceive only as evil? Are we to elect ourselves then as judges of His unknowable will?" At the conclusion of my brave words Giotto reached out and placed his hand on my head.

"Well said, young man. It is indeed so. I owe you an apology for assuming your wisdom to be in proportion to your years. In this at least you have shown yourself as wise, if not wiser than I."

"It *is* confusing, sir," I said, in the honest expectation of my unseasoned sagacity and consolation having the power to ease the burden of his doubt. At this he smiled at me again, and then bade us all good night, and as soon as he had departed the other youths all crowded round me, apart that is from Paraveredus who wandered off in ill-temper towards the city, following Messer Giotto down the hill.

As for me, I had suddenly become an object of great interest. Without trying, I had with only a few well-considered words and a modicum of divine inspiration, not only shown myself to be a source of great wisdom, but had elicited words of praise, and indeed apology from my master. This alone, despite my age and lack of skills, which thus far had relegated me along with Domenico to the lowest rung of the hierarchy extant within the *bottega*, had made of me one whose friendship was now something to be courted and vigorously pursued.

As though by Divine Revelation, the others had seen, and in concert, what in my heart I already knew - that a great and worthy future lay in store for me.

-OO-

On the following day another anonymous visitor entered and passed briefly through my life, one who was to influence my thoughts and my ideals most profoundly, though when I say this occurred on the day after my unexpected transmogrification, I realise I may well be guilty of distorting the true chronology of my story, to suit, or perhaps even to prove my own debatable purposes. Nevertheless, it was about that time, being as I have said, the end of October, nearing the feast of Ognisanti, and it was certainly close to the time of the encounter with Messer Giotto on the hillside I have just described, and which itself coincided almost exactly as best as I can now recall with the zenith of the passage of the comet across our skies. All three things fell close enough to each other anyway for me not to be able to resist, like most of my contemporaries likewise did of theirs, seeking coincidences and connections among the events which were then taking place in my life.

From the day of the visit of my master to the hill to witness it our celestial visitor had begun to recede from the panoply of the heavens, growing with each day steadily more dim and small above the horizon, until by the Octave of Epiphany of the following year it had disappeared completely and no longer played a visible part in the course of my life. That was not to be true of the strange figure (strange at least to my fanciful eyes) who came to the *bottega* that day to visit my master. After this first, though fleeting and indeed remote encounter he was to return again to my life within the space of but a few years and with this second coming, of which I shall tell later, was to influence me even more profoundly than did the momentous passing of the comet.

It was about evening time when he arrived, unannounced and unexpected, while Domenico and I were clearing up the workshop in preparation for the following day. Such was our task most evenings, we being the newest additions and therefore not yet entrusted with any of the creative work of the *bottega*, though both of us were - as was evidenced by the very fact of our having been accepted to serve and to learn under so famous a master - already possessed of some skill in drawing and in the depiction of the many and diverse things of Nature.

Our chores being nearly ended Domenico and I were indulging our childish natures, drawing grotesques and imaginary creatures with our fingers in the drying pigment which remained on the discarded palettes when we heard someone enter the *bottega* from the street. We span around together, fearful of reprimand, dropping the palettes onto the bench behind our backs. A man draped in a plain hooded cloak stood just inside the doorway. He looked first towards us and then glanced around the shop as though seeking someone, but he did not venture to speak. From what I could make out of him, for the material of his cloak was heavy and hung from his head and shoulders almost to the floor, he was of average height and build and stood very erect, like one of noble breeding, but of his age and race, and whether he was of flesh and blood or of the dead it was impossible to see.

"Good evening sir," we both said, again together, while trying to conceal our paint-stained hands behind our backs.

"I am sorry sir, but we have finished work for the evening," Domenico added, trying to inject a tone of authority into his thin, child's voice.

"I know. It is late, and I am sorry to disturb your labours, but tell me, is your master here?" the man asked, his face still concealed within the shadow of the cowl enveloping his head, his voice too coming to us shaded and muffled by the weight of the wrap of material from within which he spoke. I made to say I would go and ask if my master would speak to him, but at that moment Messer Giotto himself appeared from the room where he had been occupied all afternoon preparing drawings for a small painting on which he was to begin work the following day.

"I am here. Who is it wants to...?" he began, but stopped as soon as he recognised the cloaked figure who had so perplexed Domenico and I, and who had now thrown back his hood to reveal his face and was walking forward to greet him with open arms. At the first sight of his face Domenico let out a quiet gasp of surprise.

"It is you! I thought I recognised the voice. I understood you were leaving for Rome. But come, here in the back, where we can talk in privacy," my master continued, turning to where the two of us were standing, gawping at the mysterious visitor. He glared at us and clapped his hands, and we jumped and returned hastily to our chores as the two men retreated to the small room from which Giotto had emerged. Domenico and I stared at each other for some time after they had gone, our faces expressing a shared confusion.

"Who was that?" I asked, whispering for fear Messer Giotto might hear and return to chastise us with more than just a clap of his hands.

"You mean you don't know?" Domenico said, and I could see on his face that he was delighted to find himself able to impart some iota of knowledge to one who had so recently shown himself to be such a deep fount of wisdom.

"That…" he continued, drawing me closer and whispering even more softly as though echoing the desire for secrecy the stranger had himself displayed. "That was the famous Dante Alighieri!" We both stood, staring at each other for a while in silence, considering this momentous fact.

I had heard a few things of this Dante; that he was a nobleman by birth, but of limited means, a poet of no small reputation, and a politician of great influence who had but recently served as a Prior on the Signoria of the commune, and who was now embroiled at the centre of the dispute between the Black and White factions of the Parte Guelfa which was currently erupting into bloody battles on our streets. This latter, from what little I had heard of such things, was the reason for his intended departure for Rome. I had however never before seen him in person, nor had I seen a likeness of his face. Neither had I read his poetry then, for his verse was not considered fit reading for one of my tender years, being concerned, or so I had heard, mainly with that strange passion which men (and women too, of course) call love. And here this man was, visiting my master under cover of darkness, and in great secrecy.

"What can he be doing here?" I said, but Domenico had picked up a long-handled brush and was wielding it about him as a sword, oblivious to my curiosity.

"Did you know that he fought...as a cavalryman...at the Battle...of Campaldino...and at Caprona...and with his own hands...slew at least a score...of Ghibellines?" he said, still in a whisper, and punctuating his phrases with wild strokes of his sword-brush, then he commenced to make his own hobbled cavalry charge between the rows of benches, alternately scything the air before him and whipping his imaginary horse behind.

"No, I did not," I said impatiently. "But what can he be doing here, and why come so disguised?"

At that moment my fantasy was busily inventing all manner of schemes and villainies in which my master and this Dante might be involved. Without any help or connivance on their part, and without recourse to good cause or reason, I had proceeded to hatch a number of covert plots on their behalf - against the commune, against the Ghibellines and the Emperor. Even against the Holy Father himself! In truth, I was rapidly becoming excited at the prospect of my master, and of ourselves, becoming embroiled in such intrigues.

"Could they be planning to assassinate the Holy Father, do you think?" Domenico asked, coming to a halt beside me, and echoing the most extravagant of my own improvident thoughts.

"That perhaps," I said gravely.

"No!" Domenico protested, suddenly incensed at the possibility he had suggested now that my acknowledgment had lent more credence to it. "Messer Giotto would never allow such a thing!"

"No, perhaps you're right. Perhaps then they plan to wrest control of the commune from the Priors, and to instigate a Signoria under Messer Dante's name." Domenico stared at me in awe.

"They couldn't," he said, shaking his head slowly in disbelief. "Could they?"

"A cavalryman could," I said boldly, and we sank down, stunned by such a possibility, and sat in silence on the floor.

We were still sitting there several minutes later when Messer Dante decided it was time for him to leave. It was obvious neither he nor our master realised that Domenico and I were still in the *bottega*, hidden as we were from their sight behind the wooden benches, and so we sat and listened to their parting exchange, our tiny souls wracked in equal measures by the complementary compulsions of guilt and excitement, our hands clasped over our mouths for fear we might giggle or cry out loud and thus give ourselves away.

"When do you leave?" Messer Giotto asked as they came to the door.

"In the morning, as early as we can, if the learned doctors from Bologna can shift their idle bodies from their beds in time to join us." His voice sounded tense despite the wit of his reply. The two of them laughed together quietly.

"Take care, my friend. These are dangerous times, and you have collected enemies enough in the few years you have spent in the baiting-pit you call politics."

"That is true, and I fear too his Holiness may intend to trick us. I do not trust him. He has too many ambitions here in Tuscany, and now he has the audacity to send this Valois to plague us. Why can he not be content

to corrupt what he has in Rome and not do his utmost
to ruin the labours of honest men?"

"You know that what he does, he does only from fear.
His Papacy is not secure. Anyway, when was a Pontiff
ever to be trusted?" Giotto said, and at this both men
laughed out loud.

"You have done well to steer clear of our baiting-pit, as
you call it," Messer Dante added after a few moments.
"Would to God I had been half so wise. But sadly, I love
the commune. I would lay down my life to defend it, and I
cannot stand idly by while others seek to control
it and pervert her virtues. That is why I can never be
content just to write and pursue my studies. I must do
what I can."

"God desires we perform the tasks we are assigned."

At this they again fell silent, and although I tried with
all my might to sit and match their quietude, before even
a few moments had elapsed I found myself defeated by
my curiosity as to what they were doing. Ignoring the
great likelihood of my movements leading to our being
discovered, and ignoring too the tiny, clawing hands of
Domenico trying to hold me back, I crawled towards the
bench in front of us. Having reached this objective unde-
tected I leaned out in such a way that I was able to look
towards the door along the line of the other benches
without having to reveal more than a small part of one
side of my face. The end of the *bottega* we were hiding in
was by now almost in complete darkness, and in reality
(and according to those laws of science which can be confirmed solely by observation), there was little possibility
either of them could see us, standing as they were in the
light of a lamp which hung beside the doorway while we
crouched in the deepest of its cast shadows. That is not to
say I was not fearful of detection, being only too aware of

our great transgression in trying to conceal our presence in the workshop. In this way however I was able to see both of them clearly, and as I peered out from my hiding-place I saw Dante put his hand inside his cloak and take out a small package.

"At least I have this to remind me there are other, more worthy ideals in life, even though they have caused as much anguish as inspiration to my spirit. It is not always easy to tell right from wrong in such things. Now, though, I have this to help me and guide my path. Thank you for your efforts."

"Think nothing of it. May it serve you well," Giotto said, clasping Dante's hands, holding the package, between his own.

"I must leave," the other said, replacing the package within the concealing darkness of his cloak. "If things go wrong here while I am in Rome I hope our friendship will not have compromised you in any way."

"Oh, I doubt it. Anyway, what can go wrong? Do we not have a good omen burning in the sky above us..., and a white one at that! And it is well known that what few sermons I have seen fit to preach have been delivered from a different pulpit. They will do me little harm, whoever they may be."

Their conversation ended there, and they embraced again and said farewell, and Dante disappeared through the doorway into the dark street outside. My master barred the door behind him then returned to his room at the rear of the shop, deep in thought, and Domenico and I, able to breathe freely once more, quietly cleaned and replaced the remaining palettes where they belonged. We then crept from the *bottega*, fearful still that our presence there might be detected and punished, and went to join the others who had already retired to the dormitory, where I lay all night trying to find rest in my troubled sleep.

-OO-

The contents of that small package fascinated me and occupied my thoughts for days and weeks to come. What could it have contained, I wondered, and I have to confess my powers of invention did not then possess the strength nor the depth of experience to conjure up an explanation of sufficient credibility for my heart to accept as truth?

And what few clues did I have to go on anyway to help solve the mystery I had so effortlessly discovered? There was the package itself, which was no larger than a small prayer book, such as could be held easily in the palm of the hand. More than that about it I did not know, for just as Dante had been it too had been swathed in concealing cloth. The reality was that it was not possible for me to have sensibly hazarded a guess as to what it might contain. The object of my perverse fascination could have been anything - even as innocuous a thing as a book of common prayer!

But to confound any doubts I had, the strange and ambiguous words the two had exchanged kept returning to haunt me. They alone were more than sufficient to convince me of their involvement in some manner of intrigue. What else was I to make of their cryptic conversation if not to assign to it such a covert interpretation? Had the poet-politician not spoken of other, more worthy ideals, and of right and wrong...and how was I to tell which of his two chosen roles he had then been playing? Had the poet in him been alluding to the intellectual or spiritual; or had the politician been making a statement entirely political in its implications and aims? And what was I to make of the equally ambiguous reply of my master - that the thing concealed might serve Dante well? Was it then an implement, or a tool, that it should be used, and to good effect? Or a weapon with which to strike against one's enemies, in Rome perhaps, dealing them a mortal blow? I did not dare dwell too deeply upon the true nature of the strange object my master had created, nor to what illicit ends it might be employed.

Being that much older as I am now, and a little wiser too, I hope (or maybe it is only that I am now no longer susceptible to the hungers of the fertile and fantastical mind of a child), I know for a fact that my imagined mystery amounted to nothing. The true contents of the package I was to discover from Dante himself during my second encounter with him, and although it proved to be of great interest to me then, the small boy who cowered behind a bench eaves-dropping on an obscure conversation, and who spent the ensuing days troubled by guilt and fear, and wounded by the suspicion that his beloved master was involved in some misguided intrigue whose execution might jeopardise the very redemption of his mortal soul, would have been disappointed to have known what the truth of it really was. But of that later revelation, and what I then made of it, I shall have more to say in good time.

Before I continue though, I feel I must once more offer some excuse, for when I say that my suspicions troubled me for some considerable time to come, I must confess to the possibility that I am again guilty of making a distortion in my recording of the passage of time. For in reality events were to turn so fast in the days which followed that within a week of that time I was to be surrounded by and occupied with things much more concrete and political than my own naïve suspicions could ever have conceived. My master too was to show himself much concerned and discomforted by these things, despite his bold reassurances of his immunity to Messer Dante, so that I quickly came to push at least my deepest suspicions of his complicity in their occurrence to one side.

Because, there was of course another truth behind the visit of Dante Alighieri to our shop, and in such respect my childish fantasy was not so far amiss. As is well known, our visitor was indeed then a political animal (though later, as you will learn, if you have the patience to bear with my haphazard remembrance of things long past, he was to find some of the contentment he wished for solely in the pursuance of his Art), and at that time we all of us lived - poets, citizens, *dipintori* and their apprentices alike - in direly political times.

Domenico and I knew little of this game the adults played called politics. We knew there were Guelfs and Ghibellines (if Messer Dante had not slain them all through his valiant efforts); that one favoured the Papacy and Democracy, the other, the benign patronage of the Holy Emperor of Rome. We knew too that one sported a red lily, the other white, and that our city of Florence was a democratic republic, governed by a body of freely-elected Priors, but that conflicting interests and passions had led to a populace which - although ostensibly Guelf in inclination - was divided into two factions, calling themselves respectively Blacks and Whites. The Blacks, for reasons they no doubt understood well enough, gave their allegiance to the Papacy; Dante, being a proud man and a champion of true democracy, was therefore to be counted as a White. Even so, our knowledge and comprehension of these things was obscured by over-simplification, and was based more on hearsay and old-wives' tales than on any sound historical truths.

The reality of our own involvement in the history of our city was, of course, that Domenico and I were not yet then emotionally or intellectually equipped to understand the reasons why people came to and held such varying and conflicting beliefs. In our young eyes the world was simple and for the most part good. Looked at with such innocence it was not possible for us to comprehend the ideals and principles which underlay and dictated such choices, nor the passions such beliefs could induce in the hearts of political men. We had however seen with our own eyes the riots and the fighting, the bloodshed, and the mutilated bodies lying in the streets.

In fact, so confused was I by the situation prevailing at that time in Florence, I took recourse to asking Paraveredus, in spite of the low opinion I had of the fellow, if he might be able to shed some light on this murky subject. This seemingly ill-advised course of action was founded on my having calculated that he - being the oldest and most worldly among us - would be most likely to have knowledge of such mundane things.

"Why do the political parties in Florence call themselves Blacks and Whites?" I asked him one day when he came to instruct me in his usual brusque manner to prepare a certain pigment for him for the panel on which he was working.

"Don't you know anything, you little imbecile? It's common enough knowledge," he replied haughtily. "I really do have better things to do, but I suppose if I don't tell you I'll be waiting all day for my pigment while you worry your diminutive brains over it. It began some years ago in Pistoia. A disagreement arose between the two wives of a merchant named Concilliere who died without having had the sense to settle his estate. The descendants of one, who was named Bianca, called themselves. . ."

"The Bianchi!" I interjected, nodding vigorously in appreciation of my powers of deduction.

"Am I telling this or are you?" he asked sourly, and I nodded again, though less vigorously, in acknowledgement of his complaint. "The descendants of the second wife, to make clear the distinction between their claims, called themselves the Neri, the Blacks."

"But what does that have to do with what's happening here?" I asked, as I failed to see the relevance of this tale of domestic woe in Pistoia, the place where I was born, to the riots and street-fighting which had been going on sporadically for the past several weeks in the city where I now lived.

My dubious mentor sighed deeply at my ignorance and proceeded to relate the story of a young blood of the Concilliere family named Focaccio who, hoping to effect thereby a swift and profitable end to the problem, had first disposed of his uncle in an alleyway with a taste of steel to his throat and had then proceeded to slice off the hand of one of his cousins, which gruesome trophy he had presented to the cousin's lover disguised and garlanded as a gift. As recompense for such brave, conciliatory efforts this Focaccio had been summoned to answer to the citizens of Florence, who were more outraged by this it seems than were his native Pistoians, and he, together with his fellow conspirators were thrown into a Florentine goal.

"No sooner was poor Focaccio lying in his cell," Paraveredus continued, "than his cause - that of the Neri - was taken up by the Donati family. The Donati, if you don't know that either, are one of the old aristocratic families of Florence, and as such are supporters of the Holy Father, while the Cerchi, who are but a covey of old women and *sottoposti* from Acone, who resent interference in their affairs by anyone, especially by the Church, out of cussedness and jealousy of the Donati, espoused that of the Whites," Paraveredus concluded his tale.

"And what are they fighting about now?" I said gravely, impressed by, but still largely sceptical of what he had said.

"Don't you know anything, you worthless little flea?" he asked, becoming exasperated by my ignorance of any and all of these things, and reverting to the name which to my consternation he had taken to calling me from the day of my arrival at the *bottega*. This cognomen he had given me no doubt on account of my size, for I was small then for my years, even as I am now. You will understand therefore, with what pleasure, and with what feelings of revenge I referred to him always as Paraveredus in my every thought about him as well as to others behind his back.

"At the celebration of the Calends of May," he continued with some animation, for despite his exasperation he seemed to be enjoying the telling of his tale, "not this year, but the year before, two parties of youths, one Cerchi and other White youths, the other Donati and various Blacks, were watching the dancing-girls in the Piazza Santa Trinita. Being hot-blooded and desiring, as we young men do, to display their skills to impress the ladies, they spurred their horses against each other, to prove who amongst them was best. Inevitably, blows were exchanged in the excitement and blades were drawn, and a Cerchi nose was left so well bloodied it remained lying in the street long after its owner had retreated, red-faced from the skirmish, to seek what assistance he could find.

"A great fight then developed amongst the crowds who had gathered for the celebrations - a *farrago* which spread out into the surrounding streets as every man there rose to the defence of his colours, and which within an hour had become a full-scale riot, leaving scores of men dead or dying and their houses reduced to ashes and dust. The fighting continued for days, with the nobles ensconced in their fortress homes, directing the engagements from the eminence of their towers while the *popolani* and *Societi della Arme* of both sides erected barricades of stones and timber from which they issued forth to do battle with each other in the streets. The bloodshed continued unabated, and would have done so to this day had the civil guard not intervened."

"And they have been fighting ever since?" I asked after a few seconds had passed, overwhelmed as I was by his sudden and unexpected eloquence. So well had he related the episode, and with such passion, I had almost seen the fighting and the bloodshed taking place before my eyes.

"More or less, though until of late, and since the visits of Cardinal d'Aquasparta, the two sides have tried to keep apart."

"Were you there?" I enquired, curious as to whether this was all just hearsay or a first-hand account of what had taken place.

"Of course," he said, a smug expression coming to his face.

"And did you take part in the fighting?"

"Of course," he boasted, which, being what he was I should naturally have expected. Paraveredus would have placed himself equally happily at the gates of Hell or at the Adoration of the Magi if he thought his own participation there would show him in a favourable light.

"And whose side were you on?" I asked, playing along with his shallow pretence.

"The side which won, of course!"

"But they are fighting still," I wanted to complain, but held my tongue. I was not about to question him further on his doubtful loyalties. Young and artless as I was I had heard the logic of similar arguments expounded often enough before, and have done so many times since. Even in my youthful ignorance I knew enough to see it would take something more persuasive than my inadequate words to divert his reasoning from its stubborn course. Such passions, I knew, once enflamed, responded only to the eloquence of a brightly coloured banner, or to the self-righteous complaints of an affronted sense of honour, or to the pleas for bitter vengeance of a jilted brother or friend.

"And who is this Valois?" I asked, in the hope I might divert him before he had chance to add the vain details of his own participation in the fighting.

"Charles of Valois?"

"Yes. This Vicar, or whatever it is he claims to be."

"He's the brother of Phillipe of France."

"A Frenchman? But what is he doing here?" I persisted with my interrogation. Paraveredus looked at me coldly and I could see from his expression his patience with me was almost at an end. When he replied he spoke slowly, without emphasis or expression in his voice.

"Boniface has sent him to act as *Paciaro*, the Pacifier of Tuscany and so he calls himself the Vicar of the Papal States."

"But why send him to Florence?"

"Because he doesn't like to see his congregation murdering each other in the streets," he replied with much more animation, bending down and pushing his face into mine. "Because, stupid flea, to take life without cause is a mortal sin…or do all Pistoians go about lopping off hands and slitting throats without compunction? Now, do you think you might get me my pigment sometime today?"

and at this he turned away and returned to the far less demanding labours of finishing the preparatory work for his painting.

In such manner began and ended my first lesson in politics. As for the Pacifier of Tuscany, Charles of Valois, he was at that moment encamped, together with his army of horsemen from Picardy and his lances from God-knows-where, at the high stone fortress of Castel della Pieve, a black Guelf stronghold which stood not so very far from where I myself was standing, just outside the boundaries of our parti-coloured city.

-OO-

The tale Paraveredus told, facile though it undoubtedly was, served me well enough, containing as it did sufficient elements of the truth to explain the events which played themselves out around me during the ensuing days. The real truth of the matter however, I understand much better now. The Black-White conflict of which he spoke, although it had indeed to some extent been imported into Florence from Pistoia, had been born of much less superficial origins. Such quarrels as he described, though undoubtedly they helped to maintain the status quo of antagonism between the two parties had been merely the latest sprouting of a more deep-rooted friction which once propagated was to blossom into a confrontation of ideals which would eventually force Dante into a life of exile, and would change permanently the complexion of the politics of Florence from White to Black.

For all its relevance to the situation then existing Paraveredus might equally as well have invoked the ghost of one Buondelmonte Buondelmonti, who some one hundred years earlier had been murdered on his wedding day, and which treacherous act had been no less centred around the Donati family. Indeed, Giovanni Villani, that greatest of all chroniclers of the history of our city, was later to identify this singular episode as the provenance of the entire conflict which exists to this day between those parties in Florence who call themselves (often irrespective of, or in stubborn contradiction to their true allegiance) Guelfs and Ghibellines.

Every man, it seems, however foolish, however wise, has his own opinion of what the truth is, and of where it may be found.

As I have already confessed, my own understanding of these things was then no less naïve. I knew nothing of the machinations of Pope Boniface VIII, the man whose arrogance and megalomania it was had lain at the root of those more recent problems, nor of his plans to defend himself behind a mantle of nepotism from French aspirations to the Papal See. Neither did I know of the enemies he had made in pursuit of those ends; the Colonna family of the Trevisan Marches, who, being Ghibelline by persuasion, had supported Frederick of Sicily in his struggles against the Pope's putative and provisional ally, Phillipe II of France.

Equally ignorant was I of the events which had led Boniface to remove the benefices of the two Colonna cardinals who sat then in the Papal curia, and of the self-righteous Crusade he had preached against the family; and of how the Donati of Florence had been among the first to rally to the Holy Banner, and had fought and vanquished the Colonna at Palestrina, which once fair city they salted and ploughed into the ground. This sequence of historical events it was, and the great forces of power that are constantly at play in the world, not tales of petty domestic squabbles and crimes of personal vengeance, which had led to the conflict between the Donati and the Cerchi, the latter having sympathised with the Colonna and their dissent at the legality of the resignation of Celestine, Boniface's predecessor, and hence against the election of Boniface to an unjustly vacated throne.

The May riots that Paraveredus had described so graphically had merely provided Boniface with the excuse he had been seeking for intervention in the affairs of Florence. On two occasions that year he had sent Cardinal Matteo d'Aquasparta to promote peace between the two embattled parties, though (as even blinkered Paraveredus had noticed) his presence had proved no more than a temporary prophylactic and the fighting had resumed the moment the good Cardinal had departed for Rome. His true purpose however (or so it would seem in retrospect to those who survived it), was to have covertly favoured the Blacks to the detriment of the Whites, who then held power.

To bring about a more permanent solution to this, and to his other, equally vexing problems, Boniface had turned finally in desperation to Charles of Valois, the dispossessed brother of Phillipe II of France. To this end he had appointed Valois *'Il Paciaro'*, the Pacifier of Tuscany - a Tuscany, which in Boniface's understanding, encompassed not only Florence and its neighbouring lands but all of the troublesome States appertaining to Rome.

And now Valois was sitting, waiting patiently (and no doubt he too was watching and contemplating the significance of the recession of the comet) outside our city gates.

-OO-

A few days after the unexpected entry of Messer Dante into our lives, and while Valois was still sitting and waiting, biding his time, I found myself feeling sorely in need of company and of someone who might help me understand the things, both philosophical and political, I was struggling to comprehend, so I set out to find Domenico. As I had resolved, we had by then become the closest of friends and were usually inseparable, although on this particular day I had not seen him around the *bottega* for some time. Neither was he to be found in the dormitory, nor in the narrow streets and alleyways which wound between the high blocks of houses surrounding our work-place where he and I often joined in the pastimes of the other children when-ever our duties allowed. After much searching I even-tually discovered him on the banks of the river, amusing himself there in throwing pebbles at leaves and twigs as they were carried past him by the stream.

After we had greeted each other I also began to search for pebbles to join him in this distraction, and naturally enough (for we were both but children, despite our being engaged in learning a trade with which to make our livings as men), it was not long before our idle sport became a competition between us, as we aimed to see who could get closest to targets we nominated successively further and further away from where we stood. From what I recall, the river was running sluggish and low that day, and I soon grew bored with waiting for suitable targets, and with the winning, for in all honesty, and not least because of the physical disadvantage he suffered, I was a far better shot than he. Anyway, I had sought Domenico out, not to play games nor to best him at them but because I had more serious matters I wanted to discuss.

"Did you believe what Messer Giotto said to us that night on the hill?" I asked, finally giving up our recreation and flopping back onto the ground.

"About what? He said so many confusing things."

"About the *cometis stella* being a good omen."

"If he says it's true, then it must be so. I don't think he would..."

"What about this Vicar then?" I interrupted, for though at heart I concurred with his conclusion I needed still to voice the remaining doubts I had. Domenico considered my question for a while as he continued to toss pebbles aimlessly into the water.

Seeing his reaction, I realised then my foolishness in having sought him out as sounding-board for my deepest thoughts. Dear as he already was to me I knew Domenico had no stomach for too philosophical a discussion, and certainly not for such a profound debate as I was attempting to involve him in. Neither did he want to trouble himself too greatly in comprehending the equally confusing ways of men. It was already plain to see that my overly-sensitive friend was much better suited to the cloistered life of the monastery, to be surrounded there by the loftier ideals and thoughts and occupations of peaceful men, to be isolated from the cruel and worldly actions of us more political others, and this, I am happy to relate, was how he was to end his days.

"I don't know what I should believe," he said eventually. "How about you?"

I did not know what I should believe either. I saw the things that were taking place in the city, and I saw too how easily they could be incorporated into or interpreted in the light of common and popular belief. I had also listened to the more reasoned arguments of my master, and was inclined, despite all the visible evidence to the contrary to take my direction from him. But what of the significance of such things to the individual soul, I wondered? Did the comet come to bring a single message, be it Divine or profane, and if messenger it was, one intended for the edification of all humanity; or did it comprise a missive which differed in purpose for all who witnessed it, or which varied for each according to their Destiny or the condition of their mortal soul? Could it not be, I reasoned, that whatever portent might be embodied in its presence was amenable to personal, as well as to universal interpretation, and might therefore herald a different future for me, say, or for Domenico, than it did for anyone else?

"For myself, I see it as a good omen," I said.

"How do you mean, for yourself?"

"What I said. For myself."

"And what of the others? Messer Giotto, Messer Dante, the Vicar? Is it a good omen for them too?" he enquired, and I could see from his concern for the welfare of those others that he did not understand what I was trying to say.

"I cannot concern myself with them, or their futures?" I said, revealing a misanthropy within myself I had not realised I possessed, and which ran contrary to the more humanistic beliefs I had thought I held. The teachings of San Franciscus of Assisi held then, and have ever held great sway for me, and I have tried always, as best my poor sinner's lot has allowed, to incorporate them into the manner in which I have conducted myself, both in my commerce with God Almighty and with my fellow men.

"They are things of the world, and men of the world, and they act according to their own volition," I continued, damning with my words the probable destiny of my mortal soul. "What have they to do with me? I cannot speak for them, nor see whether the outcome of whatever happens here will be good or bad. I can speak only for myself."

"Then what makes you think this star is such a good omen for you and not for them?"

"I didn't say not for them, only that I am unable to foretell what it would bring them."

"Yes, that is what you said," he replied, though he did not sound convinced.

"One day," I began, then faltered, uncertain as to whether I should give voice to my thoughts, and being only too aware of the great arrogance of what I was about to say. I decided to speak nevertheless, trusting my soul to the understanding of Domenico, and if need be to the eventual forgiveness of the Lord.

"Domenico..., I am going to be a great dipintore, as great a one as there has ever been. Greater than Cimabue, greater than all the masters of old, greater possibly than even Messer Giotto himself. This is what the star has said to me."

Domenico stared at me as though I were a man possessed, which I suppose I was - a boy possessed by an unshakeable belief in the efficacy of his future, and in himself. After all, was I not bright, intelligent, and moreover, blessed with skills enough in my hands (and in my heart I hoped) such as would enable me to create many wonderful and beautiful things? Was I not also apprenticed to the greatest dipintore in all Christendom who would teach me an absolute understanding of my trade and how to employ those skills to good effect. Had I not already shown myself to be deserving of whatever knowledge and attention so great a man could bestow upon me?

The coming of the star, and the few words my master had said to me had served only to convince me of what my hopeful heart already believed.

"Listen Domenico, I see the world, and I see it is the world of men. And I see that though all men walk in fear of God, the deeds that are done, though they may be performed in His name are done mostly in the service and for the profit of themselves or other men. I too intend to make use of the world, but I intend to use it well, for my own, and for God's greater profit."

"Stop! Stop! Stop!" Domenico cried, covering his ears with his hands. "I will not listen to such blasphemy," and at this he stood and made to run away, but I quickly reached out, and grabbing him by the tail of his shirt pulled him back to the ground.

"What I'm saying is not blasphemy, Domenico. I'm talking only of the deeds of other men, not of the deeds of God, nor of my own."

"Then I hope He will understand you better than I and will forgive you," he said, and reluctantly settled down beside me again.

As I have said, I was, to put it mildly, somewhat precocious for a child of ten, and I offer my utterings that day as proof of that troublesome state of which I claim to have been a victim. Maybe though it is so that with the passage of time I have embroidered upon my memory of my words a little for better effect, as I have doubtless done with my reporting of all my other thoughts and utterances of that time, having made of them something far grander than was then within my actual compass. In essence though, what I have set down here is an accurate record of the things Domenico and I said to each other that day. Looking back at myself as I was, and in trying to understand what I have since become, I am unable to say whether my own heart was equipped then to take into itself all the strange and unbidden things which entered my head. Domenico for his part sat looking at me, tears beginning to fill his eyes, and shaking his own much less fanciful head in disbelief.

"You're just like all the others," he finally said.

"Why do you say that?" I asked, puzzled as to how he had made that connection between me and those others, whoever they might be.

"Because you're..." His bottom lip began to tremble as he spoke, and he had to pause to compose himself and to wipe away the moisture from his cheeks.

"Because you're making fun of me," he concluded tearfully.

"That's not true," I replied, feeling hurt myself that he should have doubted the sincerity of what I had said.

"Yes you are. You're making fun of me, just like all the rest."

"Domenico, you are my dearest friend," I said, leaning closer towards him, "and the last thing I would want is to hurt you. But, hard as it may be for you to understand, I do believe everything I have said, and that my ambitions remain honest and respectful to the wishes of our Lord. Forgive me if you find my words too harsh to accept." At this he wiped the last of the tears from his face, but it remained a blank mask, unable as he was to find within himself the forgiving smile I had hoped he might find.

"And what about me? What will the star be for me?" he asked mournfully, and he looked so miserable that water started to come to my eyes too.

"I know the star will be a good omen for you too," I said, and reaching out, I took his hand in mine.

-OO-

On the feast of Ognisanti of that year thirteen hundred and one, Charles of Valois finally entered our city. By that time the *cometis stella* had begun to recede visibly from the upper sphere of the Heavens, but despite its taciturn departure, the omens and superstitions that had been voiced by the popolani on its arrival were about to be confirmed by the events that were now unfolding around them, and that in their worst expectations, as History - or Destiny, or Providence, call it what you will - brought about the realisation of all their natural and in-born fears. As for the more reasoned arguments my master had expounded in contradiction of such common credulity, and which I myself still held to, they - in following the natural laws of opposites - were about to be proved wrong.

Domenico and I often ran outside to watch the soldiers whenever they entered or passed through our city, and we would stand and stare, enthralled by the sight of armour and weapons glinting in the bright winter sun, and would listen with cold chills running up and down our spines to the sounds of armour creaking and straining, of swords and lances striking the thighs and chests of the soldiers as they marched, and to the hard, measured tramp of their steps. I knew at such moments exactly what it would be like to be a soldier waiting to join in battle, hearing his adversary marching towards him, knowing that eerie cacophony might be the last sound I was ever to hear on this earth. Still we waved bravely at these daunting figures, and shouted to each other above the sounds of marching, pointing eagerly at the various shields and banners, trying to guess - for we had little knowledge of heraldry and insignia - to what Lord, or to which land each band of men belonged. To us, such shows of strength were no more than pageantry; exciting therefore, and for us, if not for the dark men sweating and straining inside their armour, great fun.

We loved especially the great war-horses which passed by so close we could almost touch them, their eyes proud and glassy, their coats shining with sweat under the load of man and armour they carried, and snorting plumes of thick grey steam into the air before them as they went. Sometimes they would be decked out in plates of leather and armour, at others (if their presence among us was cause for rejoicing, and not intended to impress upon its spectators the might inherent in such a coupling of man and beast and armour) their backs and haunches would be draped in gorgeous caparisons marked out in bold cheques and stripes and diamonds, or with chevrons of blue and red, and yellow, green and gold. Sometimes too, these huge beasts would snort angrily at us and shake their great plated heads in our direction, showering us with the saliva which foamed white upon their muzzles, making us jump back and scream out in our combined fear and delight.

"Is that him? Look! I see him there!" Domenico would cry out each time another knight, his face obscured beneath the shadow of his raised visor came into view, as we competed to see who would be the first to spy the great Prince, or Lord, or Bishop who commanded that particular brigade of horse and men.

"Look! There! Wearing the chevrons of gold and blue!"

"No! That's not him!" I would invariably have to answer, "Our man is clean shaven," or utter some such other denial to deflate Domenico's, and my own expectations, as soon as I saw clearly of the inferior noble who rode before us, whose spurs were of steel and not gold or silver, whose trimmings were not ermine but mole-skin, and whose squire was more poorly dressed than were Domenico and I, that he could not possibly be the mighty Lord of So-and-So, or heir to the throne of Sicilia or Napoli, or of some other distant province of which we had never heard.

On the occasion of which I tell however, we were to be given no such excuse for fear or excitement, nor for forsaking our duties for such distractions. Valois entered our city unaccompanied, and came bearing no arms other than those wits and charms rightly owing to one of such noble birth. And even if he had chosen to come upon us dressed and armed for battle, and attended by a thousand knights and their footmen, and with a thousand archers, and with a hundred engines of war, still I suspect he would have met with little resistance, for he had chosen his day to enter our city well. In his wisdom he had known that on that day of all days, when the saints in their multitude were being lauded, the thoughts of the city would be focused on celebration, and the hearts and brains and bellies of all would be full to the point of stupefaction with newly harvested wine.

It seemed therefore to the joyous and inebriated eyes of those who saw him enter that *Il Paciaro* had indeed come to make his peace.

-OO-

In the days that followed his entry Valois continued to act towards all with courtesy and forbearance, and he swore publicly to perform with equanimity the pacific task for which he had been sent. Seeing this, and seeing too the shadowed mass of his army still encamped outside their city (and understanding only too well in their new sobriety how that body of men, after several weeks of waiting, would be hungry for the heavy pulse of battle), the Priors of Florence elected to accept his authority without complaint. On the fifth day of November a Parliament was assembled and a motion carried to grant Valois full powers to act as mediator for peace.

There was one thing however that had escaped the attention of the otherwise prudent citizens of the commune. In their eagerness to yield to the peaceful ministrations of *Il Paciaro* they had failed to take into account the probable reactions of one Corso Donati, head of that Donati family of whom I have spoken. This Corso had been among those sent into exile for his part in instigating the riots that had disrupted the city during the summer of the previous year. It should have been no surprise to the Priors therefore that he would hold in small regard the alien power to which they had so readily deferred. Now, with the coming of Valois, the stage had been set for Corso Donati's return.

Not long after the parliament of peace had arrived at its decision, Donati and his cohorts stole into the city under cover of darkness, and having seized the nunnery of San Pier Maggiore and making of it a fortress, they sallied forth, again bringing disorder and bloodshed to our streets. The houses and stores of those who had ordained their exile were plundered, and the Priors themselves burned with their homes and possessions, or were driven into a penniless exile of their own. The doors of the prisons too were thrown open, so that not only the ill-served Blacks who had been incarcerated there unjustly (or so they saw themselves), but every malefactor, ruffian, rogue and lowlifer who rightly belonged there was made free to roam and terrorise the streets.

And while the dark powers of anarchy ruled, Valois threatened and swore publicly to hang Donati - if he should catch him - but took no action, and his army of eight hundred horse, and fighting men from Sienna, Perugia and Luccia remained outside the city, occupying itself in revelry, and in feats of arms and jousting, and in plundering the *contadini* and the surrounding lands. The Blacks had returned to our city, unwelcomed and uninvited, but they had now as their patron and defender the all-powerful Vicar of Rome.

-OO-

"What's to become of us?" Domenico asked plaintively of me one day, when the smoke from the burning stores and houses hung particularly dark and heavy in the air. We could see flames rising beyond the roofs of the houses opposite, and sparks and ashes were being blown towards us on the wind, and as they fell and settled against the window we feared at every minute we too might become engulfed in flames.

"I'm sure I don't know," I said, pressing close against the wall to see what I could of whatever was happening outside the sheltered world of the *bottega*. "Nobody knows where or how this will end, not even Messer Giotto."

As I peered out over the smouldering commune from our high vantage point, a group of youths, all with Cerchi black ribbons tied around their wrists and ankles, and about a dozen in number (and of a decidedly common sort, I thought), came into view at the far end of the street. Above their heads, silken banners bearing Donati arms and colours waved and fluttered in the breeze, and their cries of *"Viva Il Barone!"* came to me clearly above the besieged stillness of the commune. As they drew closer, still shouting and waving, and eventually passed below us, one of them spotted us staring down at them from our elevated position.

"Hoi, *dipintori*! Can you paint a new banner for us?" he called out. "One with a picture of Dante Alighieri's bloody head on it!" At his cry the others all stopped and started to laugh and to make ugly faces in our direction. I stepped back quickly from their sight, driven to such judicious action both by spontaneous fear for my own immediate safety, and by the realisation of the dreadful possibilities for all of us which lay concealed behind their taunts.

Could it be these ruffians had heard of the secret visit Dante had made to the *bottega*? Had they come now to make us pay the penalty for the thoughtless association our master had made with one whose politics - it was now plain to see when gauged against the new sentiments rife within the city - had been a treason of the highest degree? I began to tremble as I envisioned the terrible things these louts might do to us. What would be our punishment for such political indiscretions, I wondered, for the Lord only knew to what privations and tortures they were planning to subject us, innocent though we were?

Fortunately, and to my great relief, my fears proved unfounded, for all their great likelihood, and the youths merely laughed at us some more and slapped the one who had first called out to us on the back as compliment to his wit. Then, becoming bored with such minor sport as we two boys offered, they turned quickly away, setting off in search of some more deserving victims, continuing loudly on their way.

"*Viva Corso! Viva Il gran Barone!*" they continued to cry in unison as they disappeared from view.

Il gran Barone, Corso Donati, had always been a great favourite with such as these. They adored him, contrarily, it always seemed to me; on the one side for his aristocratic bearing, which in their base uncertainty gave them something unquestionably superior to look up to, and which he primped and exaggerated shamelessly for their benefit; and on the other, for the wit he was always ready to share with them whenever he went amongst them to rally their capricious support. Such carefully fostered adoration was to serve him well. Once the initial outrage at his sacrilegious seizure of San Pier Maggiore had passed, popular feeling had risen strongly in his support, following its natural tendency like that of all lowly things being drawn to brightness, and the cries in his favour could be heard echoing throughout the city both day and night. The few faithful Whites, leaderless as they now found themselves to be, and with no friends or allies to turn to, cowered behind their bolted doors and windows, no doubt listening fretfully to the roaring flames approaching to engulf them, and to the loud cries for vengeance and justice, and to the last desperate clanging of the Priory bell calling them to arms.

Once the louts had moved on and we had exchanged taut glances of relief, Domenico and I started to return below to where we were supposed to be working. We had barely descended half-way down the stairs when we were halted by a terrible screaming, followed closely by the sounds of shouting and of timber breaking, coming from outside. I ran back up to the window, scaling the steps two or three at a time, Domenico clambering less vigorously behind me. Looking out I saw the gang of youths who had just assailed us attacking one of the houses further along our street.

The door of the house had already been broken down and lay in pieces, and while the rest busied themselves with hurling stones and bolts of timber up at the windows, two of the youths had entered the house and were now dragging a young girl into the street, her clothing torn, and her hair fallen down around her face and shoulders. She it was who was screaming so forcefully. At the appearance of this new distraction the young men gathered around her and began to taunt her as she stood, shivering and frightened in their midst. One of the youths holding her reached around her body, and to my surprise and dismay, with one brutal movement tore open the front of her clothing, exposing the white skin of her breast and belly to all who cared to see.

Oh, what shame I feel burning even now in my face and through my being as I confess to you my own, unworthy reactions to this sublime revelation. Confess though I must, else feel the sting of it forever added to the lashing tongues of eternal damnation which will doubtless be the reward of my unfailingly sinful life. For I have to admit that amidst the fear and anger I experienced as I watched this, my soul was further wracked by overwhelming anguish and guilt. For so help me, and as hard as I tried to prevent it, I could not keep from looking at the revelation which had been unveiled before me, for never before had I seen the flesh of a woman naked and exposed in such a way. And here too I must divest myself further of my past transgressions (if my story is to remain the true and honest account I have professed and want it to be), and confess to you that even in the turmoil of that moment, my heart, and even my childish and immature body (may Heaven forgive me!), found much pleasure and excitement in what little of her innocence I was permitted to see.

For her part, the girl continued to scream and struggle bravely, striking out at her tormentors with her hands and feet whenever she could, though try as she might she was unable to escape. Then a tall red-haired youth, who until then had been but part of the crowd, and who had been content merely in watching her despoliation, stepped up to her and again to my horror, slapped her in the face. The shock of the blow halted the girl's struggles in an instant, and the youth, taking advantage of her stillness, began to caress and kiss her neck and shoulders roughly, pulling back the dark mane of her hair from her face. The girl turned her head this way and that, trying to avert his unwelcome advances, and as she turned her face to avoid him she looked up towards where I was standing, and only then did I see clearly and for the first time the countenance of her tormented face.

Picture if you can the sweet and terrified angel I saw before me, and try to imagine too the conflicting emotions which were then racing through my heart and soul. The face of the child (for she was yet but a child despite the shaping of her flesh which had raised my own to shameful excitement), was small and rounded, and her skin so smooth and white I thought it woven from finest silk or carved from purest pearl. Her features too were as fine as was the texture of her skin, her nose and lips and cheeks being all so finely moulded and set in perfect proportion around the orbs of her eyes. These too were in perfect harmony with all those other, more minor things which together constituted her total beauty, but in them and in them alone lay the true seat of her attraction, being as they were wild and dark and rounded and shaped that day by fear and disbelief. Yet I, in my equally wild and dark imaginings, saw within them all the tenderness and purity which could possibly be held within so young a mortal frame. Such then was the face I glimpsed but fleetingly, and though I know my meagre words can do little justice to her beauty, such is the memory of her which has returned to haunt and to tempt me often throughout my long and ghost-ridden life.

I stood watching all of this, puzzling over how it was I had never before seen, or if so had not remembered this angel who lived in the same street as I, and with my soul lifted high, and with my heart filled with wonder and praise for her tender beauty, and at the proof evidenced in her splendour of the skill and ingenuity inherent in the blessed Creator's hand. Yet at the same time my elevated spirit was being bludgeoned back from the higher ground it had assumed for itself to the lower regions where it more rightly belonged, being battered down and deflated not only by my fears for the safety of this angel-child I had discovered among us, but by the passions which had been evoked in my tiny sinner's body by the sight of her naked flesh. I watched, feeling at one and the same time beatified, wretched and helpless, until I saw the hands of the red-haired youth searching to find those parts of her which through respect and modesty only a husband, or perhaps a lover may visit or enjoy, and through my shame and anger at what I was seeing and feeling, I had to turn my eyes away.

When I summoned up the courage to look again the youth had turned towards the main group of his companions, and with one hand was pulling the girl towards them, while with the other he continued to fondle her naked breast. The others were by now all crowing and shouting, encouraging him loudly to his improper actions when - to my surprise and elation - the girl managed to break free of his grasp. Finding herself free of her assailants, she ran quickly from them, fleeing in the direction of our shop. As she ran towards me her eyes were raised, and I - heart-struck fool that I was, and still remain - believing them fixed on me, beseeching my assistance (though I realise now they were probably turned only to Heaven in desperation), without thinking of the consequences which might follow on such a reckless action, hurried down to the door to the street and threw it open wide.

The terrified girl ran in through the doorway, stumbling headlong in her eagerness to escape. Sadly (for my own happiness, as well as for any heroic thread my story might have aspired to), I have to relate that I was not the one chosen by Fate that day to act as her saviour. Instead, she ran straight past me, not even noticing me I believe, and threw herself, sobbing violently and begging for his protection, at the feet of Paraveredus, who - having been drawn too by the commotion - happened to be standing but a few steps inside the door. Looking up at this Herculean figure, and seeing in him precisely the hero incarnate she had been seeking, she crawled behind him, and cowered there trembling, trying to conceal herself behind the bulk of his legs. In her panic, however, she had forsaken all awareness of her naked condition, and despite her efforts to hide from her assailants, you can understand in what way (though for the sake of your own salvation I beg you not to imagine it) she was exposed shamelessly for all in the *bottega* to see.

Close to her as I now was I saw how she was even more beautiful than I had at first imagined, and again I had to force myself to turn my importunate eyes away. To this noble end I was helped greatly a few moments later - thanks be to God, for my own efforts were failing miserably - when several of the youths, also breathless and wild-eyed with excitement, came running through the door.

"Where is she?" one of them cried as they entered. It was the tall, willowy youth with the red hair who had slapped her, and whose nose I now saw, having once been broken and poorly mended, crawled like a badly-scripted "S" across the parchment of his face.

"Where's that little White witch? We want..." He stopped as soon as he saw the girl crouching on the floor, and the large frame of Paraveredus standing before her.

"Oh, it's you saddle-horse. Hoi! Good to see you," he said lightly, as though he had just come into the shop to pass the time of day.

"I doubt if I could say the same of you," Paraveredus replied coldly, disdaining the other's counterfeit courtesy.

"Why is that? I thought you were with us," the red-head said, smiling slyly, and turning to indicate the others who made up the dubious group to which Paraveredus had apparently once belonged.

"If it comes to this, then you were mistaken," Paraveredus replied, half turning to the terrified creature behind him, and without the slightest trace of emotion in his voice.

At his defiant words the girl stopped crying and looked up at him hopefully, and much of the fear drained from her face. In its stead something much closer to adulation crept across her features, and the unfathomable pools of darkness which her eyes had been till then brightened with the introduction in them of a faint yet discernible light. As for my poor heart, it experienced only a brief yet certain tremor of jealousy, occasioned by this unforeseen and most unwelcome turn of events. Nevertheless I had again found for myself an unexpected champion, albeit an unwitting one, for I am certain that in doing what he did Paraveredus espoused a cause which in no way did he envisage as being mine. In that instant though, I wished I could retract every one of the cruel and possibly unjust things I had ever said or thought about him. Fortunately, for my pride, and for my future peace of mind, I was not allowed time to say anything that I might later have come to regret.

"Now, be a good little pony and get out of the way!" the one with the broken nose said to prevent me.

"Why? Is there something here you wanted?" Paraveredus asked, smiling, and indicating the frugal interior of the shop. "A buckler perhaps, with the Donati arms painted on it? A painted screen, maybe? Something pastoral, perhaps? Or a small Madonna to put beside your bed?" The group of youths started to laugh, and I have to admit that it was one of the few occasions I was ever amused by anything Paraveredus had said.

"In my bed, more like. Now don't be an ass, you know what we want. Something much more delectable than a painted saint." As he spoke the red-headed one made curving gestures with his hands in front of him, and it was easy to see what he envisaged standing before him. Sensing the sting of shame more rightly belonging to them that they should be making her the subject of such ill-placed humour, I looked at the girl again and blushed.

"Why then should I let an ugly brute like you soil it with…?" Paraveredus started to contest.

"Because if you don't…," the youth interrupted him, placing his hand on his dagger to complete his sentence.

"Because if I don't, what?" Paraveredus interrupted him in return, and stepping forward struck him a single, mighty blow high up on his head. There was a sharp snapping sound, and the fellow groaned once, then staggered and fell backwards to the ground.

My little soul positively glowed and hummed with joy, so pleased was it to see justice dealt out so swiftly, and to such great effect. An eye for an eye indeed; or rather, a snapped nose for a smarting cheek! Whatever, I doubt if the fellow ever again slapped a woman in the face, and certainly not without an itch of the memory of that blow crawling along the length of his crippled snout to make him doubt the wisdom of his actions.

"And when he wakes up, tell him I do not expect any favours in return," Paraveredus said, turning to face the others, who all backed away from him towards the door.

Considering the matter concluded, Paraveredus turned away from them, and walked back to where the girl was still sitting and lifted her to her feet. Standing before her champion as she now was, and becoming suddenly aware of her unveiled condition, she started to blush, and began as best she could to cover her immodest charms.

As soon as Paraveredus had withdrawn, the youths rushed forward to assist their stricken leader. When he was again recovered to his senses and standing, and the blood from his freshly-broken nose had been wiped from his face, they drew their blades as one and turned towards Paraveredus. As they moved towards him, spreading out to encircle him, my newly-elected hero pushed the girl to one side, then turned and ran towards the rear of the *bottega*, and for one terrible moment I thought he was running away. When he came to the first of the benches however, he stopped, and reaching down to the floor behind it he stood again then turned to face them, a length of timber, of the sort we used to make the battens to support our panels clenched in his hands. Thus armed he advanced towards his adversaries, who I now counted to be seven in number, his not insubstantial weapon sweeping great arcs before him through the air.

"What the devil's going on here?" the loud voice of my master suddenly cried, echoing around the room, as he appeared in the *bottega* as though from nowhere. As soon as he spoke the ruction ceased.

"What do you young fools think you are doing...and here in my shop?" I had never before seen my master angry, but I was glad then to be given the opportunity to witness it in all its fury. "You Francesco, and Gatteo! You of all people should know better. You disappoint me both."

Immediately he uttered their names I recognised the two youths to whom he was speaking; I had seen them around the *bottega*, and indeed enjoined in conversation with my master many times before. At his words they both lowered their heads and slowly returned their daggers to their belts, and the others, finding themselves no longer having sufficient advantage of numbers did the same. Even the red-haired one returned his weapon, though with more reluctance, for in fairness he of them all did have some cause to seek reparation for the damage which had been done, both to his body and his pride.

"Now get out of here, all of you. Before I..." Before he could finish explaining what he would do they all turned and fled, their collective bravery flying in tatters, like their ribbons and shirt-tails flapping behind them, and dark, viscid blood dripping onto the floor from the red-haired one's freshly adjusted snout.

Outside in the street, the house was burning fiercely. Flames licked up the walls from out of the windows, and curled and crept around what remained of the wooden framing of the door. The family of the girl stood huddled together on the opposite side of the street, clinging to each other miserably for comfort and protection. The younger children were pressed hard against the bellies of their parents, and all of them appeared too frightened to either move or speak. The gang of youths were gathered around them, spitting at, and jostling and abusing them, but when the others ran, themselves red-faced and humiliated from the *bottega*, my master and Paraveredus following close behind them (and the rest of us too, who had also armed ourselves with bolts of timber to join in the battle now it was safely won), they all of them turned as one and fled.

"Thank you, sir. You saved my life," the young girl said when we returned to the *bottega*, forsaking her former champion, Paraveredus, and running this time to my master, and throwing herself at his feet in turn. My angel, it seemed, was just as fickle in her loyalties as were a great many of the city's hot-blooded youths. For his part, Paraveredus (as I suppose did I) looked most put out by this defection, for I believe he had been similarly smitten by her charms, certainly the visible ones if not the intangible one I had more nobly discerned in her, and had leapt to her defence as much in pursuance of his own venal aspirations as from any altruistic compulsion to protect an unknown innocent from harm.

"Think nothing of it child," Messer Giotto replied. "With our young saddle-horse here to protect you, you were never in any real danger." Paraveredus' spirits picked up again at this, for once, honest flattery, but mine remained low, beginning to realise as I was, how my own contribution to this drama had been a foolhardy, if entirely honourable thing to do. My rash action had put the lives of all of us in great danger, and the possibility yet remained that the youths might return with others of similar, Black-hearted persuasion, to exact from us their revenge.

"You must leave the city as soon as you can," Giotto said to the father when a few moments later he came towards us at the entrance to the *bottega*, and after the girl had run to him, tergiversating for the third time that day, forsaking all three of us, her confederacy of saviours, and throwing herself finally into her father's arms. When he had composed himself, the man simply nodded in agreement to my master's suggestion, and with much sadness and resignation gathered his family around him to leave. My master asked if they needed money. The man quietly shook his head.

"You have already done more than enough for us, for my daughter. I do not think all the money in Christendom will help us now. All we can do is put our trust in the will of God," he said, and started to lead his family away down the street.

And so that divine creature, the third unaccountable visitation I had received in the space of but a few weeks, entered briefly into my life and then departed, just as the other two before her had done. So quickly did she materialise, and then vanish, in fact, I did not even have time to discover her name. Cloistered in the *bottega*, as we were to remain for several days thereafter, fearing for our own survival, I had no way of knowing whether she and her family had made good their escape from our just and democratic commune, or if they too had become victims of its morbid hunger. I could only wait and hope that news of her death, of the removal of her blessed presence from the mortal realm, did not reach me. My soul trembled in fear and anticipation any time some outsider came, bringing tidings of what was happening beyond our doors in the loud and lawless *imbroglio* which our city had become. No such news came to me however, neither good nor bad, and in such absence I eventually persuaded myself, for the sake of my own peace of heart, that she and her family had escaped.

Yet she too, for all the brevity of her physical presence in my life, was to infect my thoughts often in the many and varied years that were to come my way. Indeed, of the three, it was she who was to affect me most deeply, and I will say here, the most purely. For unlike the other two (whose messages I have happily revised and corrupted, and have continually questioned and at times rejected, and have used as and how I wished to suit my own needs and conditions and whims), I have carried her image with me almost unaltered, as accompaniment to many of my waking moments, and as a source of inspiration in not a few of the numberless things I have thought and said and done. Happily too she was eventually to become for me a powerful and effective muse just as Beatrice Portinari had been for Dante, and the lady known as Laura was to be for Petrarca, though at that time I had no such hopes nor inclination that she should come to serve me in such a way. But here again, as always, and as I shall doubtless continue to do until my history is finally ended, I find myself running ahead of my tale.

For that, dear reader, is the conclusion of my chronicle of the passing of the comet, and of the things, both wondrous and terrible, both good and bad, that it brought to our lives. I am glad to tell that we all of us survived it - Giotto, Domenico, Paraveredus and the other members of the *bottega*, Messer Dante (though the course of his life had been irreparably altered), and myself - every one of us lived to tell the tale of what he had seen. My master, although arguably he had been disproved by events in his interpretation of the significance of the comet, had nevertheless been right in what he had said to Messer Dante that night in the *bottega*. As he had predicted, the agents of disorder had not harmed us, too occupied had they been in doing harm to each other, and in their ignorance of what they were doing, to themselves.

While we of its denizens were to emerge from that nightmare mostly untouched and undamaged, the commune of Florence itself was not to escape so lightly from its dreams of independence from Papal Rome. Within days of that time the troubles had subsided and some semblance of order had returned to the city, the self-righteous anger of the masses having been first cajoled and steered in the service of the installation of a new Black Signoria, and then - as is always the way in such things - just as adroitly subdued and appeased in order to ensure its future success. As a result, Florence was to remain in one way or another in thrall to the Papacy. Until that is, it was to be relieved of that sufferance by the infliction of yet another scourge, and one so terrible that in its throes the thoughts of men turned only to their own salvation, leaving no room in their hearts for ideals or allegiances, either to temporal powers or to other men.

-OO-

And what were the lessons I learned from that, my first introduction to the world of human politics? Firstly, and this despite my misguided opinion of my own importance (as indeed I had possessed the wit to comprehend in my conversation with Domenico, but of which brief insight I had not then taken heed), that the world revolved not around myself, or my insignificant hopes and aspirations, but around the actions and wishes of other, more powerful men. I realised then, more than I have ever since, that my only hope of attaining fortune or influence during my mortal existence was in the pursuance and fulfilment of my humble craft. Whatever influence I might hope to exert in Heaven, should I ever attain that place, for that, I reasoned, I would have to wait and see.

Then of course there were the three visitations which came to inform and confound me. What can I tell you of what I made of each of them?

As for the first, the comet, though at the time it seemed to shape the very fabric of my days and being, its influence upon me over the ensuing years was to prove no more than illusory. As you have seen though, the events unfolding around me had provided evidence sufficient to confirm me in all my misconceptions of its import and worth. As soon as I was able to see it in relation to the things which truly shaped and governed my life, I realised I could usurp such omens - just as every other person did - to support whatever purpose I wanted, and I took it therefore to be no more than confirmation of those things I had already suspected or known.

The second (though he should more correctly be termed the third, for it was during our second meeting that he would come to share with me his wisdom), Dante was to provide some little light to brighten my shaded ignorance, and with the scant consolation of knowing I was not alone in my sufferance of the joys and agonies (those sweet and painful passions whose pleasures I would not have missed for all the riches in the world), which were the gifts bestowed upon me by the passage through my life of the sweet angel-child with whom I was so deeply smitten, and who, of those three visitations in Florence, was the third.

Together, with the passage of time, I have come to look upon them, with what some might deem too prideful affection, as the great Trinity of my childhood. The first, the *cometis stella*, I see as having been the Annunciation to my virginal spirit of my then unconsummated, and soon to be shattered dreams; and just as the Annunciation of the coming of our Saviour heralded the awaited redemption of a sinful world, so the comet was to serve as *exordium* to my own far more humble catharsis, which this my equally humble story is. The second (and here I hold to my revised chronology, placing Dante last, and for you my sorely tested reader, still in the future), that I can but read as an Adoration, though in truth it was an adoration of the flesh as much as of the divine spirit I believed to have discovered incarnate within it. This debasement it may have been that was to deprive the more honest passion I felt for the spirit of its efficacy, and which for much of my life was to prove my undoing in many of the ways I ventured to use it. Sadly, the image I held of the object of my worship, though she herself was divine in nature, was and remained tainted by the more carnal memories manifest at the moment in which my passion for her was conceived.

And what of my third visitation, my second meeting with Dante? That, of course, to continue in my blasphemous analogy, was to be my Revelation, providing me with some understanding of the conflicting ardours I had found myself subject to as a result of my Adoration. But that, consoling as it was, was not the only divine wisdom which he, as supernatural agent of disclosure was to impart to me. (And I call him that expressly, to suit the purposes of my profane imagery, for though I know him to have been merely human, many spoke of him, as a consequence of his *Commedia*, as the man who had walked in and had returned from Hell.) He was to reveal to me knowledge of things within myself of which I had hitherto never suspected, and of the ambitions which motivated Dante himself in his writing, and which, though not revealing itself in him so strongly, also motivated my master in his own art. This knowledge gave birth within me to new drives and hungers, demanding as such things do to be satisfied, and which motivation I have struggled with for all my days and with all my might in my vain efforts to make it my own.

Of that revelation, and what I was to make of that received wisdom, I shall now try to tell.

-OO-

PADUA 1304-1305

"The most miserable misfortune is to have been happy once"

Boethius, *De Consolatione Philosophiae*

Such is my story so far; the first chapter of my book has been written. Whether you have found some little pleasure in its reading, that I will never know. Yet despite the doubts I have harboured while toiling in its preparation, I can but hope it is so, and that my labours have brought you both pleasure and some measure of understanding, both of myself, and of the world as I saw it as a boy at the onset of his future path through life. In this, as in all things, I remain but a servant to the needs of others.

Perhaps, though, and irrespective of its more worthy intentions, it is I who have received the greatest pleasure in the telling of my story, and in the recollection of my childhood days, and of the people I then knew. In truth, however, if I were to measure it in terms, not of pleasure given or received, but of the physical and spiritual anguish it has cost me, I must confess I have found my task far more demanding than I could ever have envisaged it to be. Who would have thought such onerous labours lay concealed in the seemingly gentle and reflective art of writing? Certainly not such an inattentive fool as I.

Was it not Boccaccio (himself a producer of many and copious volumes, and another of those bright stars who have blessed our age, and who I have seen born and blaze into glory, and whom I have long out-lived), who claimed that to aspire to the honours of this world was to the favour of those who gave themselves to the art of poetry? If that were true then I would have found the compilation of these words an effortless occupation, and would have arranged them in far better order, and far more poetically than I see myself to have done.

For it cannot be that I am alone in suffering in the pursuance of such labours; that I am the only one whose fingers grow weary in dictating to the stubborn ink the edifying course it must wend each day across the equally recalcitrant paper, or whose mind labours, also to the point of painful reluctance, as it strains to recall those miscible facts and details - the names and faces, the dates and places, the events and conversations - just as they were, and as they took place then, and not as they occur to me now, willy-nilly as I am writing, and scrambled and addled by the decades of doubt that have since passed to cloud my mind. If it is truly so, that such pains are the natural reward of all who write, I can only say from my brief and wearisome experience of that art, that I am glad to have lived my life as I have - as a painter, and in study - and not as a man of words.

So saying, with pen in hand, and with my mind replete with more than it can hold without confusion, and taking consolation in the knowledge that a thing sought with greater effort is come upon with far greater sense of reward, I resume my narrative, not on the day following where I left it, nor even during the mutable weeks and months which followed that time of fire and bloodshed. Instead, I leap through time, as though it really were of no consequence to me, to pick up the thread of my story some three years later. By then, the precocious child I had been had become a no less precocious youth, and he, and Domenico, and all the other members of the *bottega* (though not Paraveredus, for by then he had left us, though I believe he was not yet dead), had transferred together with all our possessions and various equipment from Florence to Padua where we were to assist our master in the execution of a series of frescoes depicting and glorifying the lives of the Virgin and of Christ.

This grand commission was to be carried out for one Enrico Scrovegni, knight and citizen of Padua, and was to be made in a small chapel which Scrovegni had recently contracted to have built on a site situated within the precincts of the Roman arena whose ruins can still be found in that town to this day. For that reason we came to call the chapel the Arena Chapel, despite our knowing that in the ceremony of dedication some two years previously the ground and all that would be built upon it had been assigned to the service of Santa Maria del Carita, and that I believe was then its real and proper name.

Needless to say, our transfer to Padua was for all of us a time of great turmoil and excitement, but although it was for me a marvellous adventure, I do not intend to relate here the details of that otherwise inconsequential journey. As I have said, I plan to relate the story of a much greater journey that I was to undertake many years later, and in comparison to which our passage to Padua was but a merry excursion. Suffice it to say that travelling in consort as we were, and laden down with our equipment and possessions, and in the heat and dust of the waning summer, our train did not make good progress and our journey to Padua took several days to complete.

-OO-

And how much should I tell you of the work we then did when we arrived finally in Padua at the end of the summer of the year thirteen hundred and four? For I must admit the temptation is there, and that I find it difficult to resist it, to set down all I know regarding the details of my craft and of the techniques natural to a painter - to list all of these things in their scope and multiplicity, in the hope you might find such dry facts as fascinating, and would find in such knowledge the same reward and satisfactions as did I. But I know that I must, and that it is right I should resist it, for of what use or of what interest could such things possibly be to you?

What would it benefit you to know how and where we erected the scaffolding, from which cramped rigging of ropes and beams and boards we worked to paint the highest rows of paintings and to reach the higher arch of the ceiling? Or how we set out the designs for our work upon the layer of plaster known to us as the *arricciato* (which is the second layer, and is laid upon the *rinzafatto*, and upon which is drawn the outline drawing, the *sinopia* of whatever is to be made), thus dividing the walls into the panels on which our master was to devise his creations; or how we marked out between those panels the borders and friezes which we apprentices and *pictors* were to decorate with patterns and geometrics, and with depictions of the vices and virtues, and with the faces and images of the lives of the saints, so that by the time our combined labours there had been completed, the whole of the inner surface of that chapel would come to be covered in an unbroken layer of wondrously applied and crafted paint? And what purpose would it serve in my story to make here a list of the pigments we employed in the making of those glorious pictures, and of the substances we did not use, their colours being too readily degraded by exposure to air or water, usually to impassionate black; or of the problems to be encountered in the preparation and application of those pigments, and of the tools and brushes and implements we used to achieve that glorious end?

What more than that of the intricacies of the trade I was learning do I need to tell? For in having mentioned it at all I wished only to convey something of the great joys and passions the wielding of such powers of creation aroused within me, and of the labours and skills it was necessary for us to master, and to show that although I had not been so very long with the bottega I had made much progress in acquiring knowledge in those very techniques and materials, and in the good and true application of my trade.

-OO-

From what I had heard of him (and Domenico and I were expert at unearthing such sordid information about our pious patrons), our new employer had inherited much of his wealth from his father. As the father before him had done, this gratuitous fortune had then been further increased through the practice of usury, which as you are aware is a grievous sin. Indeed, the father, Rinaldo Scrovegni, was to be placed by Dante in his *Commedia* among those many who were condemned to suffer for eternity in the deepest regions of nether Hell. The chapel in Padua was being built therefore, and our humble services were being paid for by the proceeds of this ill-assembled fortune, and it was as well when it came to such things that my master did not permit himself to be restricted in his choice of labours by any sentiments of piety or shame. As for the reasons for our labours, the chapel and the things that were to be done in it were intended to serve as penance for the trespasses of the successive generations of the family - firstly to prevent the son from befalling the same miserable ending as the father, and secondly to wrest the soul of the already dead and suffering father from the jaws of Hell. To this salutary end, Scrovegni had made it known in his contract with my master that in the paintings that were to be done in the chapel particular emphasis was to be placed upon the depiction of the sins of usury and greed.

After the ceiling had been completed, and in keeping with our practice of working always from above to below, my master began work on the wall of the chapel immediately above its entrance. There, in accordance with tradition, he painted the Day of Judgement, with Christ seated in the centre in a *mandorla* surrounded by his angels and flanked by the twelve Apostles, his hands held out in gestures respectively of welcome and dismissal, on one side to the blessed and on the other to the damned. To satisfy the wishes of his patron he had also painted a likeness of Scrovegni himself in the lower centre of this composition, kneeling at the foot of the instrument of crucifixion. There he could be seen offering a representation of the chapel to the Madonna, she reaching out to accept his offering and to lead him further along the path of righteousness he had travelled to be in her gracious presence, and from which the souls of the dead could be seen rising up to be judged.

To the right of the cross, and close by this act of repentance, the figure of Judas was to be seen hanging by the neck from his tree, his tunic torn open in the French manner of showing him, and with his bowels spilling onto the ground. I will tell you here that it was not coincidence that directed my master to paint this sorry figure (who, like the Scrovegni, had sold his soul for the profit of silver), precisely there in the vicinity of the head of our patron, whose own lips were shown parted in the act of confession, and close to the model of the chapel, and to the very jaws of Satan himself. Neither was it happenstance that had directed how these several things should all lie on the same level in that great construction. They had been placed that way deliberately, such that the eye of all who looked upon it - in revealing to the soul what simple lessons were to be drawn from such profusion - could not help but make a line of association through those things my master wished to portray as being joined by the same malign cause and remorseful intent.

-OO-

Being but an apprentice, I was not to have much contact with our patron, but I remember well one of the first occasions on which I was given the opportunity to see him and hear him speak, for it afforded me great insight and understanding, both of the manner of thinking of my master, and into the meaning of the things he was trying to create in Padua. Scrovegni had come that day to inspect our progress, and it was during the time we were engaged in work on the triumphal arch above the entrance to the choir at the rear of the chapel, that is, on the wall opposite the entrance, and which was the thing on which we worked after the Last Judgement had been completed.

From what I recall, Scrovegni was a somewhat drawn and sallow man, with high rounded cheek-bones and sunken jowls, and a fine but lengthy nose projecting forwards, which things, when combined together made of his eyes two dark recesses set deep into the paleness of his face. He was too uncommonly tall from what I remember (though this conception may well have arisen only as a result of my own diminutive stature, because from where I looked out on the world everyone was seen to be tall - even by now, poor, crippled Domenico), and he was as lean in his limbs and body as he was in his face.

As for the work he had come to witness, we had already finished the things filling that part of the lunette above the archway and beneath the higher arch of the ceiling, and there He who determines all could now be seen enthroned in His glory, dispatching the Archangel to convey His ineffable Word to the Virgin Maria. That thing being completed, my master was now occupied on the depiction of the Annunciation. This he had divided boldly into two, and had placed the protagonists, Gabriel on one side of the round of the archway leading to the choir, Maria on the other, and not as is more usual, with both depicted in the same image.

"The sense of physical connection you have created between the figures is exceptional, despite their physical separation," Scrovegni called up to my master. "There is still the sense of Maria receiving God's Word direct from the Angel." Messer Giotto put down the brushes and pigments he was using and descended the ladder to join his patron, going to where he was standing in the middle of the chapel.

"Yes, I feel the effect of the architecture works well, and is not unpleasing to the eye," he said, referring to the two turrets he had placed, one beside each of the figures, and which structures - in defiance of the laws of true perspective - projected towards rather than away from the centre of the archway, thereby seeming to draw together the two separated halves of the scene.

"Indeed. It is far from painful to look at," Scrovegni agreed. "But please, I feel we need to discuss again how you plan to complete this. Your preparatory drawings are more than clear, and the scheme appears to be according to my wishes, but I would like to see if I can imagine it here, in situ, where I can see it before my face."

I am certain everyone there that day had been aware of the presence of Scrovegni as soon as he had entered the chapel. We were all of us inquisitive by nature, and were always curious to see and to know more of this man for whom we worked. When he uttered these words however, I for one (and I doubt I was alone in my reactions) strained and listened, though feigning occupation still in my labours, to hear what my master would say in reply. Above and beyond our improper interests in the ways and habits of the elusive Scrovegni, we of the *bottega* were ever curious to know what we could of the great works in which we were involved.

"Below the Archangel of the Annunciation, the Pact of Judas will be depicted on the wall at the left of the arch," my master began to explain. "And on the other wall, below the Virgin, will be the meeting of Maria and Elisabeth. Below these will be the two vaulted chambers symbolising Death."

As I record this, I realise these words may mean little to those of you who are not as well-trained in the visualisation of form and physical space as I, unless that is you are among those who have had the good fortune to have visited that chapel in Padua. Perhaps therefore it would be wiser, before I go further in relating the conversation Giotto was to have with his patron explaining the decoration of the chapel, if I were first to describe the internal structure of that building, how the walls and windows and the things within it had been arranged.

The building itself was not large, the nave being little more than thirty *braccia* in length, and between the two side walls, eleven or twelve *braccia* in width. From the floor to the highest point of the ceiling, it was less than twenty *braccia* high. On the wall above the entrance was to be found, as I have told you, the Last Judgement, and opposite it, the triumphal arch on which my master was working, through which one passed to the choir, though at that time that part of the chapel had not yet been built. On the right-hand side as one entered, six windows had been let into the wall at equal intervals. The recesses for these started somewhat above the average height of a man and extended upwards almost to the beginning of the arc of the ceiling. The wall opposite however had in it not a single window, and this was of course an uncommon thing, for usually light would have been admitted from all directions to illuminate the interior of such a building. But as I have said, the chapel in Padua had been designed this way expressly to suit our singular purposes, which was to decorate as much as possible the entirety of the surfaces of its internal walls.

To this end each of the side walls of the main chamber were to be divided into three bands of paintings, the bottom two of which together were the same height as the recesses for the windows, and the third of which began above the windows and curved over partially onto the ceiling, being the same height as the other two. With this singular arrangement two scenes could be fitted in each of the spaces between the windows, one above the other. On the opposite wall the two bands at this level, as was the upper band, were to be divided into six equal portions, all of the same dimensions as the five panels on the other wall. The difference in the length of the surface that was to be painted, which arose by virtue of the omission of the windows, was to be made up by the insertion of five panels of decoration between the narrative episodes, and a further such panel at each end of the wall. Each of the two lower bands on these walls was to consist therefore of eleven paintings, and the upper of twelve.

The middle one of these bands corresponded to the level on the end wall occupied by the Pact of Judas, and by the Visitation, and was to contain scenes illustrating the infancy of Christ. The lower band, which corresponded to the two sepulchral chambers my master had mentioned, was to depict the images of His Passion and Crucifixion. As I have said, the upper band on each wall had been similarly divided into six panels, and these had already been given over, the one on the right to the lives of Joachim and Anna, and the other to the life of Maria and her betrothal to Joseph. Apart from the thirty-four episodes of which these three bands were to consist, there was also the Last Judgement, and the seven things that were to be painted on the triumphal arch, that is, God in His Heaven and the two portions of the Annunciation, the Pact of Judas and the Visitation, and the two chambers representing Death.

"Everything is caused by, and begins and ends with God," my master continued, pointing at the vision of the Almighty he had rendered high on the triumphal arch. "He sends the Archangel, first to Anna and Joseph, to announce to them the child that their daughter Maria is to conceive of God." As he spoke, he indicated along the length of the highest band on the right-hand wall, turning as he did towards the Last Judgement and following with his out-stretched hand the sequence of images that had already been completed there.

"We follow the lives, first of Anna and Joseph…, then of Maria…," he said slowly, turning again, and pointing now along the other wall, to return once more to the triumphal arch, "…and through her we return once more to God."

As I watched my master turn bodily to follow the sequence of the paintings, I understood how - once the work was completed - any observer who wished to grasp its meaning would have to turn himself in similar fashion to follow and comprehend the sequence of the stories that were being told. I saw too that by performing such movements, the mortal man who came here but to pray for salvation would of necessity become a part of that story's great unravelling, and in doing so could not help but find himself involved in the physical reality of what had taken place. The spectator would no longer be but a spectator; he would participate. He would walk, and be born, and rejoice and suffer, and then be born again through the love of Jesus Christ, there in those various scenes and episodes, and placed at all times at his blessed redeemer's side.

"God sends his angel again, to announce to Maria the incarnation of His spirit that is to take place within her flesh. The final episode on the side wall before we come to the Annunciation will be the Return of the Virgin, which event precedes the Annunciation and confirms that Maria has not had knowledge of a man. In the Annunciation, Gabriel is placed at the right-hand side of God, for he is the symbol of the Divine Spirit, the mean operating between God the agent and the object, which is Man. Maria is the symbol of the mortal flesh, fallen from grace to suffer death through the original sin of Eve's disobedience, though made pure again through her own obedience in performing God's will. She is therefore placed at His left-hand side."

"Is a connection to be made then between Maria and Joachim's expulsion from the Temple?" Scrovegni asked, referring to the first episode that had been painted on the right hand side wall, immediately beside the Annunciate Virgin.

"Yes, if only by contrast, for one is a scene of acceptance, the other of rejection. Maria turns towards God, her spiritual father, and away from her earthly father Joachim. Joachim's glance, as he turns to look back at the priest directing him from the Temple, is as much at her as at the priest. The physical presence of the Temple, and by inference its written laws of old, and the fact of Joachim's existence in the physical world, as symbolised by the secular tower at the right of the Annunciation, also stands between Maria and her father, keeping them apart. Father and daughter represent respectively the old Law and the new way to salvation that is heralded by the coming of Christ. The church is the mean which stands between them, though acting in a negative fashion, being as it was, resistant to such change."

As I listened to this exchange, I marvelled at the myriad correlations my master was able to discern among his seemingly purely narrative images. I had thought them little more than illustrations of the various episodes which went to make up the lives of the Holy family, but I was discovering how he had embodied in them a wealth of dogmas and ideologies, which though concealed with great subtlety within the imagery, were there to be read and interpreted by those who had the knowledge and the inclination to understand. My own new understanding of the work we were doing filled my soul with equal measures of awe and joy.

"But what of the two things below the Annunciation?" Scrovegni asked, pointing at the empty spaces on the wall. "I still do not understand why you wish to juxtapose the Pact of Judas with the meeting of Maria and Elisabeth, and why you choose to show his act of treachery other than in its proper place."

"Is it not your wish that this should serve as expiation?" my master replied, gesturing to the chapel around him. Scrovegni bowed his head.

"That is true," he said, and turned to look around the chapel to see who, if any of us, might be paying heed to their conversation. As he looked up towards where I was I pulled back behind the edge of the high scaffolding from which I was working. I do not think he saw me, or if he did he made no comment to my master, and as the others were all to be seen and heard, outwardly at least, to be involved in their labours, I do not think he noticed anything untoward.

"Depicted here on the archway, the sins of Judas will be seen immediately by all who enter the chapel, and will continue to confront them during the time they remain," my master resumed, moving closer to the left-hand wall of the triumphal arch.

"But Judas was not a usurer," his patron protested quietly.

"That is true. But he entered into a contract made at the expense of another, for his own gain, and a parallel can be made therefore between his crime and the transactions you wish to make atonement for. Adjacent to the Pact, on the side wall, to emphasise such an association, will be shown the money-lenders being expelled from the Temple. In that scene there will be two Pharisees." As he spoke he reached up to indicate the angle the side wall made with the wall of the archway. "Here, adjacent to, but standing aside from the figure of Judas selling his soul."

"And what purpose will they serve?"

"The same two personages will appear in the Pact itself, again distanced from the transaction yet culpable by their presence, and contriving through the treachery of Judas to bring their strict doctrine to bear forth its stubborn fruit. But the Pact can also be seen as a representation of the meeting of two opposing ideologies. Firstly, that of the old Law, as personified by the self-righteous Pharisees, who are striving to maintain its strict observance, purchasing the help of Judas to protect its threatened interests; and secondly, that of the new faith, and the promise of spiritual redemption to be found in Christ's incarnation in the flesh, and which - in spite of his doubts and treachery - is also embodied in Judas himself. It allows us also to see that evil exists, and has to be overcome, in both the old and the new. This confrontation between the old and new can be seen again in the Visitation. In that meeting Elisabeth represents the old world of the prophets, of whom the son she is bearing, John the Baptist, will be the last, while Maria, and the child Christ she is bearing inside her, are representative of the new."

"I am still confused. How then are we to read these things in their correct sequence when the treachery of Judas is so removed from its proper place?" Scrovegni asked, looking around him in some consternation at the blank walls.

Again my master proceeded to draw his attention around the as yet unpainted sequence of images, pointing out to him how, moving from the Annunciation, one was led first to the scene of the Visitation below it, and from there to the side walls where the life of Christ, commencing with the Nativity in Bethlehem, was to be represented in the eleven panels that were to make up the middle band I have already described. The last episode of this sequence was to be the cleansing of the Temple, and this, as you have heard, was to be symbolically coupled with the Pact of Judas adjacent to it. From the Pact, it was necessary for the attention of the observer to pass from the archway to the beginning of the lowest band of paintings, where, starting beneath the Nativity, were to be shown the events of the Passion which had ensued from that betrayal - namely, Christ before Caiaphas, His mockery at the hands of the soldiers, His passage along the road to Calgary, culminating in His Crucifixion, the Piéta and *Noli me Tangere*, and finally His ascension to Heaven. The last episode in this sequence however was not to be Christ resurrected, but of the disciples being blessed with the gift of tongues at the feast of Pentecost, from whence they went out to prepare mankind for the day of Judgement, the image of which was to be seen above the door through which all had to pass as they departed from the chapel.

Once my master had finished describing the sequence of the paintings Scrovegni took him by the arm and led him from the chapel. They passed below me and out of ear-shot, leaving me to contemplate on the things that were to come in that place, and to try to envision the various scenes I had heard described but which had not yet been brought into being on the unmarked plaster. In vain did I try to picture the characters and the various faces that would soon be shown there - their gestures, and the moments they would be enacting, the way in which their actions and thoughts would interact and come together to bring about the telling of the life, the Passion and Death, and the resurrection of our Saviour.

All I saw before me, however, was the blank expanse of unpainted walls and plaster. I did not yet possess the depth of painterly vision which my master had perfected through his own years of practice and acquiring the knowledge of his craft. All of that depiction of the sublime legend lay for me still in the future, as did the events I am yet to describe, and which, as you will see, were likewise to shape and colour the progress of my own much less impeccable life.

-OO-

Now it is not everyone who is blessed with such good fortune as to have had as teacher one as great and as skilled as I. During the years I spent as an apprentice at the *bottega* (and I was to stay with Messer Giotto until my twenty-fifth year) it was my required task to learn from him those skills which he in his turn had learned under Cimabue, as he likewise had done by dint of rote and example, and to acquire the ability to copy and emulate his style and manner of working as well and as faithfully as I could. To this end I, and indeed all of the craftsmen and *dipintori* who worked for him, were involved in daily practice and repetition of his methods, and this manner of learning was to prove so effective that when I was considered accomplished enough to work together with our master and with those others on the production of a panel, or in fresco - one of us painting the heads and faces, one the robes, one perhaps the trees and buildings, another the beasts and creatures of the field - it was impossible to see that it had not all been produced by one, solitary hand.

During the first months of my training I studied nothing more than how to draw good likenesses from Nature, and the correct manner of preparation and working of the pigments and materials I would use in the execution of my profession, and how to recognise good materials from bad. Once I had come to master these essentials (for I was taught that a man might not call himself a craftsman, nor say that of himself with an honest voice without first having acquired a full understanding of the materials of his craft), I learned how to create in fresco and in tempera the hands and feet and limbs of the human body, and the folds of materials that draped them, doing them in such a way as to suggest the human form enclosed within them, and also how to portray the face and head, replete with all its expressions, and its varying degrees of beauty, emotions and age. Somewhere in between the learning of these most vital capacities I must have learned too how to create the forms of buildings, and of rocks and trees, and the landscapes in which to enclose those human figures, and to create the illusions of depth and space upon the walls or panels on which we were working, and in which the characters we portrayed and the events they enacted were to be placed. Such lessons though, essential and as equally repetitive as they must have been, I cannot remember receiving, and it seems to me now that I have always created such illusions as if by second nature, though it must have been so that I was taught this, and have often taught the same tricks to others since.

One lesson though I remember quite clearly. It took place not so very long after our arrival in Padua, while my master was busy rendering the lives of the Holy Virgin, and of Joachim and Anna on the uppermost row of paintings on the two longer walls of the chapel. I too had played some part in the work which had thus far been completed, having assisted in making the decorative panels and borders of the ceiling, and also the ceiling itself, where I had painted several gold stars that shone there as though truly fixed in that bluest of Heavens. I had also been allowed to try my hand at the robes of the saints who looked down on our endeavours from roundels drawn in the ceiling, and these I felt I had rendered more than passably, even if in saying so I know I am guilty of the supreme arrogance of calling down praise upon myself.

On this particular day my master was working on one of the scenes from the lives of Anna and Joachim, though I can no longer remember exactly which episode of that cycle it was. Possibly it was the Vision of Joachim, or perhaps it was of him making a sacrifice, for I recall only the completed figures of an angel, and some shepherds, and several sheep grazing on a hill. In any case, and from what I remember, all that remained was for the head and face of Joachim to be painted, and his robed body and the portion of ground around him on which he sat. My task that day was simply to prepare and mix the pigments, and to keep clean and have ready to hand such brushes and materials as were needed while my master performed the work required to make the head.

By the time I had finished grinding and apportioning the necessary quantities of the various pigments, the plasterer we employed for that purpose had already laid in and rubbed down the fresh layer of *intonaco*, and smoothed and wetted it so it lay even with the rest of the finished surface of the wall. It was not even necessary for us to draw in the vertical lines and dimensions we usually made to give our work its correct proportions. It was only the head we were doing, and the *sinopia* of the body of Joachim was visible on the area of the *arriccio* which was yet to be painted, providing a reference. It was enough therefore that my master first marked out the lines of the nose, brow and cheek-bones with some *sinopia* applied on a finely-pointed brush.

When he was ready to proceed further, I began to prepare a *verdaccio* (which is made from dark ochre, lime white and *cinabrese*, mixed with black in water, without the use of tempera), and with this he painted in the shape and details of the face. This he achieved by applying the pigment most sparingly on a brush from which most of the colour had been squeezed out between his finger and thumb, and when it was done, even though he had applied no more than a few lines and areas of colour to the plaster, the general countenance of the face, and even some indications of its expression were plain enough to see. Having finished it he stepped away, to see if what he had painted was in correct proportion to the body, and to the other figures in the scene.

"What do you think, is it in good proportion?" he asked when he had finished studying it from several angles. I looked at it, turning my head this way and that, and found - even with my comparatively untrained eye - that he had made the nose a little too short in relation to the brow.

"Should the nose not be a little longer?" I said. "Or perhaps the height of the brow should be reduced."

"Is there something wrong then with how I have shown it?"

I realised then that these questions were designed only to test me, and I proceeded to explain what I knew of the proportions of the human body: that the face was divided into three equal portions, namely the height of the brow, of the nose, and from the end of the nose to the chin, and that this measure governed also the distance from the side of the nose to the end of the eye, and from that point of the eye to the ear. I told him too of the relative lengths of the face and throat, and of the parts and limbs of the body, and that because the features of the face were but parts of one greater whole they would all be seen equally distorted from the ground, and that even when shown thus foreshortened they should remain subject to the same readily observable rules and proportions.

"That is so. Everything must remain in proportion to the whole," he said, when I had finished reciting this catechism of our craft, and asking for a brush with its bristles filled with water he proceeded to wash out the uppermost portion of what he had painted of Joachim's brow.

"Is that better?" he asked once he had made his corrections, and I turned my head from side to side to appraise the changes he had made then nodded approval, though in truth it was still far from perfect. Sensing perhaps my lack of conviction, he smiled and nodded to me in agreement, and added that he would determine the final ratio when it came to painting the hair.

He asked me then to mix up some *terra-verte*, and with this he commenced to fill in the shading on the side of the face which was to be in shadow, and under the brow and cheek-bones, and beside the length of the nose. All of this under-painting he did quite sparsely, covering only small areas, again with most of the pigment squeezed from the head of the brush. The whole of the face having been picked out in this way, he then sharpened up the outlines of the features, again using the *verdaccio* I had made. I then prepared for him some lime-white and a light *cinabrese* mixed in equal proportions. This I made into a thin solution in water, and with the pink these made he touched in the lips and the bloom of the forehead and of the left cheek (for if I am not mistaken the face was to be shown in fore-shortened profile), and the latter of these blooms he placed closer to the ear than to the nose, just so that the face might acquire a greater illusion of depth.

Now the face of Joachim was not that of a young man, and I had mixed all of the colours as my master had instructed, that is a shade or two darker than would have been required for the complexion of a younger man. I now took three other dishes and in them made up portions of flesh colours of differing values, continuing as before with this practice of darkening the shades, the darkest of the three being half as light again as was the pink, the next one degree lighter again, and the third one degree lighter still. I asked my master why he painted these flesh tints in separately and directly onto the *verdaccio*, as this was contrary to what I had been told during the meagre lessons in our art that I had received in Pistoia. There I had been taught that the best way was to first give the whole face a wash of a single flesh colour, then to shape up the features by creating the shadows they formed with the *verdaccio*, and to finish it by touching in the highlights with a little colour, or with white.

"That is not a good way to work. You must take care to keep each shade in its correct position. If you do not, your work will be dull and lacking in brilliance," he said as he examined the three mixtures I had prepared, to check they were of the colour and consistency he required. Finding them to his satisfaction, he returned with them to the wall.

"With each colour the brush should follow its course uninterrupted. It should not leave the surface on which you are working, other than to blend areas of colour that are adjacent, so that the change from one to the next is not too abrupt."

Using the lighter of the shades I had made, he then began to pick out the half-tones of the face, and with the darkest, to develop the depths of the shadows. Slowly, as he blended one tone into another with sure and flowing movements of his brush, the face began to take shape, in such a way that by the time he had finished - as he had said they must - each colour ran perfectly into the next. This he continued to do over and over until the shape of the face was well constructed, then taking another flesh colour that was barely more than white, he applied the final highlights to the line of the nose, and to the eyelids and brow. The hair and beard he had left until last, and he now marked these in first with some *verdaccio*, then shaped the turns and folds of the hair in white, and also the way it fell around the head and face, correcting too in this manner the proportions of the brow. Taking next some lime white which I had darkened slightly to grey with lamp-black, he then painted in the individual folds of the hair and beard, and those parts where shadows would naturally fall. Finally, he went over the reliefs of these hairs with a sharp minever brush.

The face and head being completed, he proceeded to paint around it a golden halo, using a colour that is good for making gold known as orpiment, mixing this for himself as it was poisonous and considered too dangerous for an inexperienced apprentice to handle. When this was done, he then made good the areas all around the halo so that the new work blended in with what had already been done, and the new colours corresponded to those already existing, matching them on the wall only by the efficacy of his eye.

It is possible that on the following day I also assisted in the painting of the robed body of Joachim, but if I were to say it was so it would not be in the certainty of knowing what I said was true. In general, though, this was the way we worked throughout that winter, although it was not always I who was afforded the honour of assisting directly in the things Giotto was making, and I was often to be found occupied in much less rewarding endeavours. Nevertheless, by the spring of the following year, in good time for the ceremony of consecration of the chapel, we had - by the combined application of our various skills and resources - completed work, not only on the ceiling, and the on Last Judgement and Annunciation, but also on the whole of that upper-most tier of scenes below the ceiling, such that every one of the images relating to the Annunciation was finished in time for the celebration of that feast. As for the walls of the chapel, they had yet to be painted, and to disguise this fact and to make the interior of the chapel more worthy of such a celebration, Messer Scrovegni had occasion to write to the High Council in Venice. From there he procured the loan of several tapestries and hangings, under which trappings we were able to hide and adorn the bare intrusion of the unpainted walls.

As soon as the ceremony of consecration was over work began in earnest on the depiction of the infancy of Christ. I have to relate though that I was not to be involved for long in the production of the first of those paintings, being required instead to go to Bologna, there to purchase pigments that were sorely needed, and were not to be found in Padua, at least not of the colour and quality my master required. At first I was disappointed to have been the one chosen to run this errand, for that is what I at first saw it to be, but when I came to realise the great responsibility I had been entrusted with, I made haste to leave for Bologna with little more than a twinge of regret that I was not to be a part of those endeavours pinching at the sinews of my heart.

If the truth were to be known, my reluctance to leave Padua had been alleviated further by the knowledge that on my arrival in Bologna I was to deliver a letter from my master addressed to none other than Messer Dante Alighieri, who was then (as he was to continue to be for the remainder of his life) living under the sentence of death imposed upon him by the Black Priors of Florence. Being unable to return to the city he loved and which he had served so well, he had been forced to embark upon a life of wandering and was to be found at that time earning a living, though not one befitting his wisdom and learning, as a teacher in Bologna. Now, after my many months of speculation, I was to meet the man face to face.

First however I had other duties to perform in that city, and on my arrival there I immediately made my way to the offices of the *Arte dei Medici e degli Speziali*, to assay and purchase there the quantities of *giallorino* and *cinabrese* my master required me to buy.

-OO-

I have always had a great love of the offices and shops of the *Arte dei Medici*, having found them always (and this is true from what my memory tells me of every apothecary's shop I have ever had cause to enter), to be not only pleasure palaces for the senses, but to be places too full of wonder and enlightenment. In them, once the powers of vision have become accustomed to the veiled light which seems always to pervade those dusty caverns, one is greeted by a profusion of sensations and images almost as soon as one passes through the door. Once inside, the eyes cannot help but struggle to prevail against the all-encroaching half-light, and being but the poor and inadequate organs they are, they invariably prove wanting in their efforts to take in all at once that diverse profusion. The nose too cannot pass unseduced from its journeys through such shaded cornucopias, for it too is pricked and teased by an air made thick with the aroma of spices and unguents gleaned and gathered from the four corners of the earth. The shop I had been directed to in Bologna was to prove to be no exception to this happy rule.

When I finally discovered its whereabouts amidst the bustle and commerce of that city, I presented myself at the awned and countered porch which fronted onto the Piazza Maggiore. Finding no one in attendance there I made my way into the store behind, my senses full of expectation. Inside the air was thick and viscid, and particles of dust hung and glittered in what poor illumination fell through the shallow lights (which were not glass, but *impannate*: oiled linen stretched upon a frame of wood), that had been set into the walls on one side just below the ceiling. Barely more potent beams of light entered through the narrow doorway I had just passed through and spilled around me to cut dull planes of brightness into the chamber's shadowed heart.

Along the left-hand wall of the room a rack of wooden shelving filled with pots and jars stretched from the front to the rear - a distance, I gauged, of some ten or twelve *braccia* - to where yet more shelving stood at right-angles to this first, behind the bench at which the apothecary prepared and measured out his wares. Another, narrower rack stood against the right-hand wall and this, like the others, reached almost from the floor to the ceiling. It too was similarly laden with containers of diverse sorts and sizes. From the ceiling itself a multitude of dried and fresh herbs hung down; bunches and clasps of parsley, chervil, fennel, sage and coriander; of marjoram and dill, and mint, tarragon, and thyme, and many more I did not know or recognise, and there too hung the shrivelled skins and skeletons of snakes and frogs and lizards, and of many other creatures that go about on their bellies on the ground.

Directly before the doorway stood a low wooden table laden with various goods and fancies - bunches and mounds of dried fruits and pulses, and pots of thick bee's honey and conserves, nuts and sweet confections, and deep bowls filled with ground peppers and coarse crystals of brown, clouded sugar. Here too were cordials and elec-tuaries and sweet-smelling balsams and unguents, and viscous salves and ointments and fragrant oils. On the floor around the table stood several sacks and jars of earthenware and majolica, and to either side, more jars, of odd and multifarious designs and sizes were ranged against the walls beside the door. Lifting the lid of one, I was greeted by the bitter smell of *camellina* - a creamy, white sauce rich with cloves and cinnamon - and another I discovered to be filled with *Savora Sanguigno*, dark and bitter and, as its name implies, the colour of blood.

Moving over to the rack which stood at my right, I saw assembled the materials pertaining to my own profession: here were arranged waxes and brushes of all types and qualities, and powdered lime for the preparation of *into-naco* and gesso; rolls of canvas and parchment, and bole and burnishers and leaf for gilding: styles for drawing and writing, and many different, brightly coloured inks. I recognised there straightaway the *sinopia* with which we made our preliminary drawings, and a *verdaccio* and various haematites and ochres, and also the particular *giallorino* for which I had been sent. There too I discovered quantities of lacca, malachite, azurite and vermillion, all of which I knew to be unsuitable for our current purposes in Padua, being colours that were not to be used for working on a wall.

At the end of this rack, and behind and to the right of the main chamber of the shop was a small annex, no more than five *braccia* in both its width and depth. On entering the shop I had not realised this space existed, hidden from sight as it had been behind the corner of the right-hand wall, which angle formed one side of its entrance. Here I discovered two great ovens ranged against its far wall, one of which was burning fiercely, and stacks of timber and charcoal to fire them, and behind the corner of the recess, a trestle on which stood two glass stills and various other vessels and glass alembics and retorts. The smell of wood-smoke and sulphur hung cloying and pungent in the air. In the centre of the room yet another table bore upon it a large mortar shaped from marble, and in this, suspended from a beam which ran from above the entrance to where it was set into the wall above the ovens, a brass pestle the size of a child's forearm hung down at the end of a length of rope. In one corner an entranceway led off into a long, dark corridor, and as the equipment in the annex was also unattended, I called out tentatively along this for someone to assist me, and having again received no answer made my way to the rear of the shop to wait.

Even in the broken light which filtered through to this anterior recess of the chamber, I could see that the shelving there bore upon it the apothecary's pharmacopoeia. I was able to make out on the labels, written in a faultless Latin script, the contents of the rows of glass phials and flagons - quicksilver and arsenic, thorax and aloes, theriaca, wormwood and saffron; permanganate of potash and flowers of sulphur, and also various clysters, purges, vomits, emetics and laxatives, and many other substances possessing qualities efficacious to both the body and soul. Seeing all of this, I almost felt in need myself of some one or more of these vivifiers and medications, my senses having been dazzled almost to the point of bemusement by the great profusion I saw and breathed in all around me.

As I came to the far end of the bench however, I discovered a far less wholesome object than any of the myriad others I had been perusing, and which from the moment I saw it I doubted could ever be employed to such salutiferous ends. For there, amidst bunches of dried leaves and flowers and grasses, and surrounded by books bound in goat-skin and vellum, itself encased in a stoppered glass jar and steeped in liquid the colour of amber, and with its long, dark hair wafting thickly above it, floated the severed and perfectly preserved head of a man.

"It is the head of a Saracen," a thin, wiry voice said behind me. "You can see that much in the colouring of the skin."

"Yes...of course," I replied uncertainly, turning to see who had addressed me, and discovering before me an old man who had appeared silently from among the ovens and stills. In appearance the apothecary - for that was who I presumed the old man to be - was as stooped and wiry as his voice, and his frail frame was lost and swathed within a copious gown which hung loosely about his narrow shoulders and trailed along behind him on the floor. His scrawny arms protruded from the folds of the gown and hung crooked at his sides, and on his hands he wore a pair of fingerless gloves. His vesture, I was persuaded, had once been of the deepest red. I could see that colour in the few places where the material had not been abused and corroded by the countless years of use to which it had obviously been subjected, but through the accumulation upon it of countless dye-stuffs, spices and pigments, the greater part of it had long since been reduced to the dull and motley colours more common to the oxides of iron. A black velvet cap, likewise worn and dusted, sagged upon his head and fell down over one ear, and a long black tassel hung too down that side of his face, balancing out the shank of thin, greying hair which tumbled down against the opposite side of his face.

"Of course, the coloration is due in some part to the fluid in which it is embalmed," he continued, "but you can see it is from an infidel by the particular darkness and shaping of the eye, and by the length and straightness of the nose. A fine specimen though, wouldn't you agree?"

"A fine specimen indeed," I replied, again uncertainly, as I looked at the head, not having any true reference to determine whether it was fine or not, and seeking signs that might mark the character and origin of the man whose features these once had been. But the eyes only stared back at me lifelessly, held open as they were, I now saw, by several sutures inserted behind the lids.

And how fine a specimen could a severed head possibly be, I wondered, for - infidel or not - there did not seem much that could be deemed praiseworthy in having come to such an ignominious end? The skin, as the old man had remarked, was the colour of copper and was stretched tight across the bones of the mouth and face, exposing the teeth, fixed in a terrible grin. I found it hard to believe it could ever have been that way while quickened by a mortal spirit, for its look was but a mockery of the expressions of the soul once held within it, and which power had in days gone by doubtless bent and twisted its features into those miens and grimaces which we rightly recognise as being characteristic of human life.

"It was taken at Constantinople in the year twelve hundred and four," the old man said. "By a knight, a Frenchman I believe, from Aquitaine. It was said he fell on hard times on his journey home and was forced to sell his relic before he could proceed beyond Rome. I bought it there for my own purposes, and have had it now for the past twenty years or more."

"Then it is over one hundred years old!" I cried in my astonishment at the age of the thing, for despite the uncommon colouring of the skin, and the hideous grimace set around the mouth, the man appeared to be still in his prime, and that this face had been but recently separated from its limbs and torso.

"He has attained a form of immortality, you might say. Therein lays the skill in the embalmer's art, to make a dead thing remain as though alive. The man, had he lived, would have been at least in his one hundred and thirtieth year," the apothecary agreed. "And no doubt still an infidel," he added with a sanctimonious air. "Such as they are not easily persuaded from their inborn lack of faith."

"Is it for sale?" I enquired, deliberately ignoring his remark, for I was not inclined to make such easy judgements, seeing before me as I did, not the head of a godless infidel, but simply that of a man.

"It is if you have the money to pay for it," he replied flatly, and at that he moved closer to me and began to sniff deeply at my hair and clothing, then taking my hand in his, he lifted it up from where it hung at my side, and without a word of apology or excuse, turned it over and began to run the tips of his fingers over my nails and knuckles. Then, turning it again, he traced out the creases below the joints of the fingers and in the flesh of my palm.

"Ha! I thought so!" he muttered, and raised my hand to his nose and sniffed again. "*Dipintore!*" he declaimed, and saying this he released me from his grasp, throwing my hand from him as though the pursuance of my trade had made me the bearer of some hideous affliction or disease.

"You can tell I am a dipintore only from the smell of my skin and clothing?" I asked in astonishment.

"It does not take much to know another for what he is by the recognition of the materials of his trade, and a man soon develops other senses when that of his vision has gone."

I had not realised, nor even suspected that the old man was blind, so comfortable had he appeared in his movements, and so naturally had he behaved towards me, speaking to me and responding to my gestures and movements as would any who saw clearly with whom he conversed. I looked then more closely at his face, and seeing there what in the gloom of the shop I had originally overlooked - that the pupils of his eyes were wholly clouded and white - I began to apologise for not having been aware of the unfortunate condition to which he had been brought.

"Why would one of your years want to possess such a thing?" he asked, dismissing my words of sympathy, and pointing to where the jar containing the head stood on the bench.

Again, I was forced to marvel at his comprehension of the intricate world that lay unseen around him. How, I wondered, had he known that I had been looking at the head and not at one of the many other objects which lay scattered on the bench around it? Had it been but a well-directed guess, or was he able to recall in his mind the precise location of every one of the myriad objects which filled the shelves and tables, and which spilled out haphazardly in places across the floor? Could it be that he was able to tell where each of his customers was standing, and to where they were moving, and what trade or profession they followed, even their age and bearing, and the cut and condition of their clothing, and also at what object they were looking, simply from the combined powers of memory, and of his remaining senses of touch, hearing and smell?

I have to confess I felt humbled in the face of such mastery of the sensible universe. Perhaps though it was so that I experienced my humility all the more acutely in that I was coming at that time to pride myself - and with good reason, I believed - in my own growing ability to study and comprehend the world through the trained exercise of the one sense which this feeble old man no longer possessed, and which, to all appearances, he found totally superfluous to the execution of such a task.

"Why would anyone want to possess such a thing?" I asked.

"There are many uses for such an object - some virtuous, others not. It may be used to good purpose by those who wish to study the structure and workings of the human body, or who essay to comprehend the character of the soul it contains. Or it could serve as example to those who stray onto the path of unbelieving." He paused and pulled the motley gown closer around his body.

"There are of course other uses...potions that can be made, spells that can be cast, and as with most things, *aliquid latet quod non patet*, something always remains hidden which is not apparent. But of course, it is not right that such knowledge be made known to all," and at that he turned and started to walk back towards his ovens and stills.

"And how much would it cost?" I called after him, wanting to know the value of such an object, to appease my curiosity, "Should I wish to have it. For one of those worthy purposes, I mean."

"One hundred gold florins," he said without stopping or turning to look towards me.

"So much!" I cried, belying my poverty, for it would have been obvious to anyone, sightless or not, that I - a bound and penniless apprentice - could not possibly afford such a price, not even for an object of value, let alone for something as intrinsically worthless as an embalmed and severed head.

"It is very old...and very rare," the apothecary mumbled at me over his shoulder.

"But that is surely more than the man himself would have paid to have kept it on his shoulders so long?"

"That may be so, but that is what it costs," he said, finally coming to a halt and turning to face me. "Now tell me young man, did you come here to waste my day, or are there things here you must purchase for your master?"

Again, I was humbled, as I realised the full extent of my impertinence in having asked so many questions of something of which I had no right to enquire. In making it clear that he understood only too well that - other than to satisfy my curiosity - my sole purpose in entering the shop was in the performance of an errand for another, the apothecary had put me firmly in my place. Feeling suitably chastised I asked for the pigments I required, and as soon as he had shuffled around the shop and had gathered together from among the pots and jars the things I needed, again going amongst the profusion of his wares as though his lack of vision really was no hindrance to him, and once I had summarily checked they were of the necessary quality my master required, I handed over the coins I had been given with which to pay for their purchase and hurried out into the street.

My first task completed, and with the pigments carefully packed and stowed ready for my return to Padua (and with my pride dented, and my education unexpectedly broadened), I was free to discharge my other duty, and so I made my way to where I had been told Messer Dante Alighieri was living. I had little difficulty in finding the house where he was lodged, for I knew it to be situated adjacent to the Piazza di Porta Ravegnana, and I had been told that in that square two towers were to be found, both of which leaned markedly from the vertical, and which could be seen quite clearly from any quarter of the town. I had also heard that these towers had always leaned that way; that they had in fact been constructed in such a condition, the architects having designed them so deliberately, for no better reason than to prove it could be done. I was not sure whether I believed this latter rumour or - if it was true - whether I approved of such an abrogation. It seemed to me an arrogance, and an affront, not only to my acquired sense of convention, but also to the laws of Nature and to the will of God. However, I soon enough discovered these landmarks inclined above the roof-line, and forsaking my scepticism allowed myself to be led by their precarious beacon to the momentous encounter (momentous for me, at least) that Messer Dante and I were about to have.

As you have seen, my first introduction to that great man had been but fleeting, and had been cloaked in mystery, or rather, it had sported cloths of such confusing colours that I had taken them (in the wild imaginings of my childish fantasy), to be the trappings of a villainous character in some mystery play. This next meeting however was to be of a much more substantial nature, and I was to depart from it equipped with the indelible memory of two exchanges which took place between us, the first of which was to disabuse me of some few of the misconceptions I had held, regarding both my own past and our shared history, and the second of which was to alter, if not the course of, then certainly the outlook I was to hold upon the life which lay awaiting me.

-OO-

Contrary to my expectations, Messer Dante was most pleased to receive me when I eventually presented myself at his door, Giotto's letter of introduction clasped in my hand. I had thought it likely he might resent the intrusion as I had heard he devoted his time almost entirely to his studies, having finally forsaken politics in favour of the worthier life dedicated to the search for knowledge which he had told my master he wished for. And he was after all, despite his banishment from Florence, still a famous and important man, and what was I but a mere *dipintore*'s apprentice that I should come knocking so boldly at his door?

He greeted me however with cordiality, and having first excused himself while he read through the letter I had brought him, he then proceeded to ply me with enquiries about his native Florence, and about the people he had known there, and the places he used to frequent. As I talked to him and tried as best I could to provide him with the information he desired, it occurred to me that his exile had caused a great emptiness in his life, as he seemed ravenous beyond the point of mere curiosity to hear every scrap of information, and even of idle gossip, that he could glean from me about his beloved city. Unfortunately for him I felt I had little to relate which might sate that hunger, having been myself absent from that city for so long, and having been at the time of my own departure too young anyway to have frequented the places - the inns and Guild-halls, the great houses, the places of politics and commerce - of which he asked.

At sunset, as is the custom of all civilised and sensible men, my host asked that a meal be prepared and invited me to join him. This generous and unexpected offer I accepted gladly, being hungry from my three days of frugal travelling, and only too pleased to extend as long as possible the time I was to spend in the company of so great and interesting a man. Once the things we were to eat had been brought to us, we sat at table, he at one end, I at the other, a simple but wholesome meal of bread and fish and cheese, served with a flask of crisp Veneto wine (of which he graciously allowed me to partake, though in moderation), spread out between us.

While we ate we spoke little, other than to continue our recollections of our past days in Florence, and simply through relating to him my own experiences and memories of the place I believe I was able to satisfy at least some small part of his needs. It was plain to see from the set of his face that he was a serious and sombre man by nature, and of a truly scholarly disposition, his dark gaze calm and focused beneath the brow of his scarlet cap, his features immobile, and the edges of his mouth, the deeply ingrained lines around them, the hook of his nose, habitually turned down towards his long chin, as though he wished to ensure thereby that no mirth or frivolity should ever inflect his countenance. Throughout the meal he sat very still, his slender frame reclined peaceably back in his seat as though he was digesting my words as thoroughly as he did his food. But as I spoke he was unable to keep the light of the pleasure of recollection from kindling in his eyes, and the sides of his mouth turned up frequently from their normally implacable set. I thus continued to amuse, and to repay his generosity as best I could. No sooner had we finished eating though than our conversation returned to the events which had taken place in Florence some three years previously, and of which Dante - though he immediately reverted to a serious mood - showed himself only too willing to provide me with the details I had then been too young to understand.

To my surprise, he explained how - being himself of noble birth - he had been required to take up membership of a guild of craftsmen in order that he might pursue his desired career in politics. My surprise at this arose from the fact that the guild to which he claimed to have belonged, the *Arte dei Medici e degli Speziali*, counted among its numbers, not poets and politicians, nor students of the Arts and Philosophy, but fellows of the blind apothecary I had so recently encountered - doctors and surgeons, mercers and jewellers, book-sellers and barbers, illuminators and dentists, and even we more humble folk who essayed to make our livings as dipintori - and which diverse assemblage, in pursuance of such better interests, I was myself later to join. He had done this he said, not because he had wished to follow any of those worthy professions, but simply to circumvent the laws proscribing one of his class from participating in politics, and from holding office in service of the commune.

"I still do not understand why you were exiled," I said, as I was puzzled still by the seeming ingratitude shown to him by the citizens of Florence. "It seems to me you served the commune and her people well enough."

"It was not liked by some that I had served on the Signoria which ordered the leaders of both parties into exile. In doing so I made enemies among both factions, though I still maintain we acted solely in the interests of our city, and it cannot be said we were other than impartial in what we did."

"Not if you acted against the leaders of both sides without preference. Why then was it seen by some as an offence?"

"Not long after we arrived at our judgement, the White leaders who had been banished were recalled from exile by a predominantly White Signoria, having submitted a complaint that the place they were sent was infested with malaria. I believe it was a justified grievance, for my own friend, Guido Cavalcanti, died of that sickness soon after he was permitted to return."

"You had sent your own friend into exile?" I asked, in disbelief that he could have behaved in such a way towards one he still referred to as friend. Better proof of the professed impartiality of his actions one could not hope to find.

"As an officer of the commune I set my name to the fitting punishment for a proven crime."

"And you were among those who showed that later favour in allowing them to return?"

"No, that was done by the Priorate that succeeded the one on which I served."

"But then you are innocent!" I protested.

"Not in the eyes of those who decide such things," he replied sadly, shaking his head to emphasise this denial of his innocence. "Not here on this earth," he added, even more sadly.

"But why did you not contest the charges raised against you?" I demanded, finding it hard to acknowledge that such a man should have accepted his fate and such injustice so lightly.

"How could I when I was sitting on a horse halfway between there and Rome? They knew I would not be able to return to meet the terms of the sentence, and..." He paused, and looked down into his lap, as though he did not wish to utter the thoughts that had just come to him, or which perhaps he had been harbouring silently ever since that time.

"I almost believe that is why I was chosen to go to Rome," he continued, again with much sadness in his voice. "I believe I may have incurred the Pope's displeasure with my declaration of *nihil fiat* - that nothing be done regarding d'Acquasparta's request for armed support in Florence. I believe he may have detained me deliberately, knowing full well what moves were being set in place against me during my absence."

"But you said that the Signoria was composed mainly of Whites, just like yourself," I said in my confusion at these changing and uncertain allegiances. Messer Dante looked at me and frowned.

"Young man, you still have much to learn about politics. When all is said and done, white is but a colour, as black is but a name. Neither have much to do with the ideals and passions that consume the souls of political men."

Naturally enough, as a result of this discussion, my thoughts returned to Dante's visit to the bottega on the eve of his ill-fated departure, and my curiosity was again aroused as to what the contents of the mysterious package given to him by my master could have been. In truth, I had thought of little else on the three days I had spent travelling from Padua to Bologna, or during the time I had sat conversing of these other, equally fascinating things. Finally taking my courage in my hands and deciding to risk abusing the hospitality he had shown me, I asked if he remembered his visit to my master on the eve of his departure for Rome.

"Only too well," he replied. "And I regret both the memory and the time, for as you know, since that night I have been unable to return." He sat deep in contemplation for a while, and then spat out the seeds of the piece of fruit he had been eating onto his plate.

"But all of that is history," he said once he had finished eating. "And the history of the individual is but Destiny, and therefore cannot be changed. Now tell me, what is it you have to say?"

"Sir, I have a confession to make."

"Very well," he laughed, surprising me with his levity in response to my words. "But bear in mind I am not a priest."

"No sir...but I have a confession, and an apology to make. To you. Do you remember the two boys who greeted you that evening in the bottega?" He looked at me, at first puzzled, and then surprised, as recognition of my features dawned.

"It was you!" he cried in delight. "I have been wrestling all evening with the impression your features were familiar, and maybe I was deflected from recognition by how little you have changed in stature since then." It was obvious from his reaction that he was greatly amused at this discovery, and he sat for some time laughing to himself and all the while looking at me and shaking his head.

"But surely, that is not the extent of your confession?" he said, once he had brought his incredulity under control, and at his prompting, and ignoring his derogatory reference to my lack of height, I proceeded to tell him of my own actions that night, and of the intrigues I had subsequently fabricated for myself, and of the troubled days and nights my suspicions had caused me to suffer.

"Your improbity then was not inconsiderable, and you are right to be ashamed," he said once I had finished, and without taking the time to deliberate further upon what I had said. "And, I am glad to tell you, it was far greater than was your master's, or my own. The package you so fondly elevated to the status of mystery contained nothing but a portrait he had made for me," and at that he laughed out loud.

"Oh!" I said, or some such other bland exclamation of relief at hearing the innocence of my master, and indeed of Messer Dante confirmed, yet experiencing at the same time grave disappointment that the imbroglio I had imagined them caught up in had proved to be nothing more insidious than the innocent execution of my own craft. I had in fact, by my fabrications and suspicions, shown myself to be a far more political animal than were they.

"Come now, don't be down-hearted," Dante said, seeing my reaction. "It was a simple error of youthful ignorance and enthusiasm, and I forgive your impertinence that you should have thought so ill of me, and of your blameless master, though perhaps you should address that with him personally. So, would you like to see the contents of the enigmatic package?"

I nodded my agreement to this eagerly, and he got up from the table and left the room, leaving me alone to reflect upon the full extent of my childish folly. For that is what I had discovered my past fears to have been - a folly, and in the wildest extreme. Now that such apparently mysterious actions had been explained in their true and harmless light, the obscure words the two had exchanged that night stood only as proof of the more honest thoughts and actions I had always previously believed to be theirs. Even the disguise Dante had worn, and which had been the thing which in my imagination had first cloaked the episode in its garb of mystery, had shown itself to be exactly what it was, and nothing more - but a device to protect my master from falling prey to the political turmoil of which Dante himself was soon to become a victim. As for the package, it was about to provide its own testimony.

When Dante returned he held in his hand the object of all my past preoccupation, wrapped still in the same piece of red cloth as it had been on that memorable, yet somewhat less - or so it now transpired - momentous night. I glowed again in my shame at ever having conceived of such arcane nonsense, and at having thought so lightly of my master, and of this wise and affable man who was my host.

"See, here is your great mystery," he said, unwrapping the cloth and handing me the small portrait it contained. The image was painted on a small wooden panel without a frame. I took it from him with only the slightest hesitation, and found myself gazing upon the likeness of a lady so beautiful, whose face and eyes were full of such innocence, that on seeing it I silently also begged her forgiveness for having held her party to such heinous deeds and intentions as I had once dreamed her to be.

"She is beautiful," I said, unable to find words to express fully the depth of emotion the portrait had aroused in me.

"She was," Dante agreed, with much of his earlier sadness returning to his voice.

"Who was she?" I asked. "If I might be so indiscreet." As soon as I uttered these words I realised to what little extent my foolishness had been blunted by my recent enlightenment, and that this (for who else could it possibly have been?) was none other than the likeness of the fair lady Beatrice Portinari whose beauty had infused and shaped those sonnets and *canzoni* of his which at the tender age of ten I had been too young, and too innocent to read or understand. Now however I was a young man, in my fourteenth year, and well able therefore to share and comprehend the passions that such a face might conjure up within the heart and soul, not only of a poet, but of any man.

"An angel. A lady," he replied solemnly. "The muse of my Art."

Hearing the sadness in his voice, and having some personal experience of the pain that such a passion must have caused him I decided not to pursue the matter further. My host however proved far from reluctant to discuss his past affliction, and he proceeded to tell me of how he had first seen the lady Beatrice, and had immediately fallen in love with her, and how she had seemed to him possessed of qualities divine, and to have been noble and praiseworthy in all her ways.

"Such was the power of my emotions for her, the dominion that Love held over me," he confided, smiling softly to himself at the memory of it, "that I would faint away just at the sight of her, or even at the mention of her name." I smiled back politely, but I was confused, finding such distress as he described poor recompense for so purely conceived, and so keenly felt an emotion, so I asked him what pleasure he had found in so painful an infatuation.

"Simply in the expression of words in praise of her and her beauty. The things I came to write in her honour, and which were inspired by her, of all the verses I have made, those extended more than any others the limits of my poetry. It was as though my tongue spoke, and my pen moved of their own accord. She became my inspiration."

Listening to him speak I could not help but recall my own experience of this affliction to which Dante had apparently ever been a martyr. My own thoughts, even after the passage of so much time, remained troubled by the memory of that beatific child who I had seen but fleetingly, but by whose image I had been haunted since on an almost daily basis. My own passion, I could see, was not nearly as profound as that which had informed the sensitive soul of Dante, but on hearing such things described by another I did not doubt the anguish I felt was identical in type, if not in intensity, to those feelings within himself which he had readily identified as Love. Hearing the positive ends to which his sufferance had been directed, I began to wonder if I might not also turn my own brief experience of that dominion to similar effect in the execution of my own more humble craft.

"And are there lessons you have learned from your sufferance of that affliction?" I asked, forsaking the circumspection more rightly belonging to my position as his guest, in the hope I might gain some comfort from whatever wisdom his experience had provided.

"Yes. That although it is universal, and can be found in all things and in all places, love cannot be experienced by Man diffusely. Unlike the love that is expressed by God, and which can embrace all things simultaneously, Man's love may have but one object and one object only. Such are his limitations. A choice must therefore be made; the lesser love must be excluded, and cannot be maintained in competition with a greater."

Such profound words, you will understand, meant little to me then. Now though, being that much older and more familiar with the things my host has written - both with the *Vita Nuova*, and the *Convivio* (on which, given the things he said, it pleases me to think he may have been working at the time of my visit to Bologna), I am better able now to understand what he said. Thus do I understand now that the lady who he claimed, in his *Convivio*, had been placed in his path to distract his troubled thoughts from contemplation of Beatrice, was not herself a creature of flesh and blood, and that the emotion he professed for her was not of the kind that a man might normally hold for a woman. Instead, I know her now for what she truly was - but a device born of his own fantasy, an allegorical representation of the Lady Philosophy, precisely as Boethius before him, seeking similar consolation in his studies, had imagined her to be.

Dante had made his choice, at whatever cost to himself as had been required; the lesser, mundane love had been excluded in favour of the greater. As for myself, I had not realised that such a choice existed, and that it was necessary, even essential that it be made.

-OO-

We spent the rest of that evening in pleasant conversation, my host having been most curious to know how the work in Padua was progressing, and I was glad to tell him what I knew, feeling myself now on much more familiar ground. I was especially pleased to tell him of the things in which I was most deeply involved, and in which he showed great interest. Eventually though it became time for me to leave, as I had planned to set off early the following morning in the hope of making Ferrara by night-fall. As he was escorting me to the door, we again fell to talking of the things he had written in honour of the lady Beatrice.

"Does that remain then your purpose in writing?" I asked. "To honour and praise her memory?"

"Yes, that…and to promote and further my political ideals."

"But can that be reason enough?" I protested. "Surely those are known already throughout the land, from Genoa to Venice, and from Naples to Milan."

"And much further than that I hope!" he exclaimed, laughing out loud and slapping me on the back. "God forbid that the world should be so restricted!" At this he fell silent, and I became concerned my remark had in some way offended him. I made to apologise, but he shook his head gently and raised his hand to prevent me from saying more.

"Immortality! That is what I hope to achieve. That, I suppose, is my ultimate purpose in writing," he said, unexpectedly, as though this were the most common ambition a man might hold. I turned to him, ready to dispute the sanity of his aspirations, but he again silenced me with a gesture of his hand.

"Do you have a love of poetry?" he asked.

"Some say I have an ear for the beauty inherent in words," I replied, and that may well have been true, for I had read some of the works of Virgil and Homer, and the Sicilian poets, and had even composed some sonnets of my own, which I had read out loud to Domenico and several others in the bottega, and to their apparent delight.

"Then you have read mine?"

"I have," I replied neutrally, having indeed read and enjoyed several of his *canzoni*, but having heard also of the man's confidence regarding the qualities of his own creations, I did not wish to be drawn into a situation where I might be forced either to flatter or provoke. Neither was I certain whether he had posed a question or had made a statement of fact. Fortunately, he seemed to accept my brevity as sufficient answer.

"When I was about your age," he said, "I had as master one Bruno Latini, of whom I am sure you have heard." He looked at me, and I nodded assent to this assumption. "It was he who showed me that - besides performing its obvious functions as an instrument of learning and truth - literature could serve another, albeit less altruistic purpose."

"And that is?"

"That it could make a man eternal."

I was to say the least puzzled by so blank and so assured a proclamation. All of my powers of reasoning, everything I had ever seen or learned, everything I believed and held to be true, stood ranked against my understanding of how mere words, however grand or wise they might be, could make a mortal man immortal.

"How could that possibly be?" I protested.

"Do you think then that Virgil and Homer, or Ovid, or Lucan or Statius are dead," he asked, becoming animated, "or any of the other great minds and thinkers of the past?"

"Are you taking me as a fool?" I replied, my indignation pricked, and suspecting that this one great man was perpetrating a jest at my expense. "It is common fact those great men have all been counted among the dead for many years."

"No, my friend. You have proved yourself wise enough this evening…, if a little naïve," he said, smiling to placate me. "But to me such men live on in their words. They survive still in the pages of their books. When I read their works, I hear their voices almost as clearly as I hear yours now, talking to me in this room. Clearer in fact, for I can study their words as I will, and at my leisure, whereas yours come to me then just as quickly go, other than what little I am able to retain in my doubtless mistaken memory. But with the written word I am able to break open the outer shell of appearances and arrive at the kernel inside. I can go beyond the literal meaning of the word and letter to discover the underlying truth of what their authors are trying to say. The letter kills but the spirit quickens; it brings forth life in that which is dead."

"I see," I said, feeling only slightly mollified by his explanation. "And that is what you hope to achieve for yourself?"

"I believe to some extent I have already achieved it. I am famous, many people read my words. My thoughts are everywhere valued and praised - even though it is true my presence is not always so highly respected - and many take and use them to further their own needs." He paused and looked at me, and I could see from the fire in his eye that he was certain of the truth of what he said. "And what do you think will happen when I am gone?" he asked. I shrugged my shoulders, not knowing how I should reply. "They will continue to be read! And when they are read they will quicken the spirit of those who read them, and so will I live on."

"Yes, perhaps that is true," I replied, suddenly seeing what I had understood as an arrogance directed purely by pride, or by insensitivity, revealed now in an entirely different light. "Thank you," I said.

"For what?"

"For having made me see many things other than how I had thought them to be."

"Then for once at least I have spoken well, and to a positive end," he said, and he looked most pleased, though whether with his own words or my reaction to them, I could not tell.

"Do you remember everything your master said to me that night?" he asked when we finally arrived at the door. I nodded in silent and shameful assent.

"Go then, my friend, and may those things also serve you well," he said, placing his hand gently on my shoulder. At that we said our farewells and I departed from him, never to see him again, though he was not to pass from this earthly existence, leaving behind all his mortal torments, until the summer of the year thirteen hundred and twenty-one. His words though were to remain with me for every second of my journey back to Padua, and as my story will bear witness, for the rest of my own troubled and extended life.

-OO-

In such state did I return to Padua, my head full of wondrous plans for my future (and too with many attendant reservations!), only to discover another surprise waiting for me there. Before I had even passed through the southern gate of the town Domenico came running to meet me and, as I soon discovered, to forewarn me that something extraordinary awaited me at the chapel. I knew it was him as soon as I saw a small, dark figure coming towards me, one leg swinging in an arc from behind it, as his tousled form came hopping and hobbling along the straight and dusty road that ran from the Porta Torricelli through which I was passing to where the estates of the Scrovegni lay on the northernmost side of the town.

"Hoi! Pace! Hurry!" he started to cry wildly while he was still some distance away from me. "Hurry! You must see what Messer Giotto has done!"

At first this unexpected show of excitement caused me some concern, and I began thinking because of it that some calamity must have befallen the work in the chapel. When he came finally to a breathless halt beside me, I quickly asked if anything was amiss, but received no reply from him, only further excited entreaties to hurry along. One glance at the mischievous look on his face, however, was enough to inform me that, other perhaps than for my own well-being, I had little cause to be concerned.

On our arrival at the Arena we were immediately surrounded by the other members of the bottega, and even by some of the younger servants of the Scrovegni household, who all came running out to crowd around us. Every one of them was shouting and calling out to me just as Domenico had done, and so loudly in concert that, marooned in the midst of that great confusion I gave up trying to determine what was going on. When I was brought eventually to a halt in front of the chapel, several pairs of hands helped me down from where I was sitting, and someone among them led my mule away. I was then steered and pushed towards the doorway, and through it, into the interior of the chapel.

"Go on! Get up there!" they cried, still pushing and steering me, as we came to the foot of a ladder which stood against the scaffolding. Reluctantly, and not without some unwelcome assistance, I started to climb.

When I had reached half way up and was beyond, I hoped, the grasp of their rough persuasion, I paused to look down at the crowd of bright, eager, though now silenced faces staring up at me from below. I noticed that Domenico was standing apart from the others, leaning with his back against the portal of the door, and as my eye caught his he smiled and motioned gently with his head for me to continue. Feeling reassured by this I resumed my climb. Looking up to see where I was going I saw the face of my master peering down at me from the edge of the platform. He too smiled then turned away.

"Go on! Get a move on!" the others below resumed their urging as I came to the top of the ladder and hesitated once more before climbing onto the platform.

Again I obeyed, though still reluctantly, and stepping onto the staging saw that my master was waiting for me between where the fourth and fifth window had been let into the wall. This, I remembered, was where he had been working on the Adoration of the Magi on my departure for Bologna, but as I moved towards him along the platform, I still had no idea what might be awaiting me. My thoughts remained awash with possibilities - and those mostly bad ones - in spite of the encouraging smiles and glances I had been shown.

"Well, what do you think?" Giotto asked when I came to where he was standing, turning to indicate the painting of the Adoration which - to my surprise - I saw he had managed to complete in the few days I had been away.

"It is beautiful," I replied, barely glancing at it, for I was still much confused as to why everyone had been so excited by my return. It was indeed a wonderful thing that he had completed this panel so quickly, and so perfectly, from what I could tell from my cursory inspection, but it did not seem to me a matter of such great concern. I had often enough witnessed the speed at which my master was capable of working, and had seen too other things he had produced, and which to my mind were just as beautiful as this Adoration, marvellous though it was.

"Try looking at it with some attention," he said, laughing - as I was soon to discover - at the blindness that confusion had induced in my powers of vision. As instructed, I looked at the thing again, this time taking better stock of what he had created, and immediately understood the reason for his laughter, and for the excitement of the others. For I now saw before me, not merely the Adoration of the infant Jesus, but amidst that Holy gathering, my own image, also enshrined and depicted in that sumptuous panel. For there I stood (and it was undoubtedly I - my nose, my ears, my lips, my eyes, my brow, my likeness!), withdrawn to one side of the painting and partly concealed behind the other figures it was true, yet still my master had so honoured me as to have placed me in the company of our Blessed Saviour, and of the Virgin and the Angel, and the three Kings who had come from the East. I was astonished that he had done this, and was greatly flattered by it, especially so by the few added fingers of height he had given me, and even though he had clad me only in the plain tunic of a servant, and my sole purpose in the midst of that scene of reverence was nothing worthier than the holding of the bridle of a camel. I was even turning away from that blessed enactment, so occupied did I seem to be in controlling the temper of that, the most cantankerous of beasts.

"I am made eternal,'" I said softly, recalling the things Dante had said, as I stared in awe at my own reflection. Giotto looked at me with some curiosity.

"Let us hope that is so," he said, and laughed again.

"I seem to be having some trouble with the beast," I commented, and I too had to laugh at the predicament I appeared to be in, for my other self appeared to be more involved in controlling the will of the animal over which he had been given dominion than in the act of divine worship at which he had been so generously placed.

"It seemed appropriate. You have trouble with many things," my master replied thoughtfully.

As I stood there looking at myself, and marvelling at the great skills my master had exhibited in portraying his most unworthy apprentice, I noticed something else in the painting which in my confusion, and then delight, I had also failed to see. It was a thing at the sight of which my heart began to pound equally as hard as it had at the first sight of my own immortalisation. For there - hovering, falling, flying in the beautiful blue expanse of sky above the canopy which sheltered the infant Jesus - my master had painted, not the conventional Star of Bethlehem, but the *cometis stella* which had visited Florence in the troubled days of my youth. The very and self-same comet we had all witnessed, and which had overshadowed our lives in the year of our Lord thirteen hundred and one.

"The star... It is wonderful too," I said, again in awe of his powers of creation. "But how did you come to paint it so?"

"You remember the things we spoke of that night on the hill?"

"Yes," I replied, recalling it vividly.

"I remembered it too while I was working on the sketches for this scene. I recalled the words I quoted to you from Origen, about the guiding star being a comet, and the idea came to me of depicting it in this way." As he spoke, he pointed up at the comet, and as my eyes followed his gesture, and glancing quickly at the thing as I did, it seemed for an instant that it was real, and that it moved across the plastered surface on which it had been made.

"But is that authority enough for such an innovation?" I asked, concerned that in this one, bold departure my master might have overstepped the limits imposed upon our craft by tradition and convention. Impressed by the idea though, I certainly was, and even more so by its sublime execution. The thing glowed and pulsed with energy, its tail streaming out behind it like a sword, exactly as that of the *cometis stella* had done. A more lifelike portrayal of a celestial body I had never seen, nor since.

"Perhaps not," he said. "But in the Legend of the Saints, Jacobus de Voragine makes the same allusion, and also claims that the Bethlehem star was a new star made by God."

"But that is a book of popular legend," I persisted, if only in the hope that my arguments would force him to provide me with proof sufficient to persuade me of the correctness of what he had done.

"I am aware of that, and I was doubtful too at first, but Origen also says it was a new star, and that it had the appearance of the beard of a man." He paused and looked at me, and smiled. "And if you look closely, you will see how I have avoided having to resolve the dilemma. Within the comet I have painted an ordinary star, for those who are too stubborn or sceptical to accept such a digression. And perhaps because I too am not entirely convinced which of the two it should be."

At his direction I moved closer and peered up at his depiction of the guiding star. Within the glowing red bulb of paint that he had used to create the head of the comet I saw how he had also painted in gold the eight radiant points used to make a star in its conventional representation. It was a clever trick indeed, and one he had executed to perfection. I realised too, as I studied it more closely, that it was this very duplicity that gave to the thing its pulsing energy; that it was, in fact, the continual passage of the eye from the red of the visible comet to the gold of the concealed star, and then back again, and of the similar illusion created by the lines of gold which streamed too along the length of its tail, which caused the image of it that formed in the mind to continually advance and then recede, creating the impression that it actually flickered and moved upon the immobile plane on which it had been painted.

"Of one thing I am convinced," I said, my eyes still fixed on the image of the comet.

"And what is that?"

"That you are a great and surprising man."

-OO-

I was sitting alone on the steps of the chapel that evening when my master came out and sat down beside me. At first he did not speak, and we remained in silence, both lost in contemplation of the Heavens as they turned above us. From what I recall it was a beautiful evening, though of my many memories of that period of my life most are idyllic, distorted as they no doubt are by the passing of time and a nostalgia for a lost innocence, and for an enthusiasm for the things of Nature that with the fading of my faculties I have gradually lost. Anyway, as you will know, it is a gratifying thing to sit and consider the beauty of that towering harmony, to see the numberless stars made visible in the shadowy mantle of night, and to ponder there upon the innate perfection of God's wondrous Creation.

I sat there that evening, lost as much in contemplation of my own recent apotheosis as of the sublime Nature turning around me, with my mind at peace amidst that ordered greatness, and with my master at my side. But even then, safe among friends and engrossed in that most innocent of occupations, I fear my soul was exposed to the gravest danger. For it has been said that he who heeds too closely to the motions of the Heavens will one day hear the voice of the Moon calling to his soul and mind to wander, and that on hearing it will find himself unable to do other than listen? The wisdom of age permits me to say now that, at that moment, on that momentous day, and indeed throughout the whole of that period of my life, my mind especially was attending all too closely to the Moon's silver-tongued ministrations.

"That was a strange thing you said today," my master said after some time had elapsed. "What did you mean by it?" I cast a questioning glance in his direction as I had not heard properly what he had said, and only the sound of his voice had roused me from my reverie.

"About being made eternal," he prompted.

"Oh, that!" I nodded, and started to relate to him the things I had discussed with Messer Dante in Bologna and to explain the profound effect his words had had upon me. I explained too how the sight of my own face immortalised in the fresco had served only to convince me of the veracity of what Dante had said, and of the conclusions I had drawn from them. People would come to look at that picture in a hundred, five hundred, maybe even a thousand years' time, and through them I, Pace di Buoninsegna, would continue to live and be known to other men.

"And what would that achieve?" my master said in a more dismissive tone than I had hoped to hear.

"Nothing, perhaps. Not in any tangible sense. But since my conversation with Messer Dante I wish for nothing more than to be made eternal through the execution of my craft."

"I see," Giotto said.

"And to have done it well, and to the best of my ability," I added quickly, for fear he might find my plainly stated ambition too lax.

"But neither books, nor paintings are eternal," he said. "No more than are their authors." I turned my face away, then to the ground, to hide my consternation.

"Does it really have to be so?" I asked plaintively, as though my pleas could change it, but he merely nodded silent affirmation of this true but unhappy fact.

For what he had said was true, and the facts of it were irreversible. Everything in this world, and of this world, fades and then perishes. Proof of this sad truth I have since discovered amply for myself, not only in the passing of those many I have known, or in the gradual inclination to dust of my own wearying members, but in the many books and buildings, and the works of great and praise-worthy beauty which in the course of my life I have had the misfortune to see damaged, or corrupted, or destroyed. Too often have I had cause to mourn for those things which - either through ignorance or by accident, or who knows, by God's greater will - have been lost, both to this world, and to Posterity. Then however, as a youth embarked upon my fourteenth year, my proud heart was touched only by the concern that the likeness my master had created of me might be lost forever to that Posterity, and with it the record inherent in it of how my face once had looked.

"Is what I seek not a worthy aim then?" I asked.

"Virtue, it is said, is more admirable if practised with no thought of being admired."

"That is not what I meant!" I protested. "My desire is not to be admired, but to be remembered through the qualities of what I have achieved."

"Then take heed of the warning Boethius gave, that a man possessed of natural excellence, but who has yet to attain a state of virtue, will find the desire for fame the most beguiling of goals."

"But do you not also seek to be made eternal through the agency of the things you have made?" I asked, hav-ing first nodded appreciation of his sagacious warning, yet seeking still to hear from his lips some words of approval for the high aims I had embraced. "Do you, as their creator, not deserve to be remembered?" I added.

"Do you not want your paintings to stand as testimony to your name?"

"Are we talking of the worldly fame any man might aspire to, or the necessarily limited form of immortality you seem to hope to attain through your work being maintained into Posterity?"

"Immortality..., and that virtuously attained through the perfected execution of our craft," I replied grandly.

"An immodest ambition indeed!" he said, and immediately began to occupy himself in drawing geometric patterns in the ground with a stick he had found lying beside him.

As we again sat in silence I looked up briefly at the darkened Heavens and saw there an uncertain light burning a feeble track across the surface of the outermost sphere. At the first sight of it my heart skipped a beat, and for a moment I thought the comet of my youth had returned to scar again our skies with its awesome message. Then I saw how the thing was falling steadily towards us and not hanging motionless as that earlier *cometis stella* had done, and after a few moments it disappeared completely from view. I realised then (and with much relief) that I had been mistaken in my first fearful reaction, and that it had been but one of those transitory and inconsequential phenomena (inconsequential that is to the collective fortunes of mortal man) that could often be seen traversing the Heavens, and which wise men held to be nothing less than the joyous signs of angels taking wing.

"What do you see when you look up there, Pace?" my master asked, disturbing my fears.

"The Heavens. The sphere of the visible stars."

"And beyond that?"

"Beyond the stars is the sphere of the *Primum Mobile*, which imparts motion to all things, but which we cannot see with our eyes, only with our hearts and imaginations; and beyond that is Empyrean, where God and the Saints and Angels abide."

"And even in that knowledge you still hope to find immortality through your Art?"

"Why should I not?" I replied defiantly.

"Is it not true that all perfect things are prior to those which are imperfect?"

"Yes, that is so."

"And that man is subject to mortality as a consequence of his own imperfection, and that this has been ordained so by He, who above and beyond all else is himself immortal and perfect? Would you aspire then to reverse that immutable order?"

"No sir, I would not."

"What then, pray, do you hope to achieve?"

I did not know what to answer, so young and unconsidered was my philosophy, that already it was crumbling to dust before my master's more reasoned assault. Messer Dante's words had given me but the bare framework of something - an insubstantial idea conveyed in the space of a few sentences which in the course of three day's journeying I had built into a marvellous and towering edifice, aspiring in its unbounded potential, and so compelling for a hopeful youth such as I to behold, yet raised that high on poor and unsound foundations and erected purposefully in that manner just as those leaning towers in Bologna had been. This then was the fragile creed by which I hoped and planned to live my life. Of course I was unable to defend it; so beguiled had I been by its attractions, and so poorly had I thought it through.

The few words Dante had uttered on the subject had given me precious little of real substance with which to construct my giddy structure, and certainly not the bricks and mortar of reason to protect it from contrary elements, nor arguments with which to defend the basic premises on which it had been raised. Those I had constructed wholly for my own purposes from the fabric of my own conceit. How then could Dante possibly have provided me with such privy information? The philosophy I was at that moment being called upon to justify was not his, but - by my own needs and definitions - entirely my own.

Unlike Dante, the sower of the seeds of such aspirations as I clung to, my own goal was not to achieve fame and honour in this, my present life, nor gain blissful reward in the next. What I wanted, it suddenly became clear to me, was nothing less than to thwart unruly Death in all its cruel purposes, and that, in whatever way I could. I wanted to find a way to circumvent that Death which through its irresistible action brings about the separation of the soul from the body, making of the flesh - the vehicle through which the rational soul may express itself - nothing but worthless dust. I did not want the sum product of my days to be but a box of dust and a soul which, once liberated from its mortal harness might rise to receive its deserved rewards in heaven, or might just as easily gravitate to Purgatory or to the lower regions of Hell. Through my art I hoped I would achieve this; that through the glorious expression of that art, and of the love and humility I hoped would nurture its creation, I could perpetuate myself through the benign offices of Posterity and thereby leave behind some record, not only of my mortal passing, but of that which had once been my immortal soul.

"Did not Augustinius say that God gave Man a soul endowed with reason in order that through its use he might become as one with the angels, without the experience of death?" I offered in desperation, grasping at the one argument I could summon up which would seem in any way to justify my sorely threatened creed.

"Not if he offends God by misuse of that reason, or of the free-will that is born of it."

"But what is there in what I seek that may cause offence? My intention is to live my life, and to execute my craft only in the service and honour of His name. I do not ask for worldly glory or reward, only that my presence here, and my work, be recorded for Posterity, and for the good example of other men."

"Commendable ambitions," Giotto commented flatly, but refused to offer any further argument or response, and continued to draw his idle patterns in the sand.

"I have been taught it is right to praise and glorify God in our every thought and action." I continued, finding inspiration from I know not where, "And that such glorification is our rightful purpose here on Earth. Do we not perform that purpose better if those thoughts and actions, and the things born of them, continue to be known and praised, and to be used as example by other men? Are you not teaching me the things taught to you by Cimabue, thereby perpetuating his name?" Again, my master gave no answer, but merely nodded, and pursed his lips thoughtfully in reply.

"And is it not a sin to take one's life, as Judas did? Is not the opposite our true and worthy aim, in that we glorify God the more in the fullest possible extension of our days?"

"You may argue it so," he agreed.

"Do you think it wrong then that Margaritone put his name, in defiance of convention, to the things he considered he had done well?" I asked, citing as example in desperation at his reticence, one for whom I knew he held some regard.

"There are *dipintore* who do that, though I cannot say if it is right or wrong. I am more concerned in my daily labours to understand and portray the workings of the human spirit than with the pursuit of worldly fame. As for Margaritone, I fear he signed his name only lest he be forgotten entirely."

"What do you mean?"

"He died a bitter man, envious of the acclaim accorded to my master, Cimabue. It is even said that he regretted having lived so long to have seen the progress made in our Art, and the way in which *dipintori* are rewarded for their work."

"But he was famous in his time, and still is," I said, having seen and heard of things he created which had increased the fame and honour accruing to his name.

"That is true, and rightly so. But the fact is that such skills as he displayed did not come to him easily. He had to work hard for what little reward he received."

"That may be true for me also, and I am not afraid of hard work. Is what I seek then wrong?"

"It is not that it is wrong, certainly not if all you do is executed in strict obedience to God's greater will. But it is a difficult task you have assigned yourself." There was much concern in his face as he looked at me, and as he reached out and clasped my arm.

"You must first ask yourself this," he said in earnest. "Is your heart that pure and strong?"

Again I could not answer honestly, neither to him, nor to myself. My experiences in Florence, and too the experiences of Messer Dante, had taught me that however pure a man's intentions might be, the struggle to assert the dominion of reason over sensuality, and of sensuality over the hungers of the recalcitrant flesh, was not an easy ordinance to maintain. I shrugged my shoulders and nodded tentatively in reply, not wishing to damn myself further by putting other words on my tongue which I knew I could not defend.

"You have asked whether I also seek such immortality," my master said at last, sensing perhaps the great need in me to receive from him some small benediction for the apparently unworldly ambitions I had embraced.

"And do you?" I asked eagerly, turning to look at him fully for the first time.

"I suppose I would be pleased if I were to receive such reward for my labours, if in a thousand years my name is still remembered because of the things I have painted," he replied, and then he began to shake his head. "But that does not mean I actively seek it."

"And why is that?" He looked down at his hands, now empty, and paused before replying.

"Perhaps through fear of the disappointment failure in its pursuit would bring."

At his doleful words we both glanced at each other, and then turned our faces to the ground, humbled as we were by the honesty, and by the awful truth of his confession. What little encouragement I had garnered for myself from his initial reply had been all too quickly dissipated, and made as insubstantial as smoke by the sudden realisation of what the pursuit of my dreams of immortality must needs entail.

"There, is that answer enough for you?" he asked, and wishing me good fortune in my searching, and more immediately, a good and untroubled rest for the coming night, he stood up and entered into the chapel, there, I would imagine, to pray for the safety of our two sorely threatened souls.

-OO-

PART 2

THE KISS OF JUDAS

THE GARDEN OF GETHSEMENE

"The end of happiness is pain, and in like manner, misery ends in unexpected happiness."

Giovanni Boccaccio

By the end of the year thirteen hundred and six the work at Padua had been completed, and the *bottega* together with all its members and equipment had returned once more to Florence. In the years that followed, while I completed the acquisition of the skills and knowledge of the materials and techniques I would need to pursue my trade, and also in the years that ensued after my departure from the bottega, Messer Giotto was to work on many more important commissions throughout Tuscany. Not least among these were the decoration of two small chapels in the church of Santa Croce in Florence, and both of these - though neither were on the scale of what we had created in Padua - again proved true and lasting testaments to his skills. Indeed, it was as a result of these things, and in recognition of his unsurpassed greatness, that he was eventually appointed *Capomaestro* overseeing the design and construction of the Duomo in that city. On this worthy task he was employed until he was sadly called from among us, and before his conception for that edifice could be brought to fruition, in the year of our Lord thirteen hundred and thirty-seven.

Over the years during which I served with him I came to look upon Messer Giotto more as a friend than as my master, and I prefer to think that as those years together passed he also came to see me in a similar light. He was certainly much like a father to me, offering support and guidance in many things above and beyond the ways of our craft. My own parents had both died within a year of our return from Padua, so that not only he, and dear Domenico, but all of the people serving in the bottega became the only family I possessed. It pains me still that I was not able to be present at his death-bed. I felt it was my filial duty almost, though he had sired sons enough of his own. When I heard of his illness, I made haste to Florence, but by the time I arrived he had already succumbed, and his mortal remains had been laid to ground. I took what little solace I could from my mourning by visiting the beautiful things he had made in that city, and at each one making a silent promise to his spirit that I would devote all of my skill and time and efforts to honouring the memory of his name.

It was in Florence too that I was eventually to set out as a *dipintore* in my own right, having completed my education at Messer Giotto's side, at the end of my twenty-fifth year. In this endeavour I can do no other than say plainly that, despite those heartfelt promises I made to his memory, and despite those many I had previously made, and with equal conviction to myself, I failed miserably in all of my hopes and aspirations. Neither would it serve any purpose to ask me why that failure should have come about, nor to enquire of such insufficiencies in myself as I have discerned that might have been its cause. I cannot give adequate reason for my failure: the bare fact of it - both in the poor and lifeless execution of my craft, and in the non-fulfilment of my ambitions – must serve as detail enough.

But what is that I hear you asking; what became of the intervening years of my story? Why do I not record in its proper order the steady and inexorable passage of time? How is it, I hear you enquire, that from one page to the next I am no longer the ambitious and optimistic - if slightly arrogant and deluded - youth I was when you last caught sight of me, and am revealed now as a doubting and complacent man, matured in years, if still ostensibly in his prime, yet bereft in body and soul of the several skills and worthy qualities he once possessed?

The answer to this question is simple enough: my apparently sudden transformation had been brought about by just that sad and inexorable passage of time. And if it seems to you that those years passed by all too quickly, with no shade or memory lingering in my thoughts of their passing, then I must tell you that you have perceived it exactly as it was. For those years, and many of those that were to follow, did slip by almost unnoticed, with few pleasures and no victories or achieved goals of note to mark them, and just as hastily as they came.

My apprenticeship completed, I had departed from the *bottega* with all the skills and knowledge necessary for the successful pursuance of my craft at my command, and I was said by many, including my most gracious master, to be possessed of a compassionate and steadfast spirit, and having a gifted hand and eye. I had entered this earthly existence on the last day of the first month of the year of our Lord twelve hundred and ninety, and was therefore among those held by astronomers to be subject to the combined humours of the house of Aquarius. In that, it is true, my soul was then - as I hope it is still - blessed with a

communicative and artistic nature, and with good intu-
ition, and sound powers of reasoning and judgement, but
which has been ever corrupted by an eagerness to embrace
any unorthodox opinion that came my way. This latter
failing has been further compounded by an adherence to
such unconvention as has allowed me at times to become
too detached from the greater, external truths. Maybe
therefore, lacking a true sense of direction, or conviction
in the things I was commissioned to create, I was to find
myself unable to put my skills, and the education I had
received in their application to good and worthy use.

And what should I tell you of the mechanics of that
failure? Should I list here the commissions I was given,
and which I failed to complete either to my own or to my
patron's satisfaction; or the walls I have covered with dis-
temper, or with nothing more than a coat of arms, or at
best with pretty designs of birds and flowers and scenery;
or the shop-signs and banners, and pots, and chests and
harness I have painted merely to save myself from dying
of hunger? Or of the things I declined to do in more provident times - pleading commitment to some other work, in
some other place, to appease my patron's offence or anger
- fearing more than those things, as I came to do, to pick
up brush and pigment and by such actions abuse the
greater honour and memory of my master, and the skills
he had imparted to me and which at one time had resided
so confidently in my hands?

I suppose the sad possibility does exist that of the many
charmless things I decorated in those times of need, and
which formed too often the catalogue of my labours,
some few remain and are being put still to their worldly
purpose. But I doubt it, for often the materials on which I
worked were baser even than the designs they came by

virtue of my efforts to bear. So it is that to the best of my knowledge (and to my consternation!) but one thing remains to attest to the many and miserable attempts I made during those infertile years to find reward and immortality through the execution of my craft. In this, if in nothing else, I hope and pray I am not mistaken, and that this is all that does remain as tribute to my failure. Of my other efforts from that time, I can only hope they have all been corrected by others more worthy of having assumed for themselves the title of *dipintore*, or have been defaced or painted over or otherwise destroyed.

Nevertheless, that one indictment - a tawdry scene aspiring to the joint *cognomen* of Annunciation and Adoration - does remain, and knowing the extent and tenacity of my past ill-fortunes, I cannot doubt but that it will do so for all eternity to damn the memory of my soul. This unworthy abomination is to be found - should you wish to prove to yourself the veracity of what I am saying - in the town of Assisi, at the church of San Francesco situated there. It survives, as it was born, by virtue of my failings; no longer do I have the strength, and nor am I moved by sufficient passion against its existence to go to Assisi and hack it from the wall.

You will see now, I think, to what extent, and in what way the passing of those years had changed me by the time in which you have rediscovered me; how the dreams and aspirations I once cherished had long since been banished from my thoughts.

"Posterity be damned!" was the refrain I offered to such dreams as still came to haunt me, and to the world in which at one time I had hoped to bring them to fruition. Those heady dreams in which my soul once sung in praise of its own greatness had long since dimmed to nightmares; the nightmares had long since faded to memories of sadder times gone by, and for me - as it ever is for all men - it seemed too late to undo that which had already been done.

-OO-

As natural concomitant to my failure, poverty soon became my accustomed condition, as I sank inexorably from the position of one who - as I embarked upon my new and independent profession - had been fêted for the things I had achieved during my time in the bottega, and whose services had been eagerly sought out by wealthy patrons, to that of one who was reduced, simply that I might survive, to begging for charity and seeking alms. Thus did I come to see how the lower classes in this life, the *plebs pauperum*, suffered and struggled to eke out their daily existence, and it was not long before I found myself subject to the same deprivations and hungers, and to the same passions and beliefs as they embraced to bring some little comfort to their lives.

There were at that time in Tuscany, and throughout the lands which lay around it, many who went about preaching at the roadside or sermonising before the doors of churches and in the *piazzas* of the towns and cities. Many of these pious souls proclaimed themselves prophets, or even Messiahs of the Second Coming, beseeching all who would listen to prepare themselves for the Last Days that were soon to come. You may have heard of some of these - the French monk Adso, and Joachim of Fiore, though both were abroad many decades before the time of which I tell. One such though was contemporary to my time and province, a man known as Fra Lorenzo of Modena, of whom you may also have heard, for there was a time when his followers in Tuscany alone were numbered in their thousands, and the message he bore had instilled hope in many a lost and despairing heart.

His singular figure had appeared one day amidst the busy traffic of the commune, preaching to the poor from the steps of Santa Maria Novella, and calling upon any who would listen to join him, to take up with him the true and redemptive way of Christ. As was usual in the new and unwelcome condition to which I had been reduced, I had always time enough to spare for such distractions, and whenever I came upon him in the course of my daily wanderings in search of occupation, I would sit and listen to his sermons, and observe the crowds of impoverished who gathered around him as they grew steadily in number, and in the rapture with which they listened to the message he brought to their eager ears.

Whether it was the evocative words he used, or the manner in which he delivered them, or if it was the qualities of his voice alone which drew us to the compass of his pulpit, I cannot say, but an eloquent man, and one of great presence, he surely was. He was moreover of fearsome appearance, being more than three *braccia* in height, and so emaciated the joints of his body protruded like pebbles beneath his skin. His face too was long and gaunt, his teeth were rotten, and his azure eyes blazed beneath the shadow of his brow, and his nose was hooked and pointed like the beak of a hawk. His hair, which was the colour of flames, hung filthy and matted about his shoulders, and he wore nothing but a girdle of cloth the traitor's colour of saffron draped over one shoulder and wrapped in a knot around his loins. In his hand he always bore a gnarled staff of oak, and this he struck upon the stone of the steps repeatedly as he spoke.

The fraternal title he bore, or so it was reported to me by several I spoke to who knew more of him than I, was a vestige of the days he had spent as a Dominican friar - a *Domine canes*, a hound of the Lord - but this singular brother had long lapsed into apostasy, having found that order, despite having been founded in imitation of the apostolic life, too much devoted to those material things which denied the true and unperverted teachings of Christ. Renouncing his calling he had fled the world of men, rejecting the ways of the callous and possessive, and had hidden himself in a cave in the heart of a forest. There he had remained with neither food nor light, praying incessantly in the cold and darkness, for three and thirty days, that being the number of years our Saviour had endured his sojourn on Earth. That period of asceticism, Fra Lorenzo informed us, had led him to discover an order and meaning concealed within the history of mankind, an order kept hidden from others by hubris and spiritual blindness. This knowledge, he proclaimed to us each day, the resonance of his voice and his demeanour adding authority to his words, enabled him now to interpret the Revelations to the Apostle John in such a way as to predict the future passage that mankind's history would inevitably follow.

"Hear, all who have ears to listen," I heard him cry out that first day I came upon him, as the report of his staff striking hard upon stone echoed around the square. "Heed the revelations I bring you. Heed the words of He who is Alpha, and who is Omega. Heed the words of He who is first and shall ever be last."

After these first, commanding utterances had been spoken, and the attention of those who passed about him had been captured, he stood for a while in silence, beckoning with his arms for all to come closer, his gaunt face turned towards the Heavens as though waiting for the revelatory words of which he had spoken to be delivered from on high. Many of those who had been drawn to stop and listen, taking from him their example, also turned their faces in expectation towards the sky.

"Come! A voice shall cry out," his voice suddenly thundered about us, pitched now even louder than before, and punctuated four times by the sharper crack of the staff on the ground. Several in the crowd cried out in surprise at the immense power of his utterances echoing around us. His voice was deep and resonant - such an unexpected sound to have issued from so frail a frame - and reflected from the surrounding walls it seemed to come at us from all directions.

"Come! The voice shall cry out as the first seal is broken open, and a fearsome horseman shall ride forth in answer to his summons, and he shall be clothed in white, and be seated upon a snow-white beast, and shall be given a crown with which to conquer," he continued as soon as the echoes of his first command had died away.

"Come! The voice shall cry out again as the second seal is broken open, and another shall ride forth, clad in red, and mounted on a steed the colour of blood. And he shall be given a sword to take peace from the earth, and cause men to slaughter their fellow men." He paused, and glared around at the gaunt faces of his audience, and many of those standing before him turned their eyes away from him, or to the ground, or began to glance uneasily at their neighbours, as though they shared the guilt of the retribution of which he spoke.

"These things have all been foretold in the Revelations of John the Apostle," he said, continuing his sermon with more compassion in his voice, and holding aloft a copy of the Gospels for all to see. "And those events, and those acts of men which in the past have made you suffer, and have made of your lives what they are today, when seen in the light of understanding are revealed not as mere acts of men in History, but as living proofs that the prophecies of the higher powers shall, and have been made to come true. I tell you now, the first two seals have already been broken. A voice has called "Come!", and it has called "Come!" again. And both times, exactly as it is written, a horseman has ridden forth in answer to its command." And at this he hurried down the steps, his eyes like those of a feral animal scanning the faces of the crowd before him for prey, and within a few strides he was among his unsuspecting congregation. Once there, he laid a hand firmly on the shoulder of a sorry-looking fellow with a hump the size of a melon on his shoulder, and a dark ring of warts standing proudly on his neck, and who had the added misfortune that day to have been standing in the foremost ranks of the crowd.

"Did Frederic Barbarossa not come upon you, armed for war and clad in robes of the whitest ivory, to claim the crown of Empire for himself?" Fra Lorenzo demanded of the man, who in his utter bewilderment at what this wild visionary was asking him could do no more than nod his scurvied head in reply.

"Yessss," the prophet hissed at him, his eyes wide open, and his face pushed almost into the face of the other, though he seemed to be staring right through him, and to be addressing everyone in the crowd but him. Then, just as suddenly as he had accosted him, he released his iron grip on the man's shoulder, and mumbling a brief benediction, laid his hand on his head to bless him, then turned quickly to apprehend another unsuspecting creature among the crowd.

"And did not d'Aquasparta come, disguised in his Cardinal red, and armed with the Antichrist's Papal blessing, to take from you your peace? Did not brother then turn upon brother?" he demanded of this second, who likewise could do no more than nod to him in bewildered assent.

"You see. It is as I have said," Fra Lorenzo crowed above us, releasing the second man and bestowing upon him a similar blessing, rising to the full extent of his height, and turning once more to address the crowd. "The white horseman and the red horseman have been among us, and even as I speak, the black horseman strikes his hooves loudly at our doors."

He began to speak then of the Antichrist, telling of how it was written this base deceiver would be born a Jew in the house of Dan, and how he would enter into the world in a place named Babylon, born the son of a mother who plied her flesh as a whore, and that Satan himself would enter into her body as a spirit at the moment of his conception. Once born and enthroned, his reign would be one of chaos, a chaos that would lead to the Second Coming, and to the awaited Kingdom of the Saints. Just such a fiend had been born, Fra Lorenzo informed us, and was preaching his foul heresies among us. Avignon was the whore of Babylon who had mothered that abomination; Jacques d'Euze, the French prelate elected Pope John XXII, the unholy son of Satan she had spawned. The promised Kingdom, he assured us gravely, was close at hand.

"Come! The voice shall command again," he cried out for the third time, his own dark vociferations and the report of his smitten staff again cracking about us like thunder. "And a black horseman shall ride forth, bearing the scales of justice to measure the souls of all mankind. But though he may come to wreak vengeance, he shall be bidden by the Spirit to spare both the Olive and the Vine." At this, he paused and cast his eagle's eye among us once more.

"And do you know the real nature of that Olive, the true nature of that Vine?" he asked quietly, his fiery gaze still sweeping wildly above our heads.

"No...? You do not...? Then I will tell you," he said firmly, before anyone in the crowd had chance or could muster the courage to offer a reply. "The Olive is the bastard Church we have been blessed with as recompense for our mortal sins, the Church whose priest and clerics, in dereliction of their supposed calling, lead us in the ways of the Antichrist, and to the path of unbelieving. And the Vine...? That is the sweet wine of God's redeeming vengeance. They of all things shall be saved to last. Even as I speak, the land is purged by drought and famine, yet the priests stay fattened and sated, while all around the shepherd's flocks suffer and die. The Spirit has spoken; the Olive shall be spared for now, as shall all who are succoured by it, but God's vengeance soon shall wash over us, then all who deny His love will know and suffer His wrath."

In such tones too did Fra Lorenzo preach of the Last Days that were to come – of an Emperor who had passed from the mortal realm many years before but who was not dead and yet lay sleeping in a vault beneath a mountain, and of how, when the provident time was come, he would rise up to claim his throne, uniting all mankind around him in one true faith, driving the infidel and the unbelieving from among them, and sweeping all trace of evil from the face of the Earth. Fra Lorenzo's fiery words, and the fearful images he conjured up before us, were sufficient to instil an abject fear of impending chaos and Judgement in the hearts of all who listened, and all who heard him speak were soon convinced the final Millennium was indeed close at hand.

For what he said was true; the land was locked in the black grip of famine and poor men everywhere listened daily to the empty complaints of their bellies, yet saw plainly how the priests went about, themselves fattened and contented in that time of need, ministering liberally - if to no great effect - to the pangs of the soul, but not those of man's bodily hungers. Fra Lorenzo's new disciples did not doubt for one moment, from the things he told them, and from what they had themselves seen, that the Antichrist moved among them, and held within his power the sacred throne of San Pietro, which the hordes of Moloch had usurped to Avignon from its rightful place in Rome. As for myself, I have already told you to what unhappy state I had been reduced by circumstances and by my own vanity. I was as ready therefore to embrace Fra Lorenzo's promises of redemption for the poor, and for the meek and the down-trodden of the world, as were they.

To persuade us further of the truth of his claim, Fra Lorenzo had with him a Letter, one given to him he claimed directly by the hand of Christ. While he had lain in his forest cave, almost on the point of dying from hunger, Christ had appeared to him and had bidden him to gather around him just such as those who had congregated there to hear him speak. Only they, who through their humility and poverty had remained faithful to the selfless ways of Christ, were to inherit the eternal Kingdom of the Saints that was to come. Fra Lorenzo had come to call us, to gather us into a great army that would march joyously to the gates of the promised Kingdom, sweeping all perfidy before it, to claim there from the clutches of the Antichrist the future reward with which all of us gathered there had been unknowingly blessed.

"Do you stand ready to be weighed in the balance?" he asked defiantly of each of us, waving the Heavenly Letter before us and staring first at one then another of his spellbound congregation, and transfixing the hearts of those closest to him with the point of his staff.

"Come...! Embrace me, and embrace the truth I bring to you, and I promise you will not be found wanting. Relinquish all that you own, and your reward will be found in Heaven. Death shall be no more for you, neither shall there be hunger, nor sickness, nor pain. Immortality shall be your reward for all that you have endured."

-OO-

Several days after I first came upon Fra Lorenzo and had been listening to his now familiar words for some time, and was coming more and more to be swayed by their fervent message, a stranger came and sat beside me. He was about the same age as myself, but unlike me was dressed in the finer clothes of a merchant. At least, it seemed so to me in my impoverished state, for his jacket and cap were lined with silk and trimmed with the fur of fox or squirrel, as was then permitted to one of that class by the sumptuary laws of our commune, and he wore gold rings on his fingers and a heavy gold chain and gilded crucifix hung around his neck.

"Would you follow such a man?" he asked as he sat beside me, speaking as though we had shared a long acquaintance, or I had shown myself by my bearing to be one fully equal to his class.

"That I would, having little more to fear or lose," I replied, without hesitation, indicating the poor and threadbare condition of my clothing. "But I doubt you would do the same so gladly," I added, nodding then at the much finer condition of his. At this he raised his arm in front of him and looked at the fine cloth he was wearing, and then looked at mine, and laughed.

"Each must find his own way to God," he said. "Though I can see that yours might be a shorter way than mine. You may be surprised though at what I might do," and at that he became intent once more on listening to what Fra Lorenzo was saying.

In such manner did I make the acquaintance of Taddeo Crespi, merchant and quondam dilettante of Florence, and although in time I was to come to know him well, and to be pleased to count him as my friend, I was indeed soon to be surprised by his actions (as indeed I was by my own!), for within a week of that day we two were to be found marching side by side, he dressed now almost as poorly as I, having relinquished his wealth and rich clothing and finery for a beggar's hat and coarse linen shift, and for the hope of a greater reward in Heaven.

The body of men we joined and with whom we marched, the gaunt figure of Fra Lorenzo at our head, were taken often by those who did not understand our purpose as being among those bands of men known as *Fraticelli* who had recently been condemned by Rome for the heresies they embraced. As a consequence of this, wherever we went we were met with hostility at the hands of the agents of authority, and were similarly persecuted for what we considered to be our far more righteous beliefs. Among those we came upon however, who like us had little to lose, and for whom indeed only the greater promise of salvation was to be gained from such an association, we found much sympathy and support. Many of these hurried to join us, ignoring the threat of mortal punishment hanging over us for our supposed heresies. In this way our numbers grew daily, until we had become a great band several thousand in number wandering across the land.

Yet, if the truth had been known to those who persecuted us, as a band of men we were united more by hope for relief from a shared suffering than by any desire to closer imitate the ways of Christ. In that, if in nothing else, we and the Fraticelli parted ways. Whereas they had sought redemption for all through the strict imitation of the poverty of Christ, few of those who followed Fra Lorenzo had any possessions to relinquish, and many who joined our assembly had been driven to its cause rather by that very poverty that all had suffered in common. They all believed too what Fra Lorenzo had told them - that whatever glories waited in the promised Kingdom they had been set aside solely for those who had been disinherited during their mortal sojourn here on Earth. Assembled in our host therefore were every sort of serf and villain and labourer, and many more who through sickness or debility or treachery, or just plain ill-fortune, had found themselves consigned to the lowest of the three orders which both served and formed the community of which they were a part. Very few among that body had needed to embrace the rule of poverty; poverty had embraced them, or had been forced upon them for most of their mortal lives.

So it was that I came to join the Army of the Saints of God, for that is what we came to call ourselves, though in truth we moved with neither precision nor cohesion, and had no visible enemy against whom to rally our strength. It was as easy as that; Taddeo and I simply turned our backs on all that we had in Florence (which for him was a great deal more than for myself), and although in the beginning I was to pursue my decision with the full strength of my conviction, I cannot say I had arrived at that decision through much deliberation. Just as readily as I had taken it up, I had renounced the selfish path I had hitherto chosen, and being thus freed of the preconceptions and ambitions which had previously bound me, had found myself contented with the thought of spending the remainder of my days - however few or many they might be - in the service of the Lord.

-OO-

Soon after the feast of Ascension, in the year thirteen hundred and twenty-three, the Army of Saints departed from the sanctuary of Florence, Taddeo and I but two anonymous souls in its midst. For several weeks we marched aimlessly as one across the country, at one moment heading towards the Holy city of Jerusalem (or so we hoped was our destination), the next bearing either south, or west, or north, at each deflection from our desired goal subjugating our expectations to the unknowable vagaries of our master's visionary whims. In every town we came to, Fra Lorenzo, together with those he had appointed as his lieutenants, would expound our worthy purpose to its inhabitants, and in each place many more would hurry to join us, or sympathising with our cause but fearing the consequences of such an impetuous action, would appease their consciences with offerings of clothing and food. Still, it quickly came to seem to those who had joined the crusade at its heady inception that we proceeded without purpose or direction, and that for all his visionary fervour Fra Lorenzo was not intent upon, or perhaps was not capable of leading us to any promised, paradisaic goal.

One day, after we had been marching together for several weeks, Taddeo and I fell into conversation with some of our fellow soldiers, among who were some who had travelled widely throughout Tuscany and the Papal States, and who knew well the towns and cities of those lands, and where they lay. From them we learned of the suspicions they, and many others in our army held, and indeed that Taddeo and I had secretly ventured to one another, that we were being marched around in circles, and that the portion of road on which we were at that moment travelling we had passed along but several days before. Such intelligence did little to cheer us, and only added to the dissatisfaction we were both coming to feel at how our cause was being served. Taddeo proffered the suggestion that perhaps Fra Lorenzo had been surprised himself by the strength of the response to his calling, and that he led us first one way then the next, having no idea what else to do with the vast army of disinherited souls with which he had been so unexpectedly blessed.

"A thousand years is a long time to wait for the Day of Judgement," he said, smiling mischievously, though not without first having checked we were out of earshot of the more zealous of our cohorts. Such heresy, had it been made known, would have led to his being blinded and beaten, and left to die by the wayside, his legs broken, and his arms tethered to a wooden cross.

"After such a length of time, who knows but even its prophets might be uncertain as to what is to happen next," he added.

"Perhaps they, and we too for having followed so blindly, are but madmen after all," I responded dolefully, unable as I was to share his amusement at the possibility of our having been so misled.

Nevertheless, disillusioned though we were, Taddeo and I remained faithful to our cause, and continued to wander without apparent purpose, as every day our army gathered new disciples to its assemblage as we went. Gradually however, and doubtless as a result of the uncertainties fomenting in our hearts, and of the hunger rising in our bellies from the lack of provisions to be had for so great a host, a change came about within our fraternity, and the Army of Saints soon became truly an army of men. Fra Lorenzo even took to disporting himself like a general, going among us seated on a white charger, itself scarred and hobbled from battle, so that now he passed even higher above the heads of the lowly men who crowded round to touch him or to hear him speak. The yellow cloth he had worn in Florence was supplemented by leather breeches and a breast-plate of steel inlaid with silver, and a sword sheathed at his side appeared as complement to the wooden staff.

His sermons too became corrupted - at least they no longer spoke of the things he had promised in Florence, and which Taddeo and I and many others still wanted to hear. They seemed instead to have been tainted by the kiss of blasphemy, and to be intended now, not to persuade men to relinquish their worldly ways in return for eternal salvation, but to be addressed to those already converted among his followers, inciting them to take by force from others that which they had neither the strength nor the compunction to give of their own free will. In short, we became a band of brigands and murderers, preaching to the innocent before we robbed them that the Day of Judgement was close at hand.

"The blind must be led, the weak made strong!" became the battle cry of the bands of men who went out from among us each day, and who returned each evening, wild-eyed and bloodied, and often greatly reduced in numbers, bearing with them the tainted fruits of their righteous campaigns. In this way the great numbers of our army were kept from dying of thirst and hunger, and although at the time Taddeo and I shook our heads in consternation at what was being done in our names (and worse, in the name of God!), I understand now - though I still cannot forgive it - that if Fra Lorenzo had not so perverted his doctrine, and with it the trust of those who followed him, our Army would have faltered and fallen on the rock of starvation long before it did.

-OO-

By the height of the summer of that year we numbered, by my calculation, some four thousand souls, and had been travelling almost without cease for three months or more, having visited at least three score towns and cities, having been welcomed in few, and excluded and driven at the points of swords and lances from most. By then, for many of us, the senseless circuit of our movements was being enjoined for a purpose we were no longer able to discern. Gone were our dreams of a promised Kingdom, and of relief from our mortal suffering; gone was the fire in our spirits which Fra Lorenzo had so easily enflamed.

All of us, to a man, were tired and hungry and thirsty, and our tongues and bellies were swollen from the numberless days of deprivation we had endured. Pain and despair were the blessings which now shaped our daily existence, not the eternal joy we had been promised, nor the certain comforts we had formerly found in our beliefs. Our throats chafed and burned, not merely from the lack of water, but from the shrill cries for repentance we still managed to drag from our lungs, as much to console ourselves and to restore our own flagging spirits as to inspire those who watched and listened to join us. Our feet too were torn and blistered, and many went barefoot, or were shod only in strips of bark bound to their feet with reeds or rags.

Many were sick, and infections were rife among us, and all around men fell senseless to the ground, or threw themselves down in ever increasing numbers, their bodies wracked by violent convulsions, wailing and screaming profanities, decrying both the God who made them suffer for their salvation, and the Devil who had laid the iniquitous seeds of dissension in their souls. Every one of us too was at times stricken by the power of the sun as it beat down mercilessly upon us. In this we all suffered equally, despite the prayers and supplications many had taken to impaling on the scythes and forks and hoes they carried with them as staffs and weapons, and which they brandished above their heads, turning them towards Heaven both as plea and for protection. Those few who did not succumb consoled their fears in the belief that those who did had been otherwise inconsequent in their faith and actions, and that their own more righteous supplications would not go unheeded. And in the midst of that suffering and ever-deepening despair Fra Lorenzo went among us seated on his charger, his zealous eyes still blazing, the sun's light glinting from the silver inlays of his breast-plate, and with his fierce warnings and promises of what was awaiting those who survived the Devil's coercions, kept us true to the faith which waned and flickered in our hearts.

Thus were our days consumed in passing from one Promised Land to the next, or standing at their gates, waiting in vain for each to be delivered to our possession, while our nights were spent in fitful and pain-filled sleeping, and in dreams of a happier life, or even - at the most desperate of moments - of the sweet release of death. So it continued for days on end until we came at last to a place, the name of which I never knew, and there we discovered another army - not of God, but of knights and archers, and crowds of footmen armed with knives and cudgels - drawn up against us, their swords and lances flashing threats of vengeance in the evening sun.

"The massed ranks of the Antichrist," Taddeo said quietly beside me, and to this awed imprecation I replied some nonsense, drawn to my thoughts no doubt by vague recollections of happier days in Padua creating those wondrous pictures alongside my master, about such a crowd having come to Gethsemane to take away and imprison Christ.

-OO-

Fortunately for us (for weakened and dispirited as we were we would have given up our lives with little resistance), our enemy did not press that day to join in battle, but assayed first to sue for the peaceful dispersion of our ranks. As darkness fell emissaries came out to meet us bearing promises of provisions and safe-conduct to all who would repent their heresies and wished to return to their homes in peace. Meanwhile, our great army stood, confused and weary, and fearful of the test to which we were to be put. Four thousand souls, cowed to silence, waiting to see what response the visionary prophet whose words had caused us to be assembled there would make to the demands being made upon their faith. That night, despite the pitiable condition to which most of us had been reduced our camp was alive with noise and movement, and the thrill of impending battle coursed through all our veins. All around, camp-fires were stoked and burned and stuttered strongly, infusing the faces of all with an ungodly and angry light.

"Tomorrow we will fight for God and his promised Kingdom!" emboldened voices cried out among the contending fires and darkness.

"The enemies of God shall taste the steel of vengeance!" others voices echoed bravely, being carried to us from the various compasses of the campsite on a wind filled with spluttering sparks and smoke.

"The Army of Saints shall be vindicated!" a hundred intoxicated voices cried in unison from somewhere nearby. "Fra Lorenzo's prophesies will be consummated in blood!"

The more seasoned among us - battle-scarred veterans of other Crusades, of temporal wars fought in distant lands, discarded by their lords now they were too old or crippled by their injuries to earn a soldier's coin - sat by their fires quietly burnishing their weapons. At ease as they seemed to be with their thoughts of mortal conflict and approaching death, these sad, silent men instilled by their very calmness some little courage in the hearts of those who had never before been called upon to test themselves in battle. Throughout the night though, less brave souls could be seen slipping from the edges of our camp into the darkness, deserting our cause for the comparative safety of the night, and I have to confess it took every word, and every argument Taddeo could summon to dissuade me from joining them in their flight.

"We cannot leave now," he said, his hand clamped tightly on my arm to prevent me from leaping to my feet in deference to the commands my terrified thoughts were screaming out for my body to obey. "He promised this, that we would be tested by the forces of the Antichrist, by those who oppose us, but that if we stood our ground we would be redeemed," he continued, something of the fervour we had once shared for our cause returning to his face and voice.

"But for three months he has not fulfilled a single promise he made," I complained.

"Neither has he failed us yet."

"But what if he is wrong? What if we are not the chosen ones, and will fight and die here as nothing more than the poor misguided fools we are?"

"Then we will die in ignorance of our sins, and will be forgiven them. We cannot desert him now, not when his words are to be put to their final proof."

I realised then the extent of the conviction Taddeo held still in his faith, and that after all we had shared I could not desert him, even though I was more than ready to desert the one who had led us to this place. I told Taddeo I would stay; that on the morrow we would stand and fight, and if need be would die together, side by side. My words though were mere bravado, and when I retired for the night it was only to resume reluctant battle with my cowardice. Shaking with fear, and with my teeth chattering so hard I thought they would break, I curled up in my blanket for warmth and protection, and rocked myself, surprisingly, into fitful sleep.

-OO-

The following morning however we woke to find ourselves confronted, not by the prospect of battle, but by an enigma none could comprehend. Fra Lorenzo was no longer among us and his trusted lieutenants were also gone. His white battle-charger was tethered still beside the tent to which he had retired the previous evening, and his sword and breeches and armour were found laid out on the pallet on which he was to have slept. The Heavenly Letter was also discovered, torn and crumpled, thrown down and trampled in the mud. The wooden staff though was gone.

News of this troubling development spread quickly through the camp, and rumours flared in every quarter that our leaders had been abducted during the night by the agents of the city, and had been taken there to be tried for heresy, and there were many in our ranks who pressed that we should immediately take up arms to release them, greatly outnumbered and ill-equipped though we were. Rumour however quickly followed upon rumour, and the certainty that had seized all on discovery of this strange occurrence (and which even the martyr requires before putting himself willingly to the sword), was soon enough dispelled. We spent the rest of that day wracked by doubts in our faith, and by confusion, and with our eyes turned towards the massed lines of our enemy, listlessly waiting for news of what was at hand.

It was not until the sun was descending and evening approached that we were to be provided with an answer to our questions. Among our number there had been several who were native to that place, wherever it might have been, and having first clothed themselves from among the rags and tatters of others as best they could to avoid being recognised as members of our destitute and outlawed band, they had entered the city to see what intelligence they could gather. When they returned several hours later, the gravity of what truths they had discovered could be clearly discerned in the grim countenance of their faces.

"They've sold us out! We've been betrayed!" they cried repeatedly as they passed among us, anger filling their eyes and hardening their voices. A murmur of disbelief rose from those who had gathered around and could hear them, and as Taddeo and I were among that number we also added our voices to that quiet chorus of dismay.

"Lorenzo and his lackeys weren't taken by force. The bastards rose early and entered the city of their own volition," one of them explained when they finally came to a halt in our midst. "The traitor Lorenzo and his lieutenants are preaching against us now, and even against the cause he himself started." Again, a groan rose up from among those who were within earshot of these unhappy tidings, and cries of anguish began to rise from all directions as word of what had happened spread throughout the camp.

"They're saying we rose up against him. That they were powerless to do other than what we said. That we held them all under threat of death."

"And are they believed?" several voices asked, including my own.

"Maybe, and maybe not. Only God can know. What's certain though is they're trying their hardest to save their own hides."

"The Devil take 'em," the angry chorus replied, and the air above their heads became filled with shaking fists and brandished weapons, but the man stilled their protests with a gesture of his hands.

"Wait! Wait! All's not over. There's some there are willing to testify against him. They've heard him sermonise, and seen him in his armour, going amongst us like a Lord. That's his reward for his vanity and for having run us round in circles for so long."

"The Devil take his soul!" a thousand voices cried, but this time mine was not to be heard adding to that clamour; I was too stunned by what I had heard to join in any such curse. I had come all that way, and had suffered such hardships, only to be betrayed by the very one - or so I had believed - who had shown me the way to achieve true salvation. I began to weep, and my body to tremble, and such was my distress I would have fallen to the ground had Taddeo not put his arm around me and led me away.

"Forgive me. You were right," he said when I had recovered my senses slightly. "We should have made our way from here while we could. Without a leader we are at their mercy. We must take what we can and flee!" These last words, so unexpected from one who until a few moments before had been a most ardent believer in the justness of our cause, were music to my ears, and though I was still too distraught to speak my spirits lifted and I nodded agreement to what he had proposed.

Later that evening, as Taddeo and I gathered together what we had managed to cajole and pilfer to succour us in our flight, and as we prepared to flee the camp under cover of approaching darkness, Fra Lorenzo and his lieutenants were brought out from the city. There, on a hastily erected platform raised high on a hillock before the gates of the city so that all might see what was done to them, they were executed for their crimes. After their eyes had been put out, and their tongues extracted, and their joints cut open and the wounds filled with molten tar, their bodies were smeared in oil and set in flames. By some coincidence, or perhaps by design (though whether of temporal powers, or of some authority more Divine, I dare not conjecture), the sun was at that moment setting directly behind the hillock, so that the tableau of their deaths was played out in stark silhouette against a backdrop of a giant orange sun sinking into a blood-streaked sky.

As awe inspiring as this setting was, and much as my heart rejoiced in their punishment, I had no desire to watch the dying torments of these men who had so misled me, and so I sat down on the ground amongst the forest of legs of my fellow soldiers, my head cradled in my arms. It was not possible, however, to ignore the screams that came to me clearly above the heads of our silenced army, or to remain unmoved by the other sound that replaced it once they had finally ended - the sound of several thousand voices wailing their anguish and resentment - the most mournful sound I had ever heard.

-OO-

Once Fra Lorenzo and the others had been put to the stake, the great army of his followers, Taddeo and I among them, finding ourselves without a cause or a captain to lead us, and without food or water, began to disperse. To their honour, I must record here that the citizens of that place remained true to their word, and that none of us, other than the instigators of our heresy (for that, despite our better expectations of it, was what it had shown itself to have been), were in any way harmed. Taddeo and I, having slipped away as we had planned under cover of darkness, made our way back to Florence, and there Taddeo decided to return once more to the sanctuary of his family, and to the more certain comforts and consolations of his former life.

To explain his long absence from the city, and to conceal our involvement with Fra Lorenzo from those who might have been prejudiced by knowledge of such an association, we together concocted a tale of how Taddeo had come to visit me in Fiesole, where I had supposedly kept a small workshop, in order to commission a painting which I was to have made for him as a gift to his sister. In answer to the complaints that none in his family had known of this journey, Taddeo replied that the picture had been intended as a surprise, and had accordingly kept his doings that day a secret from them all. Returning together to Florence (we continued with our deceit), we had been attacked by bandits, who for reasons unknown had thought us other than we were. They had then taken us to their stronghold near Ferrara, and had held us there to ransom, though obviously - given the mistaken identities they had assigned to us - to no avail. We then told of how, once their error had become clear to them, the brigands had released us, having first deprived us of our clothing and jewellery, giving us suits of peasant's garb in their stead, as was evidenced by the rags we were wearing, and of how, through great hardship and several lengthy detours (which we added to our story to explain the long duration of our absence), and by the grace of God, we had eventually made our way back to Florence. Happily, at their delight in having him once more safely in their midst his friends and family did not question our shallow mendacity too closely, having

I suppose no reason to doubt us, and thus they welcomed both Taddeo and me with open arms.

To show his gratitude to me for having helped restore him to his former good fortune, and for the friendship we had shared during our time spent together in the Army of the Saints, Taddeo commissioned from me several works for himself, and for his family, and even installed me in my own workshop in Fiesole so that my circumstances would better support the details of our story, and procured too several more commissions for me from among his many friends. Fortunately (and I say this without malice, for I was grateful to receive such favour, modest though it was), his was not amongst the greater families of Florence, and those he associated with were naturally all of a similar standing, and being thus *popoli minuti*, whose tastes and refinement were necessarily proscribed by the limits of their means, they were all more than pleased with what little of my former skills I managed to bring to bear upon the execution of their demands.

Through such patronage was I restored in some measure to the position I had formerly held in the eyes of my fellow citizens, though not to one of prosperity, for my greater skills had still all but deserted me and stubbornly refused to return. Indeed, such a good friend did Taddeo prove to be that I was able to survive for a number of years, not through the merits of my own skills and reputation, but by virtue of the commendatory words he said on my behalf. Renewed once more in some measure to my former confidence, I decided to put behind me my experiences in Fra Lorenzo's army of disinherited, and to once more place my trust for my future salvation in my own hands, and never again in those of visionary men of God.

-OO-

ATRA MORS

"Woe is me of the shilling in the arm-pit,
the early ornaments of black death." Welsh
lament

I am now about to bring about another great leap in the telling of my story, an even greater one than I made before, for it is on the eve of the celebration of the feast of *Natale Domini* in the year of our Lord thirteen hundred and forty-seven that you find me next. For that, my patient reader is where I elect to again take up my story, being as that happy day was the date of my arrival in the city of Genoa, having finally embarked there at the end of five days' journey from Pisa by sea. As for the history of what transpired in the years between this time and when you last caught sight of me, I will spare you the details of my fortuitous, if faltering resurgence, and will say only that I was then in my fifty-seventh year, and through dint of my labours and the benign patronage of Taddeo Crespi (and despite my own frequent efforts to promote for myself an almost assured anonymity), I had again become better known to my fellow citizens as Pacino, artisan, *dipintore*, and resident and sometimes defender of the commune of Florence.

As I again set pen to paper to relate the events of the terrible sea-passage I had just endured, I find my words are inadequate to express the emotions I felt on finding myself once more on *terra firma*, having left behind the sea and all its mysteries and unpredictable motions. Of those five days journeying I had spent three in a state of constant fear and trepidation, and (to add physical distress to my spiritual consternation), chilled to the bone by the bitter winds which had hurried, cold and damp and snow-laden from the lands which lay to the north-east of our passage, and which bore down on the vessel upon which I was travelling - a Pisan *tarida* of fifty *braccia* and sixteen oars, bound for Avignon by way of Genoa, bearing a valuable cargo of armour and arms.

Being respecters neither of worth nor craftsmanship those winds had howled around us, coming to us from the land unbowed and uninterrupted. In their fury they had tossed us about upon the heaving back of the ocean, on the shanks of which angry beast we rose and fell and rolled from side to side, helplessly bound to its undulations, careening upon its crests and chasms like a cork awash in a tumbling *barile* of wine. To add to my misery no bed had been provided for my comfort on that foundering vessel, nor cubicle in which a man might find shelter, and so the snow fell on me where I lay on the deck and settled like dust upon the coarse fabric of the cloak and blanket I had taken with me as my only protection. From these two scant pieces of fabric I had fashioned a tent of sorts against the windward bulwark, beneath which spurious *baldacchino* I cowered and prayed without cease for two days and nights.

As was the custom my fee of passage had provided only for such space on the deck as I occupied, either prone or standing, not for food or shelter, and the master of the ship - a surly Pisan and an ungracious man by nature - had seemed not to care much either for my comfort or safety. Once my coin had been deposited securely in his purse, he did not speak to me again. Perhaps he was just an uncivil man by nature, or was too involved in keeping his vessel from foundering in the storm to pay me much heed, or perhaps (as I suspected), he had heard of what some might consider my past political indiscretions and - his sympathies lying in directions other than my own - had agreed to carry me to Genoa only in order that his own city might be freed of my presence.

For beyond my better judgement, and in defiance of the experiences of my youth (which familiarity alone should have been enough to dissuade me forever from such an inclination), I had a few years before that time become involved in the politics of the commune of Florence. It had been a reckless action to follow, all things considered, and most definitely in contradiction of that greater prudence my advanced age was supposed to bring, especially so as I had always previously managed, other than that brief, childhood aberration, to resist the attractions other men seemed to find concealed in such intrigues.

In September of the year thirteen hundred and forty-two control of the Signoria of Florence had been offered to one Gautier de Brienne, Duke of Athens. De Brienne, doubtless for his own reasons, had accepted gladly, and I, acting out of a plain desire to see justice and sanity restored to our city rather than from any particular political conviction, had served his cause eagerly. To this end I had stood, and had sometimes even fought (to my great surprise - to have wielded arms against others, and to have suffered nothing worse than cuts and bruises for my efforts, and to have done no worse injury to any other man), together with other good and equally altruistic men, as *popolano* of the White persuasion of the Guelph faction of the *vicinanza* of San Giovanni, where I then lived. My political gullibility had led me to believe that in de Brienne's office had lain the possibility of relief for the *popolani* from the bloody and endless struggles the multi-coloured factions still waged amongst themselves, and against those who supported the claims made upon our lands by the German Emperors, and who called themselves Waibelingen, or as Domenico and I had known them better, Ghibellines.

But despite the Duke's grand, and my own, more humble expectations, the summer of the following year had found us - both the Duke and I, and many more besides - fleeing the walls of the city with hordes of dissatisfied and blood-hungry Blacks clamouring at our heels. I had fled to Pisa, which was then, at least in my narrow understanding of the allegiances of cities and of the coloured banners under which their fortunes variously flourished or suffered, under White Guelph control. Where the Duke had fled to I did not know; neither did I care! I had more than had my fill of politics, just as I had previously had my fill of religion, and once safely in Pisa I again devoted my energies solely to painting, seeking in such diversion that relief from the struggles of the secular world which I had foolishly hoped to find through the exercise of those other two occupations. There I had remained for four years or more, in various degrees of health and prosperity, until by chance I happened to renew my acquaintance with Taddeo Crespi, who unbeknown to me had also fled the uncertain atmosphere of Florence. It had been through his good and constant offices that I had received a commission to make my way to Genoa, to try again to put the greater skills God had given me at an unwitting patron's command.

-OO-

In my younger days, while indulging the head-strong appetites of youth in the inns and taverns that crowded and flourished around the harbours of the great merchant city of Venice, and later in those of the less great Pisa (which fair city is sadly fallen now from its former position of grace), and even in the many inland towns and communes I had worked in or had visited, I had heard many a tale of sea-serpents and Sirens, of strange sea-bound creatures that lured unwary mariners to their doom. I had always believed these stories to be nothing more than that - but stories, no more than sailor's gossip and fantasies, idle imaginings embroidered and embellished upon during the long, lonely hours spent at sea. But I swear to you now, as God is my witness, it was the hounds of Hell that were unleashed upon us in their legion numbers in the heart of the storm in which we found ourselves floundering towards the close of our second day at sea.

To this day my dreams are visited still by the dark, bestial forms which loomed and towered above us, their rows of pearl-like teeth flashing and spitting cold, white fire upon our fragile vessel as they barked and yelped about our bows. They moaned and roared around us, their heaving bodies obliterating what little of God's provident light still fell upon us from the cloud-thickened skies. As we writhed and weaved ahead of their harried chasing, the heavy jaws of those luminous beasts snapping against the timbers of our seemingly insufficient craft, I feared at every moment we would all perish in the grip of some infernal Demon's bite. Now, seated safely here, in this dry and dusty room in Florence, far enough removed as it is from the sea, I understand those spectres for what they truly were - no more than the troubled movements of the storm-tossed ocean. But marooned on that boat, in those protracted hours of desperation, fear and superstition had given birth, and then succour to such unearthly creatures, even in mine, normally the most sceptical of minds.

Thus, did I cling miserably to this mortal existence, and for what little protection and comfort they afforded me, to the bare timbers of the deck on which I lay, as our puny vessel battled its way northwards against those monstrous seas. I had been told by some who I had previously considered friends that under favourable conditions and with a good set of oars to assist us Genoa lay no more than three days distant from Pisa, and I had therefore provisioned myself for a voyage of such a length. The adverse winds and heavy seas we encountered, however, delayed our progress, driving us back at times across waters we had already traversed. At the end of the third day I was shaking from cold and hunger, and still we had travelled no further north than to be in the Golfo della Spezia, close by the town of Portovenere, and there we were again forced to seek shelter and to lay to for the night. As darkness consumed us we dropped anchor off the island of Palmaria, and there on our troubled horizon the lamps of the Abbey of San Venerio provided some little solace and comfort to our misery, glimmering through the mists and rain clouds at the edge of the dark abyss of the night.

-OO-

The twenty-third, the day of our eventual land-fall in Genoa, had fallen on a Sabbath, and to show my gratitude to the Lord, and my repentance for having travelled, albeit reluctantly on that, His appointed day of rest, I celebrated a mass in the tiny chapel of Santa Maria Annunziata, and made an offering there of four candles to the greater glory of His name. Only later did I think to set another candle, but smaller (as I wished only to show my gratitude at having survived such a journey) to San Nicholai, patron saint of all who travel upon the sea. I had no intention of ever travelling again across the ocean; as I have said, I was already in my fifty-seventh year, and hoped I would never again have to avail myself of the services of that doubtful benefactor during what time I expected to remain upon this Earth.

To put it bluntly, I was then, as Dante would have it, *senettute* - in the age of prudence, justice and affability; or as Galen and Avicenna had determined it, I was drawing to the end of the age of diminution, approaching old age. But I ask you, was it prudence that had placed me on that ship in the middle of that tempest? Or justice that I should have been subjected to terror and discomfort in such a way? Cowering on the deck beneath my cloak and blanket, I wondered often which of the numberless sins I had perpetrated in my ignorance could have earned me such treatment at my Maker's hands.

Affable on that part of my journey I was not!

-OO-

The man who was to be my patron in Genoa was a curate to the Piscopio by the name of Bonnacorso Piombi, a relative of Taddeo Crespi by marriage on the distaff side. By coincidence, but a few days before my unexpected reunion with him in Pisa, Taddeo had received a request from him to procure the services of a *dipintori* versed in the Florentine style to paint some panels to be hung in his family chapel in Genoa. Out of friendship, and on the strength of his misguided judgement of the quality of the things I had made for him, Taddeo had gladly put my name forward.

I had in fact had the brief acquaintance of this Bonnacorso some years previously in Avignon. He had been then but a middling cleric in the Papal court, while I had been engaged upon trying to eke out an existence worthy of my skills in the painting of bucklers and shields for those petty nobles who came to that place to buy indulgences, and in the execution of imitation draperies, birds and flowers, and pastoral scenes to brighten the apartments of newly arrived clerics such as he. In his correspondence the canon had said he remembered me well, and had heard of my work, and would gladly give me his commission, but when I arrived in Genoa I bore with me a letter of introduction from Taddeo Crespi as precaution against the possibility I might be considered unwelcome by those who held power in the city to which I had been so generously called.

There I was to make for Piombi a Crucifixion, to be hung above an altar, and a *Piéta* - the depiction of Christ mortified, his body removed from the Cross and lying prostrate in the arms of the Magdalene. This latter is always a difficult and exacting composition in its perspective and likeness to life for any man to make, the body of Christ being almost naked, with all the details of its muscles and ligaments revealed, and too the bloody wounds of the Crucifixion. The relief I experienced at my safe landfall was therefore tainted by trepidation at the painterly challenge that awaited me. Both of these things, when finished, were to be placed in the family chapel in the Piscopio di San Lorenzo, hopefully to the honour and glory of my name, and I had been told too, that if the work on them proceeded as required, and I could complete both in time for the celebration of the Mass at Easter, I would further receive a commission to create several small frescoes of the life of San Francesco in the aisle of another church then being built in that city in praise of that Saint's Holy name.

But as events were to determine I was not to remain in Genoa long enough to complete a single one of these commissions. In fact, as God is my witness and will forgive my failings, work on them never began. Before the Mass of *Dies cinerum* had been celebrated, when the penitents go about on their knees, dressed in rags and sacking, their heads strewn with ashes, I was again travelling northwards, fleeing something more dreadful even than heaving seas or the mortal wrath of man.

-OO-

In the first month of that year thirteen hundred and forty-eight, not many days after my own arrival, three galleys put into the harbour of Genoa, having been driven there, as I had been, by unfavourable winds blowing from the East. This in itself was of course far from unusual, for Genoa was then, as it still is, a great and powerful city, and many merchants and factors lived and traded there. The three vessels that arrived that day, however, bore upon them a most unwelcome cargo, one which no merchant - no matter how adept or unscrupulous - could ever have turned to profit. On all three a terrible sickness flourished, and every man aboard them - the captains and crews and oarsmen, the merchants and factors and pilgrim-travellers who by

their combined misfortune had found themselves
embarked upon them - were either dead of this unknown
affliction or were close to the point of dying. The pitiable condition of those who yet lived, and the decaying
corpses of those who had succumbed, I had the misfortune to witness with my own eyes.

Rumours of a fearful pestilence raging in the Orient
had been brought to us upon the many merchant ships
which had visited Pisa during the course of the previous
year. I had heard too similar stories in the market-places
of Genoa in the short time I had been there - tales of rains
of lizards and serpents, of fire falling from the Heavens,
of fetid smoke rising up from fissures in the surface of the
Earth, which slew every man and beast it came upon. I
had heard too of a war between the Sun and the ocean,
and of mighty battles being waged between pagan Gods
and the elements in the seas that lay around the shores of
Cathay. There, it was said, water drawn up by the Sun as
vapours from that rebellious ocean had been infected by
the putrefying flesh of whales and mermen, and other sea
creatures which had perished in the conflict, and it was
said this mephitis drifted now unchecked across the face
of Creation, a miasmic cloud of pestilence and corruption contaminating all who looked upon it or whom it
touched.

Everyone I met had heard such stories, and all believed
them, having no reason - save their ignorance of the lands
in which this sickness reputedly flourished - to take them
as other than truth. Not one among them (and I include
myself amongst that large and ill-informed number) knew
much of worth about these strange people known as
Scythians and Tartars, or understood properly where in
God's Creation the fabulous land of Cathay was to be

found. I was therefore not alone in thinking it a distant and inconsequent phenomenon, a murrain afflicted upon the infidels who peopled those heathen regions, and sent to them alone as punishment for their intransigent lack of faith. Not once had I, nor had any of my acquaintance considered the possibility of such agents of vengeance having any bearing upon our own, more God-fearing lives. Yet despite such stubborn beliefs and ignorance, that cloud had arrived now to wreak its retribution upon us complacent sinners, and although no *cometis stella* had threaded our skies, and no sheets of fire had descended from the Heavens to warn us, nor plagues of frogs or scorpions had come to herald its approach, its deadly cargo washed now, or rather lay tethered tightly against our Christian shores.

The three galleys had come to Genoa from Caffa by way of Messina, their holds laden with cargoes of precious spices and silks. Fearing that not only those on board, but also the merchandise stored below the decks might have been corrupted by the sickness, the officers of the commune posted orders that nothing, neither man nor goods be permitted to leave the ships that day. Not a single voice did I hear raised against this prudent embargo, not even among those whose livelihood depended most upon it. Indeed, so effective a proscription did it prove that the only traffic to be seen between the ships and harbour was among those creatures that always take passage on such sea-going vessels, as vermin by their hundreds (sensing land perhaps, and fresh stores to plunder, and possibly themselves seeking to flee that terrible sickness), scurried from among the ships' bulwarks and timbers, and poured out in squealing turmoil along the lines and hawsers which bound the vessels to the quays.

Meanwhile the stricken sailors lay on the decks, their putrescent bodies displayed openly to all who cared to see. Many had fallen where Death had found them, or dying, and being not yet released from their suffering, were locked still in its final, painful throes. Others among them, though mortally afflicted, were yet able to cry out to God for mercy, or to beg for assistance from those who had come to the quays to witness their torment. It is my unfortunate duty however to report that neither of these blessings was to be forthcoming, for God had already despatched the angel of Death in response to their supplications, and seeing this, and fearing more for their own survival, the citizens of Genoa stood idly by, mindless of compassion or charity, merely curious to see what course Fate would follow for these unfortunate souls.

As much in doubt as that future outcome may have been in the minds of those who witnessed its unravelling, the stigmata bestowed upon those it afflicted was clearly visible for all to see. The bodies of the dead displayed dark and morbid swellings, many of which had burst and opened, bringing - so the survivors informed us - a certain and most painful death. One among them, an olive-skinned youth from Naples, removed his tunic to display the tumour that was growing in the pit of his arm. It too was dark and ashen in colour, and about the size of an apple, but unlike those of his fallen companions it had not yet opened. He laughed and joked bravely with his audience, maintaining his spirits despite the obvious discomfort of his afflictions, and informed us that he had another such *gavacciolo* - but would show this only to the women present among us - which sickly fruit was fomenting in his groin. He did not yet bear upon his person the dark spots, or *livid*, which he said would mark the disease's fatal progress, but it was plain to see that Death was seated firmly on his face.

And as we on the quays watched that macabre tableau being played out before us, and as we listened unmoved to the pleas and groans of the dying, the stench of that terrible Death and putrefaction drifted across us, making us choke and gasp for breath.

-OO-

As is often the way with mortal men, idle curiosity soon gave way to active fear. Towards the evening of the second day, as the sun settled beneath the sea's horizon, the *Gonfaloniere di Giustizia* marched to the harbour, bearing orders to drive the three offending galleys from our shores. To enforce this ordinance, he had with him a number of archers and pike-men, and horses drawing various engines of war. Once assembled on the quay-side, this assorted company, assisted by many of those who had gathered only to witness the eviction, but who found themselves now suddenly subject to the fervour of such a noble cause, began to assault and drive the offending vessels from the quays.

A torrent of arrows, some tipped with burning tar, and of rocks and stones thrown by hand or hurled from make-shift slings and by the belligerent engines, rained down on the ships and assailed those marooned upon them with such conviction that, despite their pitiful condition, those able among them were forced to man their oars and cast what sail they could to flee. It was a truly sorry sight to see men turned upon one another in such a way, and to watch those sufferers, innocent as they were of what had befallen them, being slain at the hands of their brethren, for these were Genoese vessels being driven from their own city in their time of need. As I watched this sorry spectacle unfold, my thoughts turned to how our Lord had been brought before Caiaphas, to be condemned too by his own kind. Indeed, the sight of such betrayal conjured up in my memory an image of the panel depicting that part of Christ's story which my master had crafted in the chapel in Padua. Mirrored all around me I could see reflected the same anger that my master had assigned to the faces of the Lord's accusers, though I had difficulty still in comprehending the depth of hatred that moulded those expressions and compelled their owners to commit such invidious acts, both those many centuries ago at the betrayal of Jesus, and at that moment in Genoa.

On one of the galleys fires took hold in the timbers of the *castilla*, and from there spread quickly to the folded sail, then proceeded to lick and wind its quicksilver way among the masts and rigging. Confused and weakened as they were, and being driven to despair by the treatment being meted out at the hands of men who were both their friends and kin, the sailors made what efforts they could to bring the fire under control. This they did however with little conviction beyond the necessity of their immediate survival, for I suspect they all knew by then that they were doomed.

I saw several men felled in the onslaught; one struck by a boulder hurled from a springald, which missile crushed his head against the bulwark timbers, another pierced by an arrow driven through his eye. And I have to confess that I too played some small part in that general suffering, for despite my incomprehension at what I was witnessing, neither was I immune to the frenzy of the moment - hurling a pebble (no bigger than a bean, God help me!), yet thrown with all my might, and which projectile delivered a glancing blow to the head of some unfortunate - having been driven to such uncharitable actions by honest fear, and by an eagerness to rid myself and the city to which I then owed my allegiance of the prospect of that hideous disease.

Our courageous efforts to that end, however, were to prove of no avail. Within but a week of that day the sickness was venting its powers freely among us, and raged unchecked within the walls of the city. In fact, so virulent was its hold upon us, and so many were they who had succumbed to its hunger, that soon there remained insufficient numbers among the unafflicted to maintain even the basic orders of our daily life. Each day a thousand corpses lay where they had fallen, or where their family or friends had put them, unblessed and untended in the streets. There they remained, unclean and unsainted, putrefying in the base reward of their imperfection, and corrupting through that impurity not only our vision and our sensibilities, but the very air we breathed. Even the cats and dogs and rats that roamed the streets and scoured the sewers and gutters fell prey to its ministrations, as did beasts of burden, until it seemed that the Last Days truly were being visited upon us, and that wherever one went, it was only to pass among scenes of carnage and decay.

Seeing all of this, and fearing for their own safety, many of the citizens, including he who was to have been my patron, fled the polluted confines of the city. Thus did the clergy, and the rich and ennobled unite for once in the face of common adversity; thus - again, and as was their habit - did they abandon those more humble and disenfranchised souls who in such times of need looked to them for succour and guidance, and who themselves had little choice but to remain where they were and to wait for Death to find them. And I, being likewise rich in a sense of my own worth, if not in compassion or in the commodities of this worldly existence, and having been deprived by the departure of my patron of any good reason to remain in that God-forsaken place, like the pious and the wealthy before me, I too naturally fled.

-OO-

From Genoa I fled inland to Turin, following first the road to Alessandria and Casale Monferrato, then along the banks of the river Po, making my way north of the limestone massif that lies to the east of Turin, and which also bears the name Monferrato. As I have said, it was then near the time of *Dies cinerum*, but the *campagna* through which I passed lay still in the grip of winter, the fields lying fallow and untended, and with snow spreading its somnolent blanket deep upon the ground. Even the great river was frozen over, as had been the Tanaro at Alessandria, where a great winter fair was being held in blithe ignorance of the approaching murrain, and I was therefore able to cross both of these natural barriers on foot.

Having no wish to tarry in any of these places, but desiring only to put as great a distance as possible between myself and what I had seen in Genoa, I arranged at Casale to travel westwards to Turin in the company of a merchant from Cremona. Though I had often heard it said that when travelling abroad it was wisest to do so in numbers, so great had been my haste to leave Genoa, I had not then thought to take such precaution. I had been too frightened by the thought of what might become of me if I remained to have feared what might befall me in the countryside. Anyway, I had not been the only one seeking refuge beyond the veneficious confines of the city, and would not have lacked for companionship, had I desired it. In truth, though, I had preferred to travel alone, for fear of the possibility of infection from such proximity. Neither had I wanted for protection, should the need have arisen, for as I have said, many a noble and prelate had also fled with their families and retainers to the presumed safety of the *contado*, and it had been therefore an easy matter for a lone itinerant such as myself to travel in the wake of such a train.

Despite my best efforts to escape it however, the plague arrived in Turin but days behind me, though it struck there with far less malice than in Genoa, and so, having no money to finance my flight further, and feeling less threatened by its presence than when first exposed to it (believing it to have spent its fury in the great mortality it had inflicted upon the unfortunate citizens of Genoa), I worked and rested there until after the Resurrection of our Blessed Lord. I received there anyway several commissions to paint the arms on the coffers and shields of a knight from Chiavasso, and to do a courtyard and a small room in the home of a merchant. This latter I did in *fresco secco* on plaster, with painted borders and friezes of flowers and plants, and for which I was paid two *genovini*. For the same merchant I also made a small wooden panel of the Madonna (the first time I had ever attempted this blessed subject), to which I even put my name, considering I had made it better than was usual for my efforts, and seeing in it too, much of the qualities of my master's hand. In this manner I was able to get together sufficient monies for the continuation of my journey, having decided I would make my way north-wards to Paris. There, I hoped, my past - and the failures and indiscretions it contained - would not be known to my fellow men, at least not to many among them, and

before the *Misericordia domini* had been celebrated I was
ready to resume my journey north.

As you know, I was then in my fifty-eighth year, the
anniversary of my birth having passed in the preceding
January. During the many years that even then constituted
the span of my life, I had been given cause to travel far
and wide and often, passing frequently throughout
Tuscany and in those states appertaining to the Papal See,
even as far as to Naples and to Avignon. Such journeys I
had made in every season, with never a thought to the
hardships or the discomfort such journeying invariably
entailed. But I tell you now that in all that diverse peregri-
nation nothing I had ever encountered could have prepared me for the part of my journey I was about to
undertake - neither the cold, nor the sheer terror of my
sea-passage from Pisa, nor the horrors of the pestilence I
had witnessed in Genoa.

The cold and damp of those winter seas had been as
nothing compared to the extremes of climate I was to be
exposed to in the mountains which lay between Turin
and my desired goal of Paris, and never before had I felt
such fear in the face of the elements as I was to experience then. Perhaps, though, the constant threat and spectacle of sickness and death to which I had been exposed
had weakened the fortitude of my mind to cope with
such hardships. I had seen so many struck down without
warning in Genoa and Turin, and with no apparent cause
or explanation, and of all its terrible aspects, it was
without doubt the burden of uncertainty of God's bitter
purpose in this sickness which weighed most heavily on
mine, as it did on the minds of all other men.

-OO-

To attempt the hazards of a mountain crossing in the season of snow and infertility is not an unusual thing, and I have known men who have done so even in the sharpest of winters, and who have thought little of it, but then perhaps they were fortunate in having been of lesser years than was I. Nevertheless, to achieve my goal it was necessary for me to pass that barrier, formidable as it was. I had no desire to return to Genoa, even less to go from there by sea to Avignon, to attain the easier route to Paris along the river Rhone. I therefore made arrangements to meet at Susa, at the foot of the mountains, a certain Marcovaldo of Turin, together with his factor, Tasso di Arpo, where we were to be met by the Savoyards they had employed to be our porters and guides.

At the outset of our journey northwards into the mountains the weather had been tempered by the approaching sweet season, but as we climbed higher the air became cooler and we began to feel its bite sharp upon our skin. The green meadows laced with spring flowers which had greeted us on the slopes that lay above the town of Susa soon gave way to vast fields of dazzling white snow and ice, and the lake along whose shores we walked for half a day as we approached the pass at Mont Cenis was completely frozen over, and huge greying boulders of ice fallen from the glaciers above lay dotted along its shore. Behind us the land stretched out like a grey and green tapestry, fading at its edges into a haze which marked the beginnings of the plain which lay around the city of Turin. On the evening of our second day we stopped to rest for the night beside the northernmost point of the lake, and there we huddled beside our fires and clutched our cloaks and furs around us for whatever warmth we could find.

We awoke the next morning to find that during the night thick clouds had rolled in across the peaks of the mountains, and in place of the sunlight and open vistas which the previous day had made of our climb an exhilarating adventure, dark mists hung now like veils across the faces of the rock and ice that loomed above. We broke our fast on part of the meagre rations we had brought with us, and then resumed our journey, feeling markedly less joyous than we had the day before. As we climbed, moisture began to fall from the air and to freeze and glisten upon the boulders that littered and marked our route, and even upon our skin and clothing, and it seemed to me that we must be piercing the very clouds on which Heaven itself was floating. The beards of our guides soon became white masks, barbed and bristling with icicles, and ice formed too on my own brow and on the lashes of my eyes, and the steam of my breath froze painfully about my lips and nostrils.

It was about noon when we reached the summit of the pass, and there we stopped to quench our thirst, and to rest a while before proceeding on the downward path that led to Chambery and on to Lyons. As we sat there, weary and shivering, our heads bowed against the leaden roof of the world, a wondrous thing occurred, as though we were witnessing a miracle. Even as we watched, the mists thinned and the clouds that had embraced us all morning sank below us, and we were left marooned on an island of rock floating on a sea of boiling foam. The sky above our heads was now once more of the deepest blue, pierced only by the giant golden orb of the sun, whose radiant warmth succoured both our bodies and our spirits, and as we sat there lost in silence, beatific smiles upon all our faces, three perfect rainbows manifested themselves in great arcs before us, overlapping each other like the gates of Heaven itself. It did indeed seem as though we had climbed above the world of men and had found ourselves enthroned in Heaven.

"I would gladly exchange every pleasure I have ever had just for this one moment," Tasso said to me, tears of exultation filling his eyes.

"And so would I. Are you certain some accident did not befall us on our ascent, and that we are not dead and ascended to Heaven?" I replied, laughing in my own delirium, my voice thin and weak in the rarefied air that had lightened our senses, and which served only to strengthen the impression that had taken hold in me that we had somehow passed from life into another, more ethereal world.

Our guides too were in fine humour, and they congratulated the three of us (for though both a few years younger than I, Marcovaldo and Tasso di Arpo were also well beyond their prime), on having attained the pass without mishap or complaint. The worst part of our journey was over, they assured us. Soon we would be beneath the cloud again; we would be dry, and walking once more through flowered meadows, fresh mountain-streams tumbling at our sides. Feeling much rested and strengthened by what we had seen and by such glad encouragement, we gathered together our things to begin our descent.

We had not been embarked on our downward journey for very long however before the cheerful countenances of our guides took on a more troubled mien. As we descended into the clouds once more, snow began to fall, and the surfaces of the rocks that had merely glistened beneath the settling hoar turned quickly to viscous white, and the air about us became pervaded by an unearthly orange glow, as though we were indeed descending from the Heaven we had seen above to another place where the lower fires of damnation were being kindled. As the snow began to settle more thickly, the guide ahead of me signalled for us to stop, and we all came to a halt around him.

"We must get down as quickly as we can," he said. "Not far from here is a shallow gorge. We will leave the main path and follow it. It is more difficult, but quicker, and below are caves where we can shelter should the need arise." Tasso di Arpo and Marcovaldo and myself looked at each other, and then at the guide, with some concern.

"Is that not more dangerous than to follow the path?" Tasso asked. "What if something should happen? We might never be found."

"Trust me," the guide replied. "The other way follows the ridge of the mountain for hours. We could not hope to get below this before nightfall," he said, indicating the falling snow with an upturned hand.

"But should we leave the safety of…" Tasso began to complain.

"What consolation is there in knowing you will be found when you are already dead?" the guide interrupted him. Tasso blinked once in consternation, and then turned his eyes toward the thickened sky.

"Quickly, tie yourselves together," the guide added, to confirm that the discussion was at an end, though his sharp words had already silenced any further complaint either myself or Marcovaldo might have felt inclined to make, and taking some lengths of rope from his back he handed them to us, and we began to tie them about our waists. I glanced across at Marcovaldo, for I had been surprised at his silence while his factor had negotiated the best means to ensure our safety, and saw that his face, though previously mottled from the effects of the cold and snow, had now turned quite pale.

"Come now," I said to comfort him. "We are in good hands. We have been shown Heaven. What more is there to fear?"

"Nothing, I suppose. Nothing but fear itself," he replied, feigning bravery, and then smiled at me the sickly *rictus* of one paralysed by terror.

"Follow in my footsteps and nothing will go wrong," the guide said to reassure him, his previous harsh tone softening, and once we were all securely tied to each other, he set off again and we were soon clambering from rock to rock behind him down the throat of a narrow gorge. I had been placed as second man in our train, and behind me came two of the Savoyards, then Marcovaldo and Tasso di Arpo, followed by the three remaining porters bringing up the rear. Thus arrayed, we proceeded down the gully, each carefully placing his foot, as we had been instructed, precisely where the man before him had trod.

We had only been travelling in this manner for some short time when a noise commenced above us like the sound of approaching thunder, or of a thousand feet tramping in the distance, such as I had heard many times before while marching in the Army of the Saints of God. The guide ahead of me heard it too and immediately raised his hand for us to halt. He then stood listening with one ear turned towards the mountain.

"Above us! An avalanche is brewing! The weight of new snow on the thawing snows of the winter," he whispered to me urgently. "Move carefully, and do not speak or make any unnecessary noise."

The sound from above, quiet as it had been, ceased, and I could hear only the murmur of water running below my feet, and of snow pattering to the ground as it was brushed by our passing from the branches of the few shrubs that grew in that sheltered gully. By now the snow was falling fast, and had settled and lay on the rocks more than a thumb's length deep and sat upon our heads and shoulders like cowls of silvered mail. We began to move forward again, proceeding even more cautiously than we had before.

We had not taken more than a few halting steps when the near silence was broken by a sharp cry resounding behind me. As I started at the alien sound of a human voice in that almost silent wilderness, the rumbling from above began again. I turned to see what had happened to evince such a pained outburst, and found myself confronted by the sight of Marcovaldo up to his waist in the stream. The ropes around his body bound him still to the porters and his factor, and above him Tasso clung desperately to a rock to prevent himself from being dragged to the same fate by the weight of his master. On either side the Savoyards pulled on the ropes as best they could to support him, but they too were clearly struggling to maintain their foot-holds on the snow-bound rocks, and were likewise in danger of being pulled by Marcovaldo into the stream. At that moment the lead guide appeared at my side, just as Marcovaldo began screaming for help with all his might.

"Untie yourself. Quickly," the Savoyard hissed at me. "And for God's sake tell the old goat to be quiet."

"Marcovaldo, please…not so loud," I called out in the same snake-like whisper, or some such other ineffectual nonsense, ignoring the guide's impertinence, and untying the rope that secured me to him and to the others. "You'll bring the whole mountain down on top of us!" I added, equally ineffectually, but even as I pleaded with him, the noise from above grew louder, ceasing to be but a distant rumble and becoming instead an insistent roar. The sounds of falling snow and ice rapidly filled the air around us, punctuated by the sharp crack of rocks and timbers splitting under the weight of debris pouring down upon them. An ever-deepening stream of snow and gravel began to flow around my calves and ankles, and a turbulent cloud of powdery snow filled the air. As I began to add my own cries for help to those of Marcovaldo, I felt myself being washed by the deluge towards the edge of the gorge.

"Throw yourself against the rocks," the guide cried from somewhere close beside me, though I could no longer see him through the dense cloud of snow in which we had become engulfed.

"Help me!" I screamed out, as I felt my feet being swept from beneath me as I tried to turn to follow his instruction. But as fate would have it (choosing it would seem to save me for far greater misfortunes), I did not become engulfed in the avalanche's downward sweep. As my footing slipped away two powerful hands appeared from out of the flurry of the avalanche, and grabbing hold of me, first lifted me bodily and then threw me toward the side of the gully. As I fell against the rocks I reached out desperately for whatever I could find to prevent myself from being washed away. My hands, as though by some miracle, lighted upon the trunk of a small tree.

Despairing of my fate I clasped tightly to this tenuous hand-hold praying it would not be dragged from its roots and dashed into the gorge below by my weight, or by the awesome powers which a spiteful Nature had unleashed upon us. I hung there, the sinews of my arms tearing, as the snow and ice continued to pour over and around me in an endless stream. The only distinct sound I could discern amid that unruly rush of movement was that of my heart beating wildly in my throat. There I clung, with my eyes closed, and barely able to breathe, until the weight of snow piling up on me drove my conscious spirits from their senses, and I passed helplessly into another, darker realm.

-OO-

When I regained consciousness not a sound was to be heard, and soft, fresh snow was falling on my face. Above me a huge mound of snow and ice rose up, smothering my legs and lower body and filling the section of the valley through which we had passed. There, I knew (realising what had transpired in a chilling flash of understanding), my two companions and our guides must lay entombed. I could not believe any of them had survived that icy deluge, or had they been unharmed by the fall of snow, that they could have endured its cold and suffocating embrace for long. At that instant though an equally troubling recollection came to disturb my thoughts; an image of the last moments before consciousness had been driven from my senses - of the hands of the Savoyard clinging to my clothing for his own survival, then, as the debris piled up where he was laying, of his grip slackening, and of my own futile efforts to assist him, and finally, of his hands slipping away. It was in desperation therefore, rather than in hope of receiving any reply, that I called out softly the names of Tasso and Marcovaldo, not daring to raise my voice too loud for fear any sound I made might bring another debacle cascading down upon me.

To confirm my darkest fears, I received no answer to my quiet asking. All that came back to me was the diminishing echoes of my own voice, and the sound of water gently falling. I realised then that I was alone, without guide or help or companionship, lost in a terrain I did not know, and whose malign ways I did not understand.

I did know enough though that to free myself and to continue my descent was my only chance of survival, and I began to carefully extricate my limbs from their place of confinement. After some time and with much cautious effort - for I feared my every movement might precipitate another collapse around me - I managed to roll free of my icy prison. Once released, I slid down the face of the avalanche until I came to a halt with my feet and ankles immersed in the stream.

It was beyond my powers to climb back up to the higher rocks on which we had been passing, that much I also knew, and I decided anyway that my progress would be quicker, and easier to determine, there in the clear stream-bed rather than on the slippery, ice-bound rocks above. The only other feint intelligence I had to lighten my utter ignorance of my predicament was that down was probably the quickest way to safety, and so I plunged onwards, splashing my way, frightened and disorientated, through the near-freezing waters of the stream. Mercifully, it was not long before I came upon the caves of which the guide had spoken, and ignoring the possibility that wild beasts might be lying there waiting to devour me, I stumbled into the gloom of the one that lay first in my path. The cavern was not deep, and at its rear, against a wall of rock, a bed of dried leaves and mosses had been driven by the wind. There I collapsed, shivering and exhausted, and immediately fell into a deep and dreamless sleep.

-OO-

How I survived the ensuing days I shall never know. I must have slept for the rest of that day and the whole of the night, for when I awoke, the light outside the cave was the rising light of morning, and snow was no longer falling. I went to the stream and to ease the dryness in my throat drank tentatively from its painfully icy flow, then with my thoughts cleared, and being only too aware of what lay before me, yet seeing no alternative other than to remain there and wait for Death to find me, I proceeded on my lonely journey, trusting my deliverance to the course of the stream.

After the snowfall, the weather again became mild, and the stream soon became a raging torrent, as the snowfields that lay above me began to melt in the heat of the vernal sun. Had it not been so, and had the cold and snow persisted, I know for certain I would not have survived. I cannot recall how many days I stumbled across the rocks and ice of that barren landscape, catching sight of neither man nor living creature, save the birds of the air, and those beasts that crawl and scurry on their bellies on the ground. To keep myself alive, I drank sparingly from the cold, refreshing waters of the stream, and chewed upon what few berries and seeds and grasses I was fortunate enough to discover. At night I slept in whatever cave or hollow, or barring that relative luxury, under whatever outcrop of rock I could find. By day I stumbled on, my feet torn and bloodied, my limbs weary, my lips and gums blistered from the cold, my tongue swollen and ulcerated, and my stomach empty and complaining, and with my mind beginning to embark upon its own unguided journey of wild imaginings and despair.

As the days passed unminded and uncounted, and as hunger and fatigue fuelled the growing delirium in my mind, I began to lose those powers of reason which had previously served me so well. By some strange obsession that crept upon me I began to contemplate far too deeply upon the appearance of the plague in both Genoa and Turin but days after my own arrival there. In their blind seeking for explanations for such coincidence my thoughts drifted back repeatedly to the words Fra Lorenzo had uttered those many years before telling us of the fourth seal of the scroll of Heaven, and of the two seals he had claimed had then already passed, and of the third, whose opening the Army of the Saints had been intended to herald. With no company to correct or distract me I could not shake from my mind what Fra Lorenzo had said to us: that when the fourth seal was broken a white rider would appear whose name was Death, and how that Death would be given dominion over a fourth part of the people of the Earth, and be sanctioned to lay low that number by pestilence and famine. In my encroaching madness I saw how my own skin was turning ghostly pale through the ravages of fatigue and exposure, and forsaking all at once the last vestiges of whatever reason I had once possessed, I began to believe I might be that avenging rider, come to reap the savage harvest allotted to my part.

Was I that rider of Death, I wondered, come to sever one fourth of mankind from the powers that bound them to their lives of suffering? Was I the elected agent of God, sent to prepare the unshriven and the unready for the Day of Retribution that was to come? By my own reckoning I had seen at least that proportion struck down in Genoa by that vile affliction, and in Turin an equal portion had certainly succumbed to its touch during the brief time that I was there. As hard as I tried to dismiss it, the thought kept coming to my mind and would not leave it, that Fra

Lorenzo's prophesies were at that moment unfolding through the agency of my own, albeit unwilling self.

Naturally enough, what little of my rational soul remained functioning within me screamed out in protest at such a prospect. It could not be so, it cried out in anguish. I was undeserving of such a calling; I was undeserving of such a fate. I would not allow myself to be so cruelly used, I exclaimed loudly to the unlistening trees and rocks and water. I would not be the agent of such a purpose, I cried out to an equally unlistening God.

But what of Tasso di Arpo and Marcovaldo, and the Savoyards, another, equally insistent voice within me kept whispering? They were all dead, and that through no sin or failing of their own, other than through their brief, unwitting association with myself. Whereas I - despite having undergone similar hardships and deprivations as had they, and having been exposed to the same dangers – had by some strange providence survived.

Such were the thoughts that occupied my mind as I stumbled blindly down that mountain, being led to whatever destiny awaited me by the natural vagaries of the stream. Such was the position I had exalted myself to occupy within the greater hierarchy of things as they are ordained between Heaven and Earth. It would be no exaggeration to say therefore, that by the time I was to find myself once more in the company of my fellow men, my mind was well set along the way that leads to madness.

-OO-

I have no recollection of what happened next - of how I came to be spared the logical consequence of my illogical fantasies; of how I came to find myself, not in the solitary realms of the dead or insane, but in the village of the forest peasants who had discovered me and had taken me in; or of how many days and nights I had lain there, sweating and crying out in the throes of the fever which raged through my body and in my soul. When I did finally regain consciousness, it was to find myself lying in a bed in an ill-lit hovel, an old man wearing the threadbare garments and trappings of a priest standing at my side. From the quiet murmurings, and the sounds of movement I could hear all around us, I discerned that we were not alone, and when I turned my head I saw several figures crowding at the doorway, and vague others shuffling uneasily among the shadows of the room.

"You must go, though we wish you no harm," the old priest said when he saw my eyes were open. To say the least, his admonitory words came as some surprise to me. They were certainly not the friendly and consoling ones I had expected to hear from such as he, and I wondered what I could have done, what fate or ill-omens I could have called down upon these people in my senseless sleeping to have alienated myself from them in such a way.

"We will give you a mule, and food and water, but you must promise you will leave," he continued, confirming for me that in my lassitude I had not been mistaken in what he had said.

"Why must I? What have I done to offend you?" I asked feebly. I tried to sit up, to better explain to him my strange condition, only to discover that I was too weak even to raise my head from the pillow and I immediately fell back onto the bed. At my movements the old man stepped back, as though he was afraid of me and did not wish me to come too close. He then looked around at the others who were watching and listening to what we said.

"You spoke of many things while you slept," he said, moving closer once more to my side. "I am Death, you cried. I have come to avenge the Lord! Terrible things you spoke of. Disease and pestilence, the white seeds of sickness falling from Heaven, of Death seated on a snow-white horse." He knelt down beside me and crossed his forehead, and then taking hold of the rosary hanging at his neck, he mumbled a brief prayer.

"We are simple people here; we lead simple lives. Your eyes were open while you spoke of these things. We did not believe them, and thought them merely the ranting of a madman, or the effects of fever."

"I am a sick man," I agreed, in the hope that such a reminder of my condition might evoke some sympathy from him, and from these people who, I now realised, had been drawn to my bed not by interest or compassion, but as was the priest, were stricken rather by fear at my very presence in their midst. The old man turned again towards the villagers and several among them made irritated gestures to him with their heads.

"This morning...," he continued, then faltered again, and at this further show of hesitancy a large man with the hairy pelt of some beast draped around his shoulders, and with leather leggings, stepped forward from the doorway and said something to me in a language I did not comprehend. The tone of what he said though was clear enough, and as he spoke, a murmur of agreement and of suppressed anger passed among the gathered crowd.

"He says this morning his child was found dead," the priest explained in a mournful voice when the man had finished speaking. "The boy died in his sleep, while you were lying here raving about Death. This morning we found him, with white marks all over his body. Yesterday he was working in the fields at his father's side."

"That is not my doing!" I protested feebly, shaking my head as energetically as I could in denial, and sobbing in my rage and guilt that the possibility yet remained that I had been, if innocently, and in some unknowable way the cause of the death of this child. "You must believe me. I am not to blame," I whispered, turning my face from him and into the pillow to hide my anger and shame.

"We do not know what to believe," the priest said, forgetting his earlier trepidation, and placing his hand on my arm to placate me. "It is better therefore for all if you leave."

My protests, feeble as they were, were to no avail, but even before the priest had finished speaking I had again found refuge from his accusations and from my inner turmoil in the blissful arms of sleep. I was moreover much too weak to be driven from my bed, and as no further deaths occurred to confirm their fears, I was allowed to remain in the village until the following day. At first light, however, the priest came to me and helped me from my bed and then led me outside to where a mule was waiting, laden with the loaves of bread and flask of wine he had promised. Not one among the villagers offered to assist us; they all stood some distance away with blank expressions on their faces, patiently watching as the old man helped me onto the beast. When I was more or less firmly installed upon its back the priest draped a frayed purple blanket over my shoulders and then tied my hands loosely to the reins. This done, he started to lead the mule to the edge of the village.

"Forgive me. You will understand I had no choice," he said, once we were out of earshot of the villagers. "These are simple people, and in some things I must pander to their superstitions in order to maintain what little faith in me, and in God, they have."

"You have no need to apologise, I understand," I said, though in truth I did not understand, neither his actions, nor his reasons, and was feeling somewhat resentful at the treatment I was being shown. At that moment though my brow pained me as though it was encircled by Christ's crown of thorns, and my back and sides ached and burned as from a thousand lashes, and all in all I felt far too ill and weary to complain.

"Take this," he said, handing me a cane to goad the mule. "I will pray for your safety.., and that you will find no cause to return."

"Do not worry, Father, I shall not return," and at this he slapped the rump of the mule and the beast began to amble its way out of the village. For my part, sickened and enfeebled as I was, I could do no more than cling to its neck with both my arms, and to pray with all my heart to whatever God was testing me in this way that I would not fall from it there and then and break my neck on the ground.

"This road leads to Chambéry," the priest called out after me. "I hope you will find it more to your liking there."

Beside the gate in the wicket fence that enclosed the huddle of huts, the children of the village had gathered to witness my leaving. As I passed by them they cowered behind the fencing, giggling at me in fear, but as I proceeded along the road beyond them their nervous tittering turned to open laughter and stones and pebbles and pieces of wood began to clatter all around me.

"Hail the King of the Dead! The King of the Dead!" I heard them cry out behind me, though perhaps they mocked me only with their laughter and the words I heard were no more than the sounds of the stones and tinder they had thrown, made more ominous only by the continued imaginings of my fevered mind. Doubtless as a result of my fever, and to add to my utter confusion as to why these things should be happening to me, my thoughts were filled at that moment with turbulent images of sickness and pestilence, intermingled with fleeting, though more joyous memories of my childhood, and of the beautiful things I had helped my master make in Padua.

Not far from the village I came upon a broken-down shelter, inside of which I discovered some hay and a few swatches of half-rotted fabric, which despite the season was tolerably clean and dry. Needing no physician to tell me I was in no condition to continue my journey, I tied up the mule and made myself a make-shift bed as best I could in my exhausted state below the part of the roof that was still intact. There I stayed, sleeping most of the days and nights, and gradually restoring myself to a semblance of health on the bread and wine the priest had given me, until I felt I had gained sufficient strength to resume my journey to Lyons.

-OO-

I eventually arrived in Lyons some time before the feast of the Trinity, still greatly weakened by the things that had happened in the mountains, and further exhausted by six day's travel from Chambéry. There too, as I had feared (for it seemed my earlier imaginings were to be given further substance by the continued reality of my own progress and that of the pestilence being inextricably linked, and that the cursed thing was set to pursue me however much I fled it), the pestilence struck down the first of its victims in that city within a week of my own arrival there.

I was by then far from recovered from the deprivations I had endured in the mountains, or from the ensuing fever, and my limbs ached still from the bruising the French countryside and my ass's rump (both of which had proved tough and unforgiving), had afflicted upon me, but though unfit in both body and spirit to resume my journey, I nevertheless made what haste I could in the way of preparations to leave. The tragic loss of the company I had travelled with from Susa into the mountains had left me confused and desperate, and even more aware of the dangers of travelling alone than I had been before. Yet I feared to stay in a place infected by that sickness, and being unable to find others with whom I might travel, I was left with little choice other than to set off on my own. I no longer knew which I feared most - to sit and tarry in the city amongst the dead and dying, and to contemplate there upon my own part in the dissemination of that bitter affliction, or to travel alone in an unknown land.

But how strange it must sound to hear me say that, although fed and rested, and to a great extent relieved of the fear and isolation which had first brought about their conception, I still clung to some belief in the reality of those wild imaginings, and continued to give credence to what I knew in my moments of clarity to be nothing more than fantasies concocted by a weakened and panic-stricken soul. Stranger still must it sound to hear me state that I had come to see my own progress to be linked in some way to the spread of that vile corruption, or that I, in all humility, could feel myself so cursed, or blessed as to have been chosen by God to be the bearer of His message of retribution. But so it was to seem to me, and so it was to continue throughout the duration of that summer. As I fled northwards to escape the death and suffering, so the pestilence continued to follow me, seemingly tracking my every movement across that alien landscape until finally I came to believe that I truly was its herald and not its intended victim, as reason had always led me to fear I might be.

It came to seem to me more and more that I was fleeing it, not for my own health and safety, but that I was instead travelling ahead of it, to announce to others the coming of this *atra mors*, this most dreadful Death. In Chalon, Dijon, Troyes; in every place in which I stopped or rested, or where I hoped to find shelter and respite from my flight, the plague struck there within days of my own arrival, leaving me again feeling resentful of such cruel usage of my innocent being, and fearful of its malign purpose, yet myself unharmed.

In short, I began truly to feel like an avenging angel of Death, an instrument of God's vengeful anger. But still I fled and fled, though from what I did not know, and seemingly dragging that accursed murrain with me, until at last I came to Paris, and there in that place of learning, in that city of reason, I decided to stop and to meet my pursuer, and if need be, my Maker, face to face.

-OO-

I spent the whole of that summer and then the winter in Paris, making my living as best I could, and studying as and what books I could borrow or cajole from the few friends - scribes and clerks mostly - whose acquaintance

I had fostered expressly for that purpose. I was already then beginning to feel growing inside me a hunger for a deeper knowledge of the ways of the confusing world in which I found myself travelling. I had come to understand only too well that in all things, at all times, nought happens but from a ground and of necessity, and I felt keenly my own ignorance, both of that cause, and of the higher need that fuelled it. That ignorance too, you will understand, had been honed finer by my recent experiences, and such inner turmoil as I suffered as a result of them was only to be troubled further by the scenes I was to witness in Paris during every day I resided there.

For exactly as it had been throughout my journey northwards, so it was to be in Paris, and exactly as it had been in those other places, the sickness and death commenced within but days of my own arrival. Throughout that summer, as the days grew warmer, so the rate of mortality rose in proportion. At its peak in the autumn of that year there were - according to the sundry accounts I have since read of it - as many as a thousand souls dying of it each and every day. Indeed, even that most extreme of estimates may have been founded on truth. The inn where I was lodged lay close by the Hôtel Dieu, beside the route the porters and grave-diggers followed from the hospital to the cemetery of the Holy Innocents, and every hour of the days I spent there was marked by the passage of creaking biers embarked upon their journey to that last resting place of the dead.

During the first few days of the sickness the carts that passed generally bore but one corpse upon them, and in the first weeks of summer at least, were accompanied always by trains of mourners, and by priests and their acolytes. But as the seasons turned, and as the numbers of the afflicted grew beyond all proportion, and as the priests and the good citizens fled the city, forsaking even their own kith and kin, so the cadavers came to be piled three or four high, or more, and to pass unattended and almost unnoticed. On many an occasion did I see the porters sweating away at their thankless labours, immured under the thick hoods and beaked masks they wore to protect them from the cloying vapours of putrefaction, as they struggled to despatch a cargo of six or seven corpses to their final earthly destination.

From what I saw of the victims thus paraded past my window, and of the bodies that were lying in the streets, the sickness took on another form in Paris than it had in Genoa. It did not inflict on the Frenchmen the hideous *gavaccioli* which had blossomed on the flesh of the citizens of that other city, or in those other places where the plague and I had had occasion to visit simultaneously during my journey north. Instead, a dark rash came and formed without warning, and within hours the bearer of these infernal *stigmata* was dead. With the approach of winter, as the days became again shorter and cooler, yet another change came about in the manifestation of that sickness. For all I know it was another thing entirely, and altogether different in its characteristics, and possibly even in its purpose, coming perhaps expressly to reap its harvest from among the enfeebled survivors of those other two. This later malady filled and blocked the lungs of those it afflicted, and with the fits of coughing this congestion induced, a gory *sputum* came to their lips and their skin turned blue as though from the cold of the approaching season, presaging perhaps the eternal winter they were themselves about to enjoin.

And amidst all that horror, another omen came to confirm me in my fears that the sufferings which my fellow men were being forced to endure might have come about by virtue of my own clandestine presence among them. For so were my thoughts still inclined, despite my efforts to dispel such fears through the application to my errant fantasies of the stricter laws of reason. In the month of August, when the pestilence had barely begun its cruel sweep among us, as the Sun was about to set one evening, a huge star appeared above the city. It hung for a time low upon the horizon, a great ball of bloody, fermenting fire. It seemed very near to us, and much nearer than the other stars that rotated in the Heavens, as though it floated in the sub-lunar regions, and did not belong, as such bodies ought by right to do, to the realms of the outer spheres. Neither did it move from the position where it had first appeared, but stayed there until night was fully fallen, and in this it reminded me of the *cometis stella* that had visited us in Florence, and of all that awesome apparition had brought. Suddenly though, and to the astonishment of all who saw it (and to my own silently harboured feelings of relief and misplaced elation), it disintegrated into a thousand pieces, letting fall its broken rays upon the roofs of the city, and then what little remained of it disappeared from view.

And just as I had in Florence, I again took this heavenly visitor as a personal omen, embracing self-centred optimism once more in favour of common and doom-laden belief. For above and beyond the stubborn inclination I still clung to regarding my own complicity in whatever retribution was being visited upon that city, I was convinced of the immunity to the ministrations of the sickness such instrumentality must doubtless bring. All about me though, the citizens of Paris were just as confused and frightened by this inexplicable phenomenon as I had once been, and all remained (with better reason perhaps), as ignorant of its true purpose as was I.

-OO-

When the pestilence returned to torment the people of Paris in the spring of the following year, thirteen hundred and forty-nine, I decided to leave that city at once and to make my way eastwards. To my relief, I had by then and to a great extent been able to rationalise and shepherd from my thoughts those unruly fears I had nurtured regarding my own role in the dissemination of that great mortality. There in the city of reason I had learned during the course of the winter how the sickness had struck with equal vigour in other towns and in lands I had never had occasion to visit. I could not therefore have been its agent, I reasoned, not unless I was but one of a host of similarly desolate souls who had been together elected to bring God's justice to the world of men. Just as easily as I had summoned up those spectres into being was I able to dismiss them from my life. In this one thing, if in nothing else, I have been more than constant - in the ready embracement, and then equally fleet rejection of such designs, patterns and motives as I have at times discerned at play in the world around me, and which I took as being the abso-lute cause and reason of my life.

Many of those who arrived in Paris throughout the winter, and who had journeyed from the east, had said no trace was to be found there of the murrain which now apparently lay to waste all of France and Italy, and had spread as far as the Kingdom of England and to Aragon and Castille. I decided therefore to make my way to the lands of the Holy Emperor, there to test my renewed faith in my innocence of the propagation of that sickness against the virtue of its unsullied peoples, and in the hope I might find respite there finally from my weary and guilt-ridden flight. For a change, Lady Fortune seemed to favour me in this decision, and I was able to travel to Metz in the company of a band of pilgrims who were making to Strasbourg, or so I believe had been their destination, for at Metz I fell in with a group of fellow craftsmen who were heading north towards Mainz, and there I decided to throw in my lot with them.

That, of all the things that befell me, and of the many months I spent embarked upon it, was without doubt the happiest part of my journey, as I travelled north and eastwards through lands not yet troubled by the pestilence which by all accounts laid to waste the rest of civilisation, and in the company of men among whom were many who knew and understood and employed in practice the materials and methods of my own trade. These men, I was surprised to discover, I was able to recognise as such simply from the scents of pigments that remained on their skin and clothing, even before they had declared themselves to me as *dipintori*. At first I was confused as to what it was that seemed so familiar about them, but once I had identified the cause, the ghosts of those well-known and comforting smells filled my thoughts with happier memories and images to obliterate those of the awful winter I had just endured. I could not help recalling too the blind apothecary I had met those many years before in Bologna, making me smile to myself both at my callow presumption and ignorance then, and at how greatly the intervening years had changed me, and had brought to fruition in me facilities I had not until then realised I possessed.

My new-found companions, I soon learned, were making their way to Prague, to find work on the great cathedral being erected there, and during the time I spent in their company I was repeatedly pressed by them to continue with them to the end of their journey, to join them in the execution of that great work. Although they had met me but a few days previously and knew little of my abilities other than what I had chosen to tell them, several of them said they would vouch for me, and for my skills (for in recounting to them my history I had not divulged the longer chronicle of my failures), and they were certain anyway that the services of one who had served in the *bottega* of such a master as Giotto di Bondone would be richly rewarded anywhere for the employment of his skills. By the time we were approaching Mainz I had been almost persuaded by their suggestion, and had decided that if nothing was to be found in that city to keep me, I would indeed proceed with them to Prague to see what employment I could find on the construction of the new cathedral.

-OO-

We arrived in Mainz on the feast of San Bartholomeus to find the place, not in celebration of that saint's day, but in turmoil, with most of its citizens filling the streets in protest, many bearing arms. When we enquired as to the reasons for this unrest we were informed that the previous day the Jews there had taken up arms against some of the men of the city. Some amongst our informants did admit, if reluctantly, that the Jews had done so only to defend themselves from the mob which had descended upon them baying for their blood, but whatever the cause or reason, in the fighting that had ensued some two hundred Christian souls had perished at their hands. So it was that as we entered the heart of the city, it was to find ourselves being pressed upon on all sides by the many who were pouring onto the streets demanding retribution, and as we passed among them we could not keep ourselves from becoming inextricably caught up amongst their fervent movements, or from being drawn by them to the part of the city where the Jews lived.

At first, being a stranger to that place and its customs, I could not understand why such an assault as we had heard described should have been made against the normally peaceable community of the Jews. While it was true that many feared and mistrusted them, and despised them even for their lack of Christian faith, and that as many more made use of them in their venal capacity as usurers, and had reasons enough therefore for wishing to see them harmed, it was most unusual (in Florence and Tuscany, at least) that the innate animosity felt towards them should be given so vehement and active a voice. When we enquired further as to its causes however, we were soon informed - it being a matter almost of pride among those we asked, and who had taken part in the assault - that they had been inspired to their actions by the presence among them but a few days previously of a band of those fanatics who at that time were to be found travelling abroad, and who called themselves the Brethren of the Cross.

As you will know, Fra Lorenzo's Army of the Saints was far from having been the only band of men who in troubled times have gathered together under the guidance of some inspired leader or visionary, and who have found themselves infused (often enough mistakenly, as I myself had been) with the Divine Spirit of the Lord. In the course of my journey towards Paris I had come upon several such groups of men who had been roused to religious fervour by the spectacle of the sickness that struck relentlessly all around them. Together these bands of fanatics had similarly called themselves the Brethren of the Cross, or the Flagellant Brothers, this latter appellation having been acquired by virtue of the acts of self-immolation they performed, in re-enactment of the flaying of Christ. Such acts they performed gladly as penitence both for their own, and for the sins of others, and without complaint, wherever they went.

I was by then thus more than familiar with the rituals the Brethren performed, the pious passion with which they carried them out, and the reciprocal fervour it incited in those who watched. I had myself watched in horror as they laid their bodies on the ground, assuming positions and gestures intended to represent the sins they wished to repent – the form of the crucifix, to signify adultery; three fingers of one hand raised in the air, for perjury - not only for their own sins, but for those of all Mankind. I had marvelled too at their passive acceptance of the lashes laid upon their naked flesh by their master. Often, it had seemed to me, as I studied their expressions, as their flesh was torn open by the strokes of their master's flail, that their faces showed something closer to gratitude, extasy even, than the pain and anguish one would rightfully expect.

The band of masons and pictors I was travelling with had even encountered such a group, about eighty in number, in a place called Bingen, on the banks of the river Rhine, not far from our destination in Mainz. There had been in fact little of remark in their orderly progress, and save for the quietly intoned prayers of the master marching sternly at their head, two lieutenants in close attendance at either side, they had proceeded in silence, their heads cowled beneath white robes, their faces turned in penitence to the ground. Indeed, it was only out of curiosity, and a jointly felt need for distraction from the tedium of our own extended march that we had decided to accompany them as they proceeded to the town. As we descended through the narrow streets that wound along the lower slopes of the valley beside the great river itself, the bells of the church had rung out loudly to herald their approach, and the people of that place had hurried from their homes to see the strange gathering that had appeared unexpectedly in their midst. Arriving before the main church of the town, the Brethren had proceeded to form a circle, and had then stripped off their robes until all were wearing but coarse linen skirts or breeches, their discarded garments gathered in the centre of the orbit they had formed. Once assembled thus, they had commenced to march round and round, marking the rhythm of their steps with the words of a popular Flagellant hymn. With each stanza the tempo of their singing and their marching had quickened, while those gathered to watch clapped their hands and stamped their feet to match the cadence of their movements, and it had not been long before my companions and I had also joined in this loud canon of encouragement.

"Spare us! Spare us!" the Brethren had then all cried in unison, and at a signal from their master had thrown themselves as one to the ground. Once all were arranged in their various positions, the master had proceeded to move among them, thrashing each with a leather whip where they lay, the duration and severity of application being in proportion to the gravity of the sins each had portrayed, or so I had come to understand.

"Arise! And be cleansed by the virtue of the martyrdom you have assumed," the master cried to each as the spiked thongs of the scourge bit deeply into their flesh.

"Arise! And from this day guard yourself against all further sin!"

This performance, persuasive enough as it was, was to be be repeated that afternoon, and again that evening. This I knew was the custom among the Brethren – that their ritual should be repeated three times each day. In such manner would they continue their purgation, or so one among them had informed me after one of my earlier encounters with the Brethren, as he tended to the open wounds that laced his chest and shoulders, and to the dark blisters of previous scourings which festered brightly between the gashes of freshly seeping blood. Their calling, the wretched man said, was to perform these rites for three and thirty days and a half, in imitation of the years Christ had spent here on Earth (just as Fra Lorenzo had measured the days he claimed to have spent in the wilderness), and that the movement was to continue for the same number of years, at which time the true Messiah would appear and the promised Millennium would finally begin.

As you well know, I had by then become sceptical of all and any such promises of the imminent approach of Messiahs, and of the powers ascribed to such mystical numbers, however compelling their argument might have been. I had heard similar promissory eschatology before, and to my cost, and although it had been couched then in different terms, and had been directed to a different cause and audience, I was not about to allow myself to be again so readily swayed by its dubious message. A powerful and salutary experience though, it had certainly been. I had, however, already seen and experienced enough of such things, and I contrived to persuade my companions that we should continue our journey and not remain in that place for the later enactments of the spectacle, and that we would more easily find better and more attentive lodgings for the night in some other place, one not blighted by the presence of such pious and fervent men. Happily, they had all concurred with my reasoning, and we had left the Brethren to attend to their whips and wounds and prayers and had proceeded on our way towards Mainz.

So powerful an experience had it been, however, that armed with knowledge of the recent presence of such Flagellants in the city I had little difficulty in understanding how the citizens of Mainz should have been enflamed by their preaching to their present passion against the Jews. In seeking to explain the pestilence which raged already in many of the neighbouring cities, and which (to my own consternation, having thought myself finally free of its dogged pursuit), was beginning to make its presence known in Mainz itself, the Flagellants claimed that the Jews had poisoned wells to bring about the sickness, and had sold food to Christians which had been similarly despoiled. They even claimed them to have poisoned the air by injecting into it powders of basilisk that had been sent from Seville by the rabbis there expressly for such a purpose. Proof of their guilt and complicity was to be found, they said, not only in that they did not draw water from the wells others used, but took theirs instead from rivers and open streams, but also by the equally inescapable fact that they above all others had remained unharmed. A great conspiracy was at hand, the Brethren maintained, one to which every Jew was party, and of which all had been forewarned; a conspiracy to overthrow Christendom and to install the

Antichrist to power and to erase all faith in a Christian God from the face of the Earth.

As for myself, I gave little credence to such charges, having heard them, or many like them, too often before. From my sojourn there, I also knew that the professors of Paris held the Jews to be entirely innocent of both the cause and the propagation of that malign disease. Sadly though, my companions were to prove themselves far less generous in their easy judgements. Or perhaps they did not comprehend the Jews as such, but like most saw them instead as eternal strangers, unholy fiends who in their arcane rituals desecrated the Sacred Host, and who kidnapped and tortured Christian children and drank their blood to give themselves the human appearance they assumed in order that they might move freely among men. Anyway, to judge by their reactions, they seemed to be all equally as incensed by the accusations levelled by the Flagellants as were the more rightly aggrieved citizens of Mainz, and as one they insisted - despite my protestations - that we continue with the mob to the Jewish quarter to ensure that justice would be done.

"Why are you all so eager to blame the Jews?" I asked one of them, whose name was Johannes, as we ran along together with the crowd. Like myself, he was a *dipintore* (though from what I could gather from what he had told me, he worked still in the old, traditional style, and knew little or nothing of the innovations introduced into our shared art by my master), and during the time we had spent on the road together, I had become closest to him of them all.

"This sickness was brought about by God's will, not theirs?" I stated flatly, belying the equally certain doubts I had earlier held regarding the provenance of that disease.

"Maybe so, but as in all things His instrument is always to be found here on Earth."

"But why should he employ the Jews? Why not the lepers, or any of the other outcasts who have been similarly blamed? Why so honour them, who crucified His own Son?"

"Perhaps that too was by His choosing," Johannes replied. "Do you not see how they remain unharmed, hidden away in their *borghettos*, while everyone else succumbs? How can that be unless they are party to what is happening, and have taken precautions to protect themselves?"

"It is said they do not deny prior knowledge of it," I interrupted him. "An astrologer among them predicted the advent of such a plague, but when they tried to warn others, they were not believed. What more could they have done?"

"Would you believe any of a race who willingly gave up Jerusalem to the infidel, and who betrayed their own Messiah, the Son of God?"

"You have just claimed that such things are the will of God," I commented. "And the Flagellants, while also proclaiming the pestilence is the will of God, in the same breath they assert it is being propagated by the infidel Jew."

"Then perhaps He also wishes for us to be the instrument of His revenge, for all they have done. Perhaps God in his benevolence wishes to provide us with plain cause and reason to carry out His will."

I had every intention of continuing with this debate but before I could respond to his specious arguments we found ourselves amongst a huge crowd drawn up before the quarter where the Jews lived in seclusion from their fellow men. As we arrived among them a great cry of "Hep! Hep!" went up, and the sounds of fighting and men suffering injury began to rise at the front of the crowd. This strange salutation, I later discovered, was an acronym of "*Hierosolyma Est Perdita*! Jerusalem is lost!" the cry of anguish the Crusaders had uttered on hearing that the Holy Sepulchre had been betrayed to the Saracen by the hand of the Jew. Now though, it was being raised merely as a call to murder, and for vengeance against the many and innocent descendants of those past and deceitful few.

Located as we were at the rear of the crowd I was unable to see much of what was taking place. Before me lay the mass of men who had gathered in that crowd, their staffs and scythes and axes wielded high above their heads, and the whole scene was cloaked in smoke from those buildings that were already burning, and in clouds of dust thrown up by a thousand pairs of trampling feet. Beyond that sea of baying heads and brandished weapons, the grey buildings of the Jewish *borghetto* rose up before us like the tiered and gloomy walls of Hell, and clouds of ashes and glowing embers drifted across and fell upon us, blown from the rising inferno on the wings of the wind. The smells of the conflagration - of charred wood, and of straw and reed burning, and of roasting flesh - fouled the air, and seared deep into my eyes and nostrils, and its bitter pungency reached down to and touched the very sinews of my soul.

After a while the crowd ahead of us began to press forward into the narrow streets and alleyways of the *borghetto*, and Johannes and I soon found ourselves witnessing at close hand the vengeance being wreaked upon the unfortunate Jews. Scores of their dead lay littered on the ground, their skulls split and their faces smashed and slit, and from many a torso the limbs had been torn and severed, and their bellies split open, and their entrails dragged out in stinking excesses across the ground. Inside the *borghetto* itself every dwelling we passed was by now being consumed by flames. Framed behind the doors and windows I could see clearly those who had once lived in them in peace, standing or kneeling now in prayer, or clinging to each other for comfort as the avenging fires grew and roared around them and peeled away first the layers of their clothing then bit deeply into their boiling flesh.

At some point during our passage through the carnage and flames Johannes and I became separated from each other, as indeed we two had been soon parted from the others of our company by the fractured movements of the crowd. I was feeling anyway faint and sickened by what I had seen, and I turned from the main thorough-fare along which we had been passing and found myself in a narrow alleyway. There the houses had not yet been set alight, but those who lived there were running hither and thither in panic between the buildings which rose high on either side of the cobbled street. Beside the door of one, a woman stood with two infants cradled in her arms, and taking me no doubt for one of the mob come to wreak his vengeance, at the sight of me she backed away in fear. When the children too began to wail and scream I raised my empty hands towards them, to show I meant them no harm.

As I came near to where the woman was standing I looked inside the building and saw there an old man with long grey hair and beard, and with a coloured shawl draped around his shoulders, going slowly about the room, setting fire to his possessions with the torch he held in his hand. I could not understand why he should be doing this, not with so many gathered there eager to wreak a similar destruction, and stepping up to the threshold I called out for him to stop. Maybe he did not hear my pleas above the sounds of the conflagration rising around him, or he did not understand them, or perhaps he simply chose to ignore them, but whatever the reason he continued about his business without acknowledging my presence, even as the hems of his gown and the tassels of his shawl began to be consumed by flames. The woman came up to me then and laying her hand on my arm to silence me, she smiled sadly at me through her tears, then stepped back through the doorway, the two children still in her arms, and walked towards where the old man was kneeling now in a position of prayer, and they too became engulfed in the heart of the flames.

I could not bear to watch as they were consumed by that inferno, but as I ran from there I saw they were not the only ones who had chosen to sacrifice themselves in this way rather than suffer humiliation and torment at Christian hands. What had the world come to, I wondered, as I fled that frightful place, that men - rather than turn to each other to share and ease their burden in the face of a suffering all knew and must together endure - should look to each other instead to apportion to them the blame? What unfathomable wash of guilt must lay submerged deep within them, drowning all sense of ratio and reason, and poisoning the very flux of humanity that flowed within their souls? For, having once accepted, as most then did, that the sickness was being visited as punishment for the individual sins of its victims, it was not easy to comprehend why any should wish to transfer to another the burden of his own transgressions, and to assign to them the punishments to which he himself was due.

My own thoughts too, of course, were not entirely free of feelings of guilt for the things I was witnessing, for despite my better judgements, I still held slight doubts as to my own culpability in the dissemination of that sickness in whose name these Jews were being mustered to their doom. Just as Simon the Cyrene had been pressed to carry the cross of our Lord on the road to Calgary, and as Christ himself had been condemned to die that others should be redeemed by his blood, I could not help but again feel that the Jews were being made to assume that day a burden of guilt more rightly belonging to me. Either way, I could not bear to remain any longer to witness that subrogation, and I began to make my way from that place as quickly as I could.

Near the point where we had first entered the *borghetto* a number of women and children had gathered and were engaged shamelessly in stripping the corpses as they lay in the streets. Even in my haste to flee I noticed how they were searching in the mouths, and even in the fundaments and other orifices of the bodies of the victims, seeking there I suppose, any gold or valuables the Jews might have secreted in such profane places, even as their lives were being threatened by the mob. I hurried past these brutal acts of intrusion, not daring to look too closely lest I cry out in despair, but my sense of outrage was deflected from this latest horror when I noticed a priest going about in the smouldering shell of one of the buildings, raking through the still-glowing embers of the fires. So perplexed was I by this, that a man of the cloth should be engaged in activities more suited to the mindless rabble, that I stopped to see what he was doing there.

"Just is the Lord in His ways, and upright in all His doings," I heard him murmur as he swept aside the ashes and cinders with his feet, and as I watched, he bent down, and not without some struggle lifted something up from among the debris and dust. At first, as he brushed and blew the ashes from it, I could not make out what it was that he had discovered, but then in an instant of recognition I would rather not have had, I realised the object was the charred remains of a human hand, and that his struggle to retrieve the thing had been to remove it from the arm and body to which it had been attached. I had seen many things that day, sufficient to have reduced a more sensitive man to madness or despair, but such few sensibilities as still remained unsullied in my heart were reduced to disbelief by what I was now witnessing. As I stood and watched, not knowing whether to weep or pray, the priest snapped off one of the fingers from the hand, and blowing the ashes from it, placed the ring that had encircled it into a pouch that hung from his shoulder, and then threw the remaining bones to the ground.

"Everything comes from Him, the only One, whose reasons are not to be explored," I heard him say as he crossed himself, and then patting the pouch contentedly, and returning once more to his searching, he disappeared among the ruins.

Again, I wanted to cry out in despair at the things I was witnessing, and to denounce such sacrilegious behaviour in a priest. But surrounded as I was by so many God-fearing people, all of whom were feverishly engaged in similar acts of desecration, I feared such dissent would only make of me yet one more victim of the ignorance and hatred I had seen vented on these equally innocent others, and cowardice, or reason perhaps, stilled my voice. Swallowing my righteous anger, and feeling dismayed by what I had seen, I made to flee not only the ruined *borghetto* but that hateful city itself.

As I stumbled my way through the narrow streets and alleyways of that place, trying to escape being drawn once more into the maw of the mob, their victorious cries still resounding behind me, I made what efforts I could to discover the whereabouts of my lost companions. Such efforts though were to no avail. In the midst of that chaos they had disappeared without trace, and I prayed that they too had possessed the foresight to make their escape from the horrors that were being perpetrated there in the name of God. I decided anyway to make my way alone to Prague, allaying such doubts as I had regarding the wisdom of such an imprudent undertaking with the hope I would come across Johannes and the others in the course of my journeying, or failing such good fortune, that we would be reunited once more in Prague. Anyway, I set off from Mainz in all earnest, for contrary to the better things I might have expected of it, I had discerned little in that city to persuade me to remain.

-OO-

Some few days after I had fled from Mainz, and from the gross inhumanities I had seen perpetrated there, I found myself passing through the heart of a forest, on the road that led from Wurzburg to Nurnberg. The way on which I travelled was broad and well maintained, but since leaving Wurzburg I had met but a handful of travellers and had not met a single one journeying on it that day. I had by then put from my thoughts as best I could the bitter memory of the things I had seen in Mainz and was beginning to feel again, not only the absence of company to cheer my journey, but the growing fear I had known before of being alone and defenceless and far from the protection of the law and fellow citizens as I had again unwittingly found myself to be.

About the time the sun had reached its highest I came upon a small clearing with a stream running through it, and as I was feeling tired from my morning's travelling I decided to rest and to wait there to see if some pilgrim or other might come along to share and lessen my journey. At the edge of the trees a shrine and a small wooden shelter had been erected for the use of weary travellers such as I, but at the centre of the clearing the stream widened to form a shallow pool flanked by banks of finest gravel, and as this appeared to me a much more inviting prospect I knelt down there and plunged my face into its refreshing embrace. When my thirst had been quenched and my blood cooled, I removed my cape and making of it a pillow, stretched myself out on the ground, and it was not long before I drifted off into sleep.

I could not say how much later it was when I awoke, having been roused from my slumbers by the sounds of human voices and of horses approaching. When I had finally managed to bring some order to my senses, and knew once more who and where I was, I sat up slowly, trying not to seem too alarmed by the appearance in that isolated spot of the group of men I saw coming towards me out of the trees on the opposite side of the stream. Three of them were mounted on horseback, and each of these had a sturdy wooden staff laid across the shoulders of his mount, and another five or six proceeded beside them on foot. All were clad in rags and the skins of animals, and their beards and hair were long and unkempt. All too were clearly armed, and as soon as I saw them I knew them for exactly what they were - the idle sort who made their livings preying on the hard-won bounty of others - and I realised then that my life (if not my possessions, for apart from the clothes I was wearing, and a few tools and books and pamphlets, I did not have any) was in the gravest danger.

When I sat up from where I had been lying unseen, the approaching men reacted to my movements as though by instinct, and two of the footmen ran off to either side to outflank me, while the horsemen spurred their horses towards me in a trot. My only chance to escape them, I remember thinking, was in the thickness of the forest; that exposed as I was in the middle of that clearing I would simply be cut down. Of that much I knew even in my panic, and I jumped up and started to run towards the cover of the forest as fast as my pounding heart and aging limbs would allow. As I ran I heard their voices shouting and howling behind me and the sounds of their horses bearing down upon me. The next thing I knew my legs were pulled out from under me, and I found myself sprawled flat on my face on the ground.

I struggled vainly to my feet, greatly hampered in my efforts by the weighted ropes which had been thrown around me to bring me crashing to the ground, and which bound my arms still to my side. As I wrestled to free myself two of the footmen threw themselves upon me and began to punch and kick me with great relish, and this they continued to do until they were satisfied I had been sufficiently subdued. This too easy yet still painful objective accomplished, they then hauled me to my feet and dragged me towards the edge of the forest whose hoped-for sanctuary I had been trying to attain. There they spread-eagled me against the bole of a tree, my arms pulled back behind me, with my head and hands held fast against its trunk.

A few moments later the three mounted men drew up before me. Climbing down from their horses this unholy trinity advanced towards me, their dark hair and beards shadowing their faces, their harsh wooden staffs clenched firmly in their hands. They came to a halt a few paces in front of me, and the one at their head began to look me up and down with some disdain. Eventually he spoke, and though I could not understand a word of what he said, I understood only too well the tone of his voice, and the cruel force in the hands which held me pinioned in my position of crucifixion against the tree.

"I am a poor man!" I cried out in the language I had possessed from birth, and at this the one who had spoken began to laugh out loud.

"You're a long way from home, my friend," he said in a tongue, which - despite his accent and the poor manner in which he spoke it - I recognised as my own.

"I have only a few small coins. Take them, they are yours!" I added in my relief that whatever else might happen to me, I would at least be understood, and motioning with my head to where my pouch hung lightly at my side. Taking heed of my invitation, the man reached forward and took the pouch and opened it, then poured out its miserly contents into the palm of his hand.

"A poor man indeed," he said, counting out the coins, and then laughed again.

"I am a *dipintore*, making my way to Prague. I hope to find a living there..., but you are welcome to what little I have," and saying this, I began to smile at him foolishly in the feeble hope of thereby gaining his sympathy, but he ignored my words and my ridiculous, ingratiating grimaces and instead turned away and began to speak to his companions in his own incomprehensible tongue.

"Yes. A poor man indeed, and even more poor now than you were a few moments before," he said, when he eventually turned back to face me, discarding his earlier humour, and jingling my meagre coins in his outstretched palm. "Sad to say, it is not enough. I think we must find some other way for you to repay the hospitality we have shown."

At these words my heart sank, and to confirm my fears of what was to become of me, the lout stepped forward and struck me in the stomach with the point of his staff. As I retched and struggled to draw breath they all began to laugh, and then a steady rain of blows began to fall on me, first upon my arms and legs and body, and then upon my unprotected head. I remember thinking as my body danced to the rhythm of their assault, that - cruel and uncouth as they were - these men were not without skill in the way they set about their business. Painful as they were, and sharp enough to draw blood from whatever of my naked flesh they encountered, not one of the blows they laid upon me was delivered with sufficient force to kill. They wanted their pleasure from me, and they knew well enough how to prolong it until all had enjoyed their fill.

In spite of their grim restraint, blood soon began to pour down my face and flood my eyes. Its iron taste filled my mouth, and I feared for a time I would die from drowning rather than from the grievous wounds being inflicted upon my flesh.

I do not know if I did cry out loud in my anger and pain, or if it was only my body I heard silently crying the agonies it was suffering. It is certain though that no one other than my unlistening assailants heard my pleas for mercy and that no friend or champion came rushing from the forest to spare my life. As I hung like crucified Christ against the tree an image came to my thoughts, transporting me back to where it seemed to me the wondrous journey of my life had begun. A vision of that terrible day in Florence flashed before me, only now I imagined the angel-child for whose virtue I had put all our lives at risk standing before me, our roles reversed, she holding open the door of the *bottega*, offering its sanctuary to me. As my senses clouded, I envisioned myself passing through that door and into the comforting embraces of my master, and of Domenico and the others, even of Paraveredus, and then turning from them to find that blessed child standing at my side.

When the men with the staffs had done with me, and I was on the point of losing consciousness, I was allowed to fall to the ground, and was left, but for the grace of God, lying there for dead.

-OO-

But as you know from the very fact of this my chronicle, I did not die. God, in his ineffable mercy, kept me alive to fulfil whatever purpose it was for which He had first quickened my mortal substance with a sensitive soul. When I eventually did regain consciousness it was to find myself lodged in a monastery close to the city of Nurnberg where I had been taken in and my numerous wounds tended to, and where I had been restored to the realms of the living by the benign attentions of the Eremite brothers who prayed and studied there. At first I could not comprehend why I had been shown such charity by so unworldly an order, but my surprise at this (and the elation and disbelief I had felt on finding myself still among the living) was far outweighed by the pleasure I was to feel on discovering the reason why I had been so favourably received.

After my assailants had beaten and robbed me, even of my tools and pigments, of which I am certain they had no use or need, nor for that matter any comprehension of their function, and had stripped me of my clothing, and had left me in the forest for dead, I had been found by a passing merchant and his train. Not knowing what else to do with me this Samaritan had brought me to the monastery, and although no one there had known who I might be, the Eremitani had agreed to take me in and to administer the Last Rites to me in my final moments, for none who saw my condition had believed I would survive the night. As the gore and tears and mud were being wiped from my face, however, one amongst them - recognising my features despite the changes the passing years had wrought - had cried out first in joy, and then in despair at my sorry condition, and had fallen to his knees as best the gross deformity in his leg had allowed. He had then offered thanks to God for having delivered me to that place in my hour of necessity, together with bitter and anxious supplications for the safety of my soul. By the workings of the cruel and unknowable twists of Fate, Domenico, the dearest friend of my childhood years and I had been united once more, having been parted for so long.

"Do you not know me?" I had apparently cried out as Domenico knelt beside me bewailing his contending sorrows and joys, or so he was to tell me later, for it seems the familiar sound of his voice had possessed the power to draw me up momentarily from out of the depths of the senseless condition in which I had hitherto lain.

"Do you not know me? I who am risen in defiance of Death?" I had cried.

At my unprovoked exclamations the brothers had apparently all crowded around me, for they had been greatly surprised, and much relieved to see such sudden vitality revealed in so bloodied and lifeless a form. The next words I uttered, though, had sent them all scurrying just as eagerly from me, to hide in muttered prayer behind their clicking beads and lowered cowls.

"*Noli me tangere*! Do not touch me!" I had cried out, again unknowingly, evoking a presence far nobler than my own unworthy self, and no doubt drawing on the knowledge I had acquired during my work in the chapel in Padua while, lost in the tumultuous depths of my delirium, I unwittingly relived my plague-driven fantasies of the previous year.

Having thus terrified my pious deliverers from their senses, I lapsed once more into unconsciousness. In this blissful state I was to remain, neither dreaming nor feeling, lost in restful and healing oblivion, for three whole days and nights.

-OO-

PART 3

THE CLEANSING
OF THE TEMPLE

NURNBERG, SEPTEMBER 1349

"Midway this journey through life we are
bound upon, I found myself in a dark wood,
Where the right path was wholly lost and gone."

Dante Alighieri, *The Inferno*

One morning, after I had recovered somewhat from
my beating and had regained some of my strength,
Domenico came to visit me in the cell where I had been
so generously lodged. The purpose of his visit had been
to enquire after my health, but as he showed himself
interested to hear my history in more detail (and as I was
equally eager to tell it to someone in all its complexities,
if only to better order it in my own thoughts), I related
to him the story of my flight from Genoa to Paris, and
of how I came from there to the forest where I was
ambushed, and of the strange and irrational fears I had
come to nurture during much of that protracted journey.
When I had finished relating my story, he sat in silence
for some time studying his hands considering what I had
said.

"There is a book here I think you might find of interest," he eventually said. He then asked if I would like to
see it, and I nodded agreement, my curiosity having been
greatly aroused by the possibility of this book providing
some or any enlightenment of my past history, however
arcane it might be. Domenico stood up and left the

cubicle, and when he returned several minutes later he held a large, leather-bound volume cradled in his arms.

"I do not even know if it is right you should see this. Take care with it. It is of great value," he said, as he placed the book on the small table which stood below the single narrow window which lit the room.

"More valuable than any of the other priceless volumes you must have here?" I asked, laughing gently at this show of intrigue, and twisting my head to one side to see what markings I could discern on the bindings of the book that might shed some light on its contents. "And why, in the name of God, should I not be allowed to see it?" I added. At my brash words Domenico placed a finger to his lips to silence me.

"Remember you are lodged in a house of God," he said quietly in admonition.

These simple words of castigation immediately reminded me of that time in Florence many years before when a younger Domenico had been similarly pained by what he had held to be my blasphemy. Then he had tried to block my words from his ears and to run away from the things he had not wished to hear; now he chose, and more wisely I considered, to stem the cause of his discomfort directly at its source. It was clear to see that both his spirit and character had grown greatly since I had seen him last, and I was pleased for him that such a change had come about, finding him to be now, to my delight (for I have never in my life had a friend who was dearer to me than he), not the deferential and timid youth I had known, but a man of great humility and presence. Sadly though, the passing years had done little to ease his physical restriction, his leg having remained as bowed and deformed, and his gait as restricted as it had always been.

"It is a book of oriental medicine," he continued, "and there are those who would claim it contains much that is profane. We do not advertise the fact we have it here, and knowledge of your having seen such a work, certainly as a stranger here in Nurnberg, could conceivably do you harm."

"But it is written in Latin script?" I asked eagerly, ignoring his warning, and fearing more than the ignorance of others that such a tantalising thing once presented for my edification might prove to be nothing more to me than page upon page of meaningless symbols.

"Transcribed from the Arabic by my own hand," Domenico affirmed, and then blushed slightly at the realisation of having succumbed, in uttering these words, to the venial sin of pride. I shook my head slowly at his unwarranted humility.

"Why can you not be proud of the gifts God has given you?" I asked, as he bowed his head and began to mumble a brief prayer of atonement for his perceived vanity. "Why apologise for taking delight in what He has given gladly for your use?"

"Because I am unable to twist the truth inherent in His works to suit my own ends in the ways you have done," he said, then he paused, and looked at me sadly. "And as you apparently continue to do. Tonight, my friend, I will pray for the safety of your soul."

"Feel free to do so," I replied too curtly, and much more harshly than I had intended. His words, I knew, had been offered out of concern rather than in reproach, and it was not my meaning to repay the years of friendship we had shared by giving offence in reply to his honest judgements, nor by demeaning his faith, and having no wish to discuss further the doubtful condition of my soul, I quickly turned my attention to the book.

In truth I had expected the thing to be but another volume of obscure facts and unattainable knowledge - an object of learning and of great intrinsic value, no doubt, but no different, other than in the class and arrangement of the thoughts and ideas it contained, than all the other equally esoteric volumes that were to be found lining the walls of a hundred monasteries and universities throughout the world. As soon as I opened it however, I realised that I held in my hands, not simply a book, but a work of art of the highest order, in itself an object of immense worth, irrespective of the value of the knowledge its words might contain. It was moreover, a thing far more beautiful than anything I had ever, or could ever have produced myself, even had I been asked to attempt it on the greater scale of a panel, or on the wall of a chapel, and even had my errant passions not thwarted the good application of all my natural skills to the execution of such a task. Domenico had every reason to be proud of the products of his craft. The training he had received from our master, though it had not been put to its intended purpose, had served him more than well.

I tried to imagine how many hours of labour he had devoted to the creation of that wondrous book, for every page I turned to was filled from margin to margin, and from head to foot with a precise and delicate script. The illuminated capitals which graced the head of each page were bold masterpieces of invention, the letters themselves having been exquisitely formed and coloured, and adorned with ornate scrolls, and with depictions of tiny human figures posed variously in gestures of bliss or fear or supplication. These uncials were graced too with fanciful creatures that curled and crawled along their stems and curves and branches, so that the letters seemed to be not just symbols conveying the sounds and meaning of a living, vibrant language, but to be themselves alive. The margins too were filled with glosses, and with delicate drawings of the plants and herbs which had been otherwise described in the wording of the text, and with diagrams of the sundry parts of the human body; and how those parts came to be affected by each sickness and condition, and how such corruptions were to be treated, and what instruments and preparations were to be used, and in what manner, to achieve this salutiferous end.

Seeing such beauty before me brought tears of both delight and sadness to my eyes - delight at how Domenico had brought such science and learning so beautifully to life on the surface of the velum, and sadness at the recollection of the many things I had hoped to achieve in my own art and had thus far signally failed to accomplish. Confronted so boldly by such perfection I had to turn away to prevent my tears from falling upon and damaging that most gorgeous work.

One thing was clear to me even through the veil of my contrary tears - that Domenico carried out his labours with a passion and a conviction that my own work sadly lacked. The love he felt for the knowledge conveyed in the alien words he had transcribed, and for the eloquent images and phrases he had employed to translate such esoteric learning into something even the most humble of souls might comprehend, could be clearly seen and sensed in the glad decoration of those pages by even the meanest of spirits. To him such work had been an act of devotion not of labour, other that is than a labour of love - for God Almighty, and for all of His Creation, and for the gifts that he, humble and crippled Domenico had been given with which to make intelligible to others the sublime mysteries that lay concealed within the workings of the world. My own work had been a gargantuan struggle by comparison, and in its arrogance, a base insult, both to God and to His wondrous Creation. In a moment of insight I realised then that perhaps this was so simply because (unlike Domenico, and despite my past youthful protestations to the contrary) I had laboured ever to create an image of a love that I did not truly feel, and that the reason I did not feel that love truly was simply because it was not my own. It was a passion rather – or an affectation, one might more accurately say - one I had acquired from my master, both out of devotion to him and through many years of practice. In that process of rote replication, it had become for me something other than what it was meant to be - a mere simulacrum of my master's much truer Art. An art that was entirely his own, fashioned from the substance of his own heart and soul.

"I think you will find the first chapter of most interest," Domenico said, ignoring my show of emotion, and at his instruction, and to hide my confusion, I turned back to the beginning of the book.

"There the author claims that disease originates from an imbalance of spirits in the organs of the body - from what our physicians would describe as a *dyskrasia* of the humours which together constitute the temperament of the individual soul. He says that the cause of a sickness can often be ascribed to selfishness, or an excessive occupation with money and reward. When such an imbalanced perception of the value of the self over others occurs, the spirits become impaired in their functions and disease arises in the flesh, and the operation of that part of the soul which affords us reason may become hindered."

"What sort of pagan nonsense is that?" I exclaimed, thinking his own reason had been impaired that he should offer such insanity to me as truth, and as explanation of my past experiences.

"I warned you the book contains much that might be considered arcane," he said. "You disappoint me though. I thought you of all people would approach such ideas with an open mind."

"I do, but...," I began, but then faltered, and was relieved when Domenico chose to ignore my complaints and to continue with his own argument.

"If the assumptions made in that book are based on truth, and if Man is indeed a microcosm of the world in which he moves, then such a pestilence as we are witnessing would of reason and necessity come to afflict us now, precisely at this moment in history when every man seems more than overly occupied with himself and with his own needs and desires. Are you not yourself a prime example of that selfish preoccupation, as was your friend Dante, who - to judge from the evidence of his scribblings - was of a decidedly sickly sort, and often suffered physically as a result of his unruly emotions? The same is true I fear of that *novus homo,* Petrarca, whose conceits I am certain you equally laud and admire."

"What do you mean by my selfish preoccupations?" I asked, once his diatribe had run its course and I had recovered from my surprise at the vehemence of the indictments he had raised against me.

"You professed to me once your desire to devote your work to the promotion of your name in Posterity as well as to the greater glory of God. I thought it blasphemy then, and from what little I know of you, and from how little I see you have changed, I think it blasphemy still. Do you not see that the world you move in is centred only on yourself? You have filled your heart so full of selfish ambitions there is no room left in it for God to find a place to reside in."

"That is not true, I try to live my every day in His service."

"Where then is He to be found? I do not see him in your life, and my powers of insight are usually keen enough to detect the slightest trace of faith in even the most shrunken and wasted of souls." I looked at him blankly, unable to reply or to defend my own meagre and irreverent faith in the face of his unquestioned devotion.

"You do not pray; you do not attend Mass," he continued. "Nor do you go to confess your sins, few as they may be. Neither do you fulfil your professed desire to put God into your art, from what I have heard, nor allow Him the slightest opportunity to enter into it. You have spent your days painting blazing comets, and trying to enshrine your soul within the gaudy flesh of your creations. You have made yourself into your own God, and have prostituted whatever skills you once possessed to the service of that selfish end."

"But isn't this theory that you are propounding also a heresy?" I protested, ignoring this attack upon my faith, and upon my work, and waving my arms in the air, then slapping the binding of the book to give more emphasis to my argument. "Is it not commonly held that this sickness has been sent by God as punishment, and that as such we should accept His judgement and His sentence passively, and not try to explain it in terms of our own misguided choice?"

"That is the common belief," he replied flatly.

For a moment, as he spoke, I was reminded of our master Giotto, not only in the tone of what he had said, but in the manner in which he had delivered it. He had captured exactly that way Messer Giotto had possessed of seeming to agree with whatever was being said while at the same time bringing it into ridicule. It was strange to see these characteristics of my former master revealing themselves in another, and I wondered whether Domenico was also able to see such traits and mannerisms of our teacher similarly manifest in me.

"You were in Paris," he continued in a manner that was entirely his own, "and which would you rather believe, common superstition, or the considered judgement of the learned professors there, who I am certain had come to their conclusions while you were still residing there? Would you dispute their verdict that the sickness had as its cause an adverse conjunction of the planets, and which the King of France and every other sensible man now chooses to believe? My theory, as you call it, says only that the selfishness of the individual may lead to their being more susceptible to the influences of such things should they arise."

Whether through the frailty of my condition, or the weariness of confusion that crept up on me at that moment, or simply through the realisation of impending defeat, I suddenly felt fatigued by our discussion. Whatever the reason, I could do little more than shake my head feebly in reply. Domenico looked at me with a grave expression on his face and also began to shake his head.

"Forgive me," he said, taking my hands in his. "I have been foolish, and selfish too. I should have taken your condition into consideration. It would have been better had we not discussed this matter now." At that he said he had to leave me anyway, as he was expected in the *scriptorium*, it being then almost *terce*, the hour at which the working day for the monks began, but that he would return again that evening after supper had been taken. He bade me farewell, and expressed the wish that I should study the book well - if my condition and strength allowed - while maintaining an open mind about its contents, and that I might thereby gain something of value from my readings. I thanked him again, and sank wearily onto the bed, and fell asleep so quickly that I do not remember him leaving the room.

-OO-

As he had promised Domenico came to visit me later that evening, and by then I was feeling again refreshed and ready to face his arguments. He too was in good humour, and finding me much revived, and at my insistence he immediately resumed the vein of reasoning he had employed earlier to try to explain to me the vicissitudes of my life.

"Perhaps it was not all just a product of your imagination. Perhaps the sickness was indeed drawn to you, and to use you as its vehicle, by virtue of that kindly inclining which draws together both the cause of a thing and its effect."

As you well know, such a possibility - that the pestilence should have been drawn to my person just as the iron moves in sympathy towards the lodestone - no longer held much attraction for me. I had debated, and had rejected such a sympathetic coupling between myself and the *atra mors* during the long, contemplative months

I had spent in Paris during the previous winter, and had indeed been persuaded further of this more rational position by the very judgement of the professors there that Domenico had cited earlier. Hearing such a notion voiced by another though, I found myself again being seduced by the very improbability of such an explanation, and I sat deliberating on its likelihood for some time until Domenico disturbed my contemplation by asking under which sign of the zodiac I had been born.

"Aquarius. In the house of Saturn," I replied tentatively, being suspicious of where this new line of questioning might lead.

"You see?" he said, clapping his hands in delight, as though my answer proved beyond doubt the veracity of everything he had been saying. "Your natural element is therefore air, and those born under that sign are of a sanguine temper by nature, which is the very temperament said by the physicians to be most likely to succumb to the current disease. In Aquarius that element is in the first house, and in that position it has the strongest influence upon the aspects of the body, and of life itself. The second house, I believe, concerns wealth and worldly gain."

"But I have never concerned myself with worldly gain!" I protested mildly. "That is the second time you have alluded to a supposed vein of avarice within me, yet I have hardly ever a *soldi* to my name, and neither care one jot about it, not if I have food enough to eat, a place to lie in, and materials with which to paint. Surely you are confusing me with Messer Giotto!" We both smiled at my last remark, for it was well known how our former master had feasted well from the harvest of his labours and had used part of such rewards as he received to purchase looms and parcels of land. These properties he had then rented out, providing himself and his family with a not inconsiderable income for a number of years.

"Oh yes!" Domenico retorted. "I remember it now! You were the one who desired to work only for Posterity, not for personal gain. Then off you went to Bologna, going away from us a naïve and divinely-inspired youth, and came back a week later with a feather in your backside, a wiser, yet far more foolish man." We both laughed aloud at this, and I especially so at Domenico's unexpected vulgarity, though his words were of course much more painful to me, being as I was the butt of their sarcasm.

"And how does that sudden memory fit into the strictures of your precious theory?" I asked, still laughing.

"That I do not know. And it is not my theory, however precious you might find it. Perhaps there are just too many adverse influences acting upon those aspects of your life. Perhaps that is why you have failed to achieve your ambitions."

I looked at him in surprise at the knowledge he seemed to possess of my miserable efforts as a *dipintore*, for I had not touched too deeply on the matter of my failings while relating to him the story of my flight from Genoa, other than of my unfulfilled commissions there. It came to me then that he had made similar comments that morning, but I had been too weary then, or had been perhaps too concerned with the attacks he was making upon my character to have paid them too much heed.

"How is it you know so much of how my life has gone?" I asked.

"You were my friend, the only one in Florence who showed me true friendship, and I have always concerned myself with how you have fared. You are not the only craftsman to have travelled this way seeking employment on the cathedral, and I have had news brought to me as and when I could, and have heard things said, though of course I have not seen it for myself."

"Then you are fortunate to have been spared that pleasure," I replied bitterly, and though at first I was reluctant to relive that part of my history, at his insistence I began to elucidate for him the sad chronicle of the frustration of all my past artistic ambitions. Once I had finished relating to him that long and painful litany, we continued to discuss my past and the unmitigated failures it contained until Domenico had to leave once more to perform the office of prayers at *compline*. In fact (and to my shame and regret, for Domenico also had a history of which I would have liked to have learned more), we were to talk of little else during the time I was to remain in that place recuperating my health. Gradually, though, and through the offices of his benign guidance, and by the mere fact of his presence providing me with a means to retrace, and to see through the eyes of another the reality of the shadowy remove of my youth, I came at last to realise and to understand much of the root and extent of my past follies.

And what were the facts of the history I then rediscovered for myself? That I had submitted to the sin of vanity? That I had wanted to make myself immortal, and that solely as a consequence of my own actions, and not by virtue of the reflected glory or the magnanimity of another? Such insight, worthless as it had been, I had long possessed. Even before I had entered the *bottega*, I had decided I would not be but another poor reflection of my master, as any other apprentice would have gladly aspired to be, aping blindly the tricks and artistry he taught them, yet incapable of forming individual expression, or of putting any part of themselves into the things they made. For better or worse, I, Pace di Buoninsegna, had set far higher goals for myself.

What I had wanted was nothing less than to create my own art, my own style, perhaps even my own creative universe, though I would not then have admitted willingly to having embraced such a heresy. What I came to realise during my time in Nurnberg was that - exactly as all the others who passed through the bottega had done (and who, other than Domenico I had disdained to a man for their innate lack of singularity) - all I had ever been capable of doing was to likewise copy that which my master had already done. Perhaps for one of lesser vanities that would have been no small thing to have attained, for when all is said and done, by the time I departed from the *bottega* I could perform that exercise more than well, and far better than could most. But then, neither did I possess the insight, nor the sensitivity and wisdom of my master, nor possess a true vision of what things I wanted to create, and try as I might to apply such mimic skills as I had acquired to the expression of my higher emotions, my efforts to that end were naturally doomed to fail.

To explain better the true extent of my limitations, I must return once more to that picture of mine I told you of which hangs in a chapel in Assisi. In it, I too had tried to create an impression of the wondrous comet I had seen in Florence, just as my master had done in Padua. What I showed there, however, in the brash farrago of ideas that purported to betray both the Nativity and the Adoration (following some arrogant and misguided whim of mine to combine the allegorical birth of my dreams with the scene of my apotheosis in the Arena), reveals instead, not my skill, nor the love I should have held for the God who had ordained and created such a spectacle, but my abject lack of faith both in my abilities and in my profane beliefs. That bold star, which had burned so brightly in the Heavens, and in the aspirations of my childhood, and which had shone uncorrupted in my memory even as I worked on that painting, glimmers now as but feeble testimony to my failure, stilled and lifeless on that wall.

I too had wanted to show the thing as something more than a mere star - a *cometis stella*, a heavenly miracle replete in all its glory. I had even had as vindication for depicting it in such a way the authority of the learned sources my master had quoted in justification of his own departure from convention, and had too his own perfect rendition as example, which all had praised and none had professed to doubt. Still I had not dared to convey my honest convictions to the application of brush and pigment to plaster, though what the reasons for the thwarting of my good intentions may have been, I had never been able to determine.

Could it have been that on some level within me, one never voiced or acknowledged openly, I had lacked the courage to commit to the untouched surface of the wall, and thus to my cherished Posterity, the boundless heresies that were brewing deep inside my soul? Or had I already realised then (though I could not see it), that all I was doing was nothing more than bland imitation of all that Giotto had done previously and to perfection? Or indeed, more sadly for my ambitions, that the perfection he had achieved could not be surpassed by anyone, so sublime had it been. In which of these possibilities the true reason for my failure lay, I could not then say, or even if it might rather have been found in some other place - unseen, unsensed, and unsuspected - lacking as I did the greater courage of my convictions. The only thing I did know with any certainty was that what I managed to create in Assisi was not a *cometis stella* in all its portentous glory, but a mediocre star conjured up by means of the crude tackle of convention I had carried always with me and made less blessed by the vain addition of a gaudy Devil's tail!

So it is that in spite of my having sought a far more substantial testimony to my passing in the sublime execution of my craft, the likeness Messer Giotto had deigned to make of me in the Chapel in Padua remains my only true claim to immortality, and even in that one thing I had been shown looking away from the blessed scene being enacted before me, as though I was unable to look fully at the bounteous glory that has ever been presented to me. I do not need to tell you how that sad indictment alone could never have been sufficient to satisfy the self-regarding hunger of my dreams, nor to have prevented my passage through life from having been anonymous, and therefore, by my own reckoning, of little worth.

-OO-

The evening before I was to depart from Nurnberg, Domenico came to talk to me one final time. My wounds were by then sufficiently recovered for me to travel (though the shadow of them continues to this day to throw its pall across my mortal frame, and echoes of the pain to both my body and my spirit still return regularly to rouse me from my sleep). I had decided to continue on to Prague, in accordance with my original intention, though I had no idea what I would do there or how I would earn my keep. My faith in my abilities as a *dipintore*, and even in my purpose on this earth, had dwindled almost to nought. All I knew was that

I had to continue my journey, to face whatever Fate had been assigned to me.

"What should I do now?" I complained to Domenico, voicing my concerns. "All I know is how to paint, and yet it seems that everything I paint is worthless. How am I to carry on? How am I to survive?"

"You could stay and join us here." I shook my head slowly at this suggestion, and the corners of Domenico's lips curled lightly in amusement.

"No, I think not," I said. "As you pointed out, I am not the most pious of souls. I could not bear the rules and strictures. Nor the ungodly hours you keep."

"You would find habit is a great regulator. It's not such a hardship once you become accustomed to it. Tell me, though. I am curious. What was the best thing you ever painted?" I had to think about this for only a short time before the image of the last thing I had painted in Turin, prior to fleeing from the plague, rose up in my memory.

"A Madonna on a wooden panel. In Turin," I replied.

"Was it done well? Be honest with yourself."

"Yes, I believe so."

"And why do you think that?"

"The handling of the colour was controlled, and it was a true likeness to…," I began, trying to expound the technical qualities of what I had done.

"No. Not that," he interrupted. "Why do you think, of all the things you have made, that one turned out so well?"

This time I had to think more deeply about what I had done. As I had tried erroneously to explain, the image was indeed more life-like than anything I had hitherto done - the flesh more like real flesh, the form of the body more solid, with something of a living spirit visible within that crafted form, especially in the eyes. But was that the product of pure craft alone, or of Providence, or had there been some other factor or agency guiding my hand to execute the task so well? I tried to recall what thoughts and images had been active in my head, and too in my heart and soul while occupied in painting that panel. Certainly myriad instances of the horrors I had seen all around me, and also the lingering memory of my troubled sea passage, but surely, I reasoned, neither of those could have aided me in the production of an object of beauty. Neither could my burgeoning doubts about my abilities in the art I was professing to have mastered have fostered such a worthy product.

Then it came to me. A realisation of the one thing that had been there, an integral part of my being, for the greater portion of my life, and which, for various reasons (which I hope to have explained to you in the telling of my story), I had tried my hardest to ignore. It had been there always, underlying nearly all of my thinking and feeling: the serene purity of the image of that sweet and innocent child, burning brightly in the deepest recesses of my being. The innate beauty of her soul which I had been blessed enough so fleetingly to perceive, and which I cherished still in my memory, and which had ever been a beacon to my thoughts. That was what had prompted me, I realised, once I allowed its power to operate unfettered through me. That was what had led me to perform my single act of sublime creation.

"Do you remember that day in Florence, when the gang of Black youths chased the young woman into the bodega and Paraveredus fought them off?" Domenico nodded solemnly.

"I remember," he said. "It was a terrible day for Florence. And almost for us too."

"Yes. Yes. I know. I was impetuous, foolhardy."

"That you were," Domenico interjected, nodding his head slowly, amusement deepening the lines around his eyes.

"But do you remember the girl?" I said impatiently. Finally seeing some glimmer of reason in my actions I had little time for such mundane considerations.

"Yes, I remember her, and I also recall you were quite touched by her. You talked of barely nothing else for the next month."

"I was indeed touched, to the depth of my soul, and I have carried the memory of her with me ever since." I paused before saying what I had to say next, knowing it was a thing of great import, and therefore not to be admitted lightly.

"Domenico, I believe she came to me in Turin as my Muse. Just as the lady Beatrice came to Dante Alighieri. That is why I made the painting so well. It was an image of her that I was painting. Not just her physical being, but of everything she has come to represent for me."

"It was an image then of something you truly love?"

"Yes, indeed. At least, I believe it was so."

"And she had never come to you in this manner before?"

"No. As I said, she has been in my thoughts constantly, but never before had I... Why do you think that should be, that she should have come to me then, and only then?"

Domenico placed one arm across his lower chest, the hand clasping his side, with the other elbow rested against it, and the hand of that arm raised to stroke his upper lip, then he turned away and began to pace slowly round the room. As my eyes followed him, it occurred to me that my original assessment of his deformity had been amiss, and that time had in fact eased his impairment, or he had learned how to compensate for it, the over-eager hobble of his youth having now become but an almost graceful irregularity in his gait. He had made three or four circuits around me before he finally came to a halt (to my relief as I was starting to feel dizzy from following his movements, and still had painful bruises around my neck and shoulders), and turned back to face me.

"Perhaps you had been too frightened to use her memory in that way before," he said. "It could be considered a profane basis for the creation of such a sacred image. Perhaps your fear of committing heresy held her beneficent powers at bay, and it was only when your fear was focused on things more immediate and awesome - the plague, the sickness and death all around you - that she was able to come to you in that way. Perhaps you had to be truly confronted by your own mortality before you could see any greater truths and allow them to enter freely into your soul."

"Do you think she will return?" I said, with more than a slight sinking in my heart. I feared she had come to me but that once in Turin and would not return again, for I still believed, echoing Domenico's speculations, that I had somehow abused her memory by using it in such a way. I also hoped, naturally enough, that the dire circumstances he had outlined as possible cause for her transformation from unrequited love to guiding light would never again arise to blight my life. A solemn look passed across his face, and he came closer to me.

"Pace, there is something I have to tell you." His eyes were full of concern and were fixed steadfastly on mine. I stared back, feeling numbed by a prescient knowledge of what he was about to tell me.

"The girl and her family..., they did not escape." My head fell forward at his revelation and a sharp gasp of air escaped my mouth. Anticipation had not dulled the pain of this news, though some part of me must always have acknowledged that, despite my assumed conviction to the contrary, such had most likely been the case.

"What...? What happened to them," I managed to ask through the fog of sadness that had engulfed me.

"They were caught, and hung, along with sixty others in the Piazza Maggiore."

"How do you know of this? Why did I not know?"

"I overheard Paraveredus telling one of the others. I thought it better if you did not know. I could see the effect she had on you, and thought to protect you by not saying. I even asked Paraveredus not to speak of it to you. Can you imagine? Insignificant and timid Domenico, asking a favour of him? I have to say, he was surprisingly obliging. I think he may have been saddened by the news of her death almost as much as you would have been, and his self-righteous arrogance would have made him reluctant to have shared his sense of loss with you."

As he spoke my thoughts were alive with recollections of that day in Florence – the crowd of Black youths in the street, my first sight of her, her beauty, her public embarrassment; the fight in the bottega, the unexpected courage and nobility of Paraveredus, and the stern, calming presence of my master; then my last, longing sight of her, huddled protectively in the arms of her father. It all still seemed so real, almost tangible, and still beyond my powers to change a single thing that had occurred. All I could do was nod feebly to Domenico in acknowledgement.

"Perhaps I should have told you. Can you forgive me?" he said.

I looked back up at him, and saw before me again the young and seemingly defenceless child who had befriended me those many years ago. His eyes still held that same trust, and that same awe (though what I read as awe was more likely his own distrust, I now realised), at the unworldly things I held within me, though in truth it was I who was now in awe of him, of the wise and noble being he had become. I was touched that he should have thought to protect me; that he, my poor, crippled Domenico, as I had once thought of him, had indeed been able to protect me from such pain.

"Of course I can forgive you. Maybe only now am I able to honour her memory properly. If I had known then, the bitterness I would have felt would only have destroyed it all."

"I thought it was for the best."

"And it was. So, tell me, do you think she will return to me?" I asked, my fears that I might have betrayed her having only been deepened further by knowledge that she was no longer among the living.

"If you allow her to, and if your love for her is truly pure. Now you may cherish the memory of her as a pure disembodiment of her spirit. You no longer need to wrestle with your baser desires. And there too, I think, you can discover the answer to your original question. You should continue with your painting. It would be a pity not to use your skills, and the guiding power of that spirit, and what's more, it would be an insult to the memory of Messer Giotto if you did not. You know he would not forgive you. I am certain those skills are still yours to command, but as in all things, it is essential to focus only on that which you truly love. Enshrine the memory of her spirit. Try to pass that down to your precious Posterity, not the vestiges of your vanity. Who knows? Maybe one day you will come to be known as

Pacino, Master of the Madonna." He smiled broadly at this suggestion.

"Now it is you who are making fun of me," I said.

"Possibly," he said. "I have had to wait a long time for the opportunity," then he turned and departed from my chamber, leaving me again to ponder on all the things we had spoken of over the preceding days.

-OO-

Thus, was my conversion to a humbler state of grace made complete. Having been shown the extent of my errors under the wise tutelage of Domenico, I swore therewith to abandon the chapel in which I had so long knelt at the altar of vanity, and to relinquish forever the religion of self-love I had so foolishly embraced those many years before, firstly in the house of Dante in Bologna, and then in the chapel in Padua, the images on whose walls had given colour and substance to, and indeed had shaped and encapsulated the essence of my self-centred dreams, and of my life. No more, I resolved, would I assay merely to copy and emulate those wondrous things my Master had painted; no more would I pursue the gratification of that ill-placed vanity through the perversion of my God-given craft, and of my faith.

And so my life has run. Since that time I have devoted my days only to the creation of depictions of the Madonna (my Muse indeed having returned to me as and when I had need of her, just as Dante had intimated, having become by some strange mechanism an integral and joyous part of my being), and in reading and study, and in the occasional transmission to others (naïve and hopeful, and egotistic youths mostly, just as I had once been) of that for me once all-encompassing craft. Since that day my hands have neither wielded brush, nor ground earths, nor mixed pigments, other than in dissemination of my skills and knowledge, and in the true depiction of Her virginal majesty, and strangely enough, now I no longer crave or actively seek it, it seems that some fame and honour has again gradually accrued to my work and reputation, and that the name of Pacino of Florence, humble and putative Master of the Madonna, may well indeed come to be passed down and remembered after I am gone.

As for the apprentices I have had working for me, and have taught, I have done what I can in the service of their education, though whether my labours to that end have served them well I cannot say. Nevertheless, I have stuck to my avowed task (though at times I have despaired at their abilities more than I ever have at my own), having found strength for the task in the hope that such instruction as I gave may have prevented at least one among them from having fostered the same deluded expectations as I once held, and thereby might have avoided the pain of failure pursuit of such dreams must bring. Of that sad possibility I had been warned by my own master in Padua, but had not taken heed.

The hand of the surgeon is hard, but it is healing. I bear the scars of his sovereign remedies upon me. I have learned my lessons well.

-OO-

FLORENCE, MICHELMAS, 1378

"The visible things of Him of the Creation of
the world are clearly seen, being understood by
the things that are made." Paul, *Romans 1:20*

My story has taken much time in its writing, as in its
living; I write now as I live - slowly, both from weariness
of body and of mind. In such restrictions I know I have
no right to complain, and despite the discomforts I have
suffered in bringing my labours to fruition, and
regardless of those times when it seemed I would not
have the strength to complete them, my task is almost at
an end. In this at least I have been granted everything I
have asked; He who determines all has been most
gracious, more gracious certainly than I have been to
Him throughout my disobliging life. Now all that
remains is for me to set down what conclusions I have
drawn from the things I have been shown, in the hope
that such wisdom as I have gained from them might be
of value - to you at least, if not to me, now that it is too
late for me to put such lessons to any effect.

Yet why is it that I feel I am not yet ready to make
such easy judgements, now that by my own admission
my story is coming to its natural end? Why do I resist
still the call of eternity's insistent whispers, when with
every day it becomes more obvious that my body and
soul draw ever nearer to the end of their unnatural
pilgrimage through life? Could it be that deep inside I

feel it is not yet ended, that hope remains while breath still quickens my being? That other, more enduring lessons may yet be learned, maybe even in this process of dissolution and decay we call dying, or in the events that are at this moment unfolding outside this room?

For nothing changes; the world remains subject to an endless and irredeemable process of change. Nothing remains the same, other than change itself, and the only certainty we may have is that a thing which has once been altered cannot be restored. Nothing is constant, certainly not the whims of mortal man; only the hubristic passion with which he pursues them. Men are born and then grow old and die, and in between their coming and going they seem irrevocably bound to do their utmost to change the ways of the stubborn world into which they have been spawned.

In this, as it is ordained, and as I have found to my cost, all must fail in their vain ambition.

-OO-

So, as Death draws ever nearer to my dulling sphere of decrepitude and ignorance, I find I am able to draw little comfort from remembrance of those things which once gave me such pleasure in my youth. Neither can I take solace in the faith in God which was supposedly the power which brought about their creation. Nor have I been able to free myself entirely of such feelings of betrayal as my experiences have endowed me with - not merely through the coarser treacheries of Charles of Valois and Corso Donati, and of de Brienne, and Fra Lorenzo, or in the grip of the pestilence whose victim and vehicle I had once imagined myself to be, but also through the subtler exercise of the unknowable ways of God Almighty, who even now leads me to face Death fearful of the retribution which surely awaits me, yet leaves me unprepared and unrepentant, seeing as I do no sins other than my faultless ignorance for which I should be called upon to repent.

And how far should I go in my self-righteous condemnation? Should I impeach here too the skills and innovations displayed so ably by my master, and which in great measure he imparted through his teachings to my unworthy self? Did my master betray me in that his teachings had promised so much, yet left me with human Art inadequate to achieve the ambitious end they had enflamed? Or was the imagined redeemer betrayed rather by the wilful passions of the redeemed? For it was I, the apostate pupil, who was to prove himself the Judas to the knowledge entrusted to him by his Master, and that not even for the reward of silver, but in the pursuance of something intangible which I believed to lay concealed within the workings of my mortal soul?

What then, pray, am I to make of such duplicity as seems ever to have presided over me throughout my life?

Even now, marooned and powerless as I am in my time of desuetude, I am being called upon to witness a Church which is governed, not by one, but by two Prelates - the one, Urbanus VI, who since the death of Gregory (whose passing, if you remember, graced the opening pages of this book), has maintained the Papal throne in its rightful place in Rome; the other, Clement VII, the *quondam* Butcher of Cesena, who with the wealth and power of French cardinals to support him claims those same powers for himself in the greying citadel of Avignon.

Do two Gods then await my death, enthroned in their separate Heavens?

But enough of such idle musings. I should be able to put such petty thoughts and doubts behind me. No longer can I proclaim my innocence, nor attempt to ascribe to others the blame for my own and wholly predictable failings. I see clearly now that in all things and in all ways I have been betrayed only by my own human nature, which like all natures is constant and undeniable, but which I have aspired always to elevate myself above.

To that fallacious end, I have too, for what it is worth, remained celibate, even on those occasions in my youth when I was tempted to surrender to the seduction inherent in the light of a female eye. Even then did I refuse to allow the sensuality to which all men are subject its brief dominion over reason, and over the more wilful portions of the flesh. It has not troubled me that since that time I have had neither cause, nor desire, to lose myself in pursuit of those unquestionable pleasures. The one small regret I do have in respect of such matters of the heart and of the flesh, is that my solitary experience of the dominion of Love was never consummated, and that the greater portion of my life had passed before I was able to use the powers inherent in such an affliction to good effect.

Fortunate indeed are they who, in the face of such passions can turn such baser weakness to strength. *Quod me non detruit me nutrit*; that which does not destroy me feeds me, or so it has been said. In my life, as you have seen in the reading of my story, I have borne many things and have somehow, by the grace of God or by good fortune survived them all. But something is gained and something is lost in every day's endeavours, in every transaction, be they venal or sublime. In that, though, who can say whether my soul has been nourished or made shrunken and thin by my daily trials and tribulations? That, only God - or the Devil - may know or decide.

Now, though, I must rest. With the passing of the years my flesh has become subject to other, more persuasive weaknesses. Now, even the simplest of tasks leaves me weary; the effort of writing takes its toll upon my bones. I must lay down my pen and put aside these pages to try to find the ease of slumber. When I am revived, I will read again what I have written, and make what amendments I must while time remains to correct those things I have recorded wrongly, and while the lights of memory and intellect and reason glow still if but dimly and ever receding in the darkening recesses of my ageing soul. Then I shall return, to try to impart to you an old man's concluding vision of all that his life has been.

-OO-

FLORENCE, THE FEAST OF SAN FRANCISCUS 1378

"Death villainous and cruel, pity's foe,

Thou ancient womb of woe,

Burden of judgement irreversible!"

Dante Alighieri, *La Vita Nuova VIII*

I am returned, but not as promised, to make apologies for my worldly deeds and actions. Little time remains for such indulgences now. While I have been absent, ruminating in the somnolent days of my senility, debating what further claims, if any, I should make in defence of my life, a terrible thing has occurred to thwart such intentions as I had.

Mother of ironies, ineffable mystery! Confounder of such petty conceits as a man may carry within him. The comet of my youth has returned!

Once more the thing hangs silently against the Heavens, as it did those many years ago. It hangs there now, motionless yet seemingly eternally in motion - a heavenly signifier of all that is unknowable, come once more to test our ignorance of God's paternal will.

Now, however, although it hangs against the sky exactly as it did in my infancy, no longer am I able to take it as the positive omen I took it then to be. For with it too have come the seeds of sickness. The world outside my room has fallen silent; the streets are empty, and fear once more pervades the hearts of all. The plague, the *atra mors* from which I once fled, and whose herald I once feared I might be has returned.

And so I sit here in my room, alone and comfortless, accompanied only by my books and possessions, waiting to see whether those *gavaccioli* I have seen flowering a thousand times upon the flesh of others will blossom soon around my own neck and armpits, and those same dark buboes writhe beneath my skin, Will my own limbs tremble and dance in time to its fevered music, locked in a *tarantella* performed too late to distract approaching Death?

Whatever! No longer can I run from it – no longer am I able! - neither to flee, nor to precede its awesome passage. Thus, do I resume my scribblings, my thoughts confounded by fear and anticipation. The hour has come to bid farewell.

-OO-

Who knows, perhaps I shall die as did Petrarca, found by the old woman who comes to feed me, seated in my chair, my head laid as though in sleep upon the pages of my book. And if I do, what should I or the world make then of the long and vainglorious extension of my days? Should I claim for myself some small superiority in having so long outlived him, and in having outlived Boccaccio, also now some three years dead? And what laurels should I strew about myself for having so long survived Villani, and likewise my fellow artists Pisano and the brothers Lorenzetti, all of whom perished some three decades past of the self-same disease which now threatens to jangle my sinews and invade my bones?

But cease! What purpose can it serve to spend my caudal hours in idle gloating? I had thought to have long since put such vanities behind me, but even as Death turns his unfaltering gaze in my direction, it seems the hubris of humanity drives my soul still to assert its presence.

So, cease, I say, this futile digression! There is no gain to be found in it. Soon enough I too shall be as dead and nameless as are they.

-OO-

What more is there to say? I sit here not knowing what awaits me, yet in such precious moments reminiscing upon the first appearance of the *cometis stella* in my life, seeking desperately among my memories of that happier time for confirmation of that which I then believed so fervently - that the thing had come to announce to the world my own brilliant nascence as a *dipintore*. Now though, try as I might to assign to it some small relevance to my own existence, I see only that it, and the work my master then did in Padua, heralded the passing of the old style of painting, and the birth of a new style, whose nativity I was privileged to have attended (and indeed to have been immortalised in by the gracious hand of my master), but which my own labours have done insufficient to promote.

Of so many things have I been mistaken; in so much has my ignorance determined the way I have used the things I have been shown. Perhaps then, all I can claim with certainty of this new appearance is that it comes to announce my own culmination, seeing as I do now in such blind comings and goings nothing but reminders of the repeated cycles that all life is bound to follow, and of the irresistible forces of God and Nature, against which the efforts of Man are to no avail.

I will not sermonise; I have no right. I who have despoiled all that I have been given may not deign to tell others how they should or should not live their lives!

-OO-

With every hour I grow more wearied, yet still I ramble on, remaining to the last true to my history of stubborn resistance, ever pitting my vanities against that which cannot be changed. What more of my life, of my faultless arrogance, is there to say?

The end of my story approaches; the hour has come to conclude this chronicle, this abbreviated record of my unnecessarily extended days. Of needs, a myriad thoughts and episodes have been omitted in its telling. Still I continue to add to it, accounting my failures like beads on an endless rosary of despair. Will this, my desperate history never end?

It was Bonaventura, was it not, who defined the various ways in which a man might make a book? (Is that so? Was it he? Of such sparse facts as I once possessed I am no longer certain!) If it is so, if it was indeed he, which of those four worthy functions that he defined - *scriptor*, *compilator*, commentator, *auctore* - have I fulfilled in the creation of this coupling of words and actions that I am presenting here as the accumulated record of my days?

In my daily passage across the face of this Earth, as I have wandered on my path from birth to death, I have by my own reckoning filled nothing more than the first and most lowly of those positions, having been but a scribe, or *scriptor*, adding nothing and changing nothing, living my life according to the words and laws of equally lowly men. In the execution of my craft - that is, in my labours as a *dipintore* - I have been nought but the second, a *compilator*, putting together passages which were not my own, but were assembled according to the bidding of my patrons, employing what skill I possessed in borrowing freely (as I had been taught to do), both from the Good Book, and from the Book of Nature, and from the great styles and traditions of the past, and from my great and inimitable master, and from his masters before him, whose combined Art my own hand had neither the eloquence, nor the skill to follow or to emulate, let alone to surpass.

And what of this chronicle I am now in the process of completing? Have I not been in this but a commentator on the sundry things I have been shown? That was certainly my intention those several months ago when I began - to set down the words and actions of those I have known, placing them together with my own, yet setting theirs in prime of place, their deeds having been far more deserving of being handed down to Posterity than were my own.

And so, it would seem that I have failed - not only in the scribbling of these pages, but in the execution of my Art, and of my life. At no time and in no manner can it be said that I have attained that most exalted of functions, that of *auctore* - one who places his own utterances in prime of place, using the words of others only as confirmation of what he has seen, and of the lessons he has drawn. In everything I have tried, in all I have done, I have failed to achieve the one thing I have spent the full and generous allocation of my days trying to be - the master and creator of my own way and destiny, the sole author of my life.

-OO-

I am grown too weary. I cannot write further, neither is there anything more to say. My thoughts, ever wayward, are no longer mine to control.

As the beckoning star of my destiny falls, as the sky dulls and lowers above my personal Day of Vengeance, I imagine I hear the sounds of the seventh seal being opened, and the clattering hooves of an avenging angel striking hard as he rides forth to claim my soul.

Pain, I fear, shall be my last and most garrulous companion.

The final words have been written; the last trace of pigment applied to the readied ground. Through the inadequate record of my Art, through these, my humble words, may my life and my being be remembered.

If it be so, if my life may be so blessed, so shall I live on.

The book is finished. Through its offices may I, Pace di Buoninsegna, sometimes known as Pacino, *dipintore* of Florence, ever continue to be known.

Per gratiam Dei.

GLOSSARY

Arricciato, arriccio – the second layer of plaster on a wall prepared for fresco painting

Arte dei Medici e degli Speziali – Guild of doctors and specialists, including apothecaries and painters

Atra Mors – L. dreadful death; a contemporary term for the plague

Auctore – author, sole creator of original written text

Baldacchino – a canopy of state typically placed over an altar or throne

Barile – barrel

Borghetto – originally, a settlement outside a city's walls, a ghetto

Bottega – workshop, artist's studio

Braccia – a unit of length, usually 66 or 68 cm but varying between 46 and 71 cm; lit. arm's length

Cadenza – an improvised ornamental passage of music

Camellina – creamy, white sauce rich with cloves and cinnamon

Canzone, pl. canzoni – song(s) or ballad(s)

Capomaestro – a master builder; one overseeing the construction of a building

Cinabrese – term for a skin colour in early Renaissance painting; a bright red earth, suitable for both water colour and tempera painting

Cometis stella – literally, a comet star

Commedia – "The Divine Comedy", Dante Alighieri, 1320; narrative poem representing the soul's journey towards God

Compilator – similar to a scribe, one creating or assembling a text to order, copying from others

Compline – last of the daily canonical hours for prayer, the Prayer at the End of the Day

Contadini – in medieval usage, the worked land

Convivio – "The Banquet", Dante Alighieri, 1304-1307; a kind of vernacular encyclopaedia of knowledge in Dante's time

De Consolatione Philosophiae – "The Consolation of Philosophy", a philosophical work by Boethius, a 6C Roman statesman; considered the single most important and influential work on Medieval and early Renaissance Christian thought

Dies Cinerum – Day of Ashes, Ash Wednesday

Dipintore, pl. dipintori – artist(s), painter(s)

Domine canes – Dominican order, created by St. Dominic; colloquially, The Lord's Hounds;

Dyskrasia – a concept in ancient Greek medicine; an imbalance in the bodily humours

Exordium – L. beginning or introductory part

Farrago – a confused mixture

Fraticelli – Lit. Little Brethren, Franciscan monks, extreme proponents of the rule of Francis of Assisi, especially with regard to poverty and wealth of the church

Fresco - a painting done rapidly in watercolour on wet plaster on a wall or ceiling, so that the colours penetrate the plaster and become fixed as it dries

Fresco secco – a fresco painted on dry plaster

Gastaldi – an officer of the Commune, the civil authority in cities

Gavacciolo, pl. gavaccioli – tumour(s) in the groin or armpit, symptomatic of the plague

Genovini – a gold Genoese coin

Giallorino – a yellow pigment, a yellow oxide of lead

Gonfaloniere di Giustizia – prestigious communal office, Justice of the Peace

Il gran Barone – The Great Baron

Imbroglio – a confused or complicated situation

Intonaco – the final, fine layer of plaster on a wall prepared for fresco painting, on which preparatory drawings are made and the paint applied

Mandorla - a pointed oval figure as an architectural feature, enclosing religious figures

Messer – master, a title of respect

Natale Domini – Birth of Christ, Christmas

Nihil fiat – L. Nothing comes from nothing

Noli me tangere – L. Do not touch me! Said by Jesus to Mary Magdalene when she recognized him after his resurrection. Depictions of the scene were common in Christian art

Novus homo – L. New man. In ancient Rome, the first man in a family to serve in the Roman Senate

Ognisanti – All Saints

Per gratiam Dei – By the grace of God

Pictor – artist, painter

Pieta - a picture or sculpture of the Virgin Mary holding the body of Christ

Plebs pauperum – poor, common people

Popolano, pl. popolani – the people, shopkeepers and artisans, united in various guilds

Popoli minuti – similar to popolani, but not among the higher echelons of their class

Primum Mobile – L. Prime Mover; tenth and outermost sphere of the Ptolemaic universe, thought to revolve around the Earth and cause the other nine spheres to revolve with it

Prior - ruling magistrate of medieval Florence

Quondam – that once was, former

Referamus gratia Christi – L. by the grace of Christ

Rictus – a fixed grimace

Rinzafatto – the coarse foundation layer of plaster on a wall prepared for fresco painting

Savora Sanguigno – a bittersweet, blood red sauce

Scriptor – scribe, copyist

Scriptorium – a place for writing, a room in medieval European monasteries devoted to the creation of illustrated manuscripts

Senettute – old age, senescence

Signoria – a government run by a lord, or despot replacing republican institutions either by force or agreement; a characteristic form of government in 14th century Italy.

Sinopia – dark reddish-brown natural earth pigment; used on the initial layer of plaster for under drawing; the term came to be used for both the pigment and the preparatory drawing

Societi della Arme – local militia, officially sanctioned to fight in political disputes

Soldi – money generally; a small low value coin

Sottoposti – petty officials, examiners

Tarantella – a rapid whirling folk dance often accompanied by tambourines

Tarida – a sea going vessel used in the Mediterranean for carrying implements of war

Tempera – a fast-drying, durable painting medium consisting of coloured pigments mixed with a glutinous binder such as egg yolk; also refers to paintings done in this medium

Terce – Third Hour; third of the daily canonical hours for prayer

Terra-verte – a green pigment, derived from an iron silicate with clay

Trecento – abbreviation of millitrecento, 1300; the 14th century

Valgus – a deformity, a curvature of the bones in the leg

Verdaccio – a mixture of black, white, and yellow pigments resulting in a grayish or yellowish brown; used for defining tonal values, or for creating an initial underpainting

Vicinanza – vicinity, in the sense of a local civic division; a parish

Vita Nuova – "The New Life", Dante Alighieri, 1294; an expression of the medieval genre of courtly love written in a combination of prose and verse.